The Lion Within

Angela L Gold

So what shall I do? I will pray with my spirit, but I will also pray with my understanding; I will sing with my spirit, but I will also sing with my understanding. 1 Corinthians 14:15

The Lion Within
© 2021 Angela Goldstein

All rights reserved. No part of this book may be reproduced in any form or by any means without the prior written consent of the Publisher, excepting brief quotes used in reviews. For permission requests, email the author at Angela@angelalgold.com.

This is a work of fiction. Names, characters, places, and incidents either are the product of the author's imagination or are used fictitiously, and any resemblance to any actual persons, living or dead, events, or locales is entirely coincidental.

Book Cover Design by
SelfPubBookCovers.com/AndrewGraphics

ISBN: 9798517039545

Chapter 1

January 12, 2078

Cruising down the dreary, gray-tiled hallway on autopilot, Rory Rydell screeched to a halt at a glimpse of a small purple capsule. It was out of place on the medicine cart since Aztavix was rarely dispensed in the hospital. Her heartbeat quickened.

No one is around. Take it. Ruby needs it.

Perspiration beaded across her brow despite the cool morning temperature. A quick survey up and down the hallway confirmed no witnesses at the early hour. A quick scan of the corridor revealed no surveillance cameras to capture the moment. Still, she was exposed. The fluorescent lights blared, "Don't do it!" She ignored their warning and stealthily approached the stainless-steel cart. Focusing on the unattended purple capsule, she summoned her courage to no avail. Stealing was wrong, punishable by incarceration. Her heart beats reverberated in her ears.

Take it already. If this one capsule vanishes, it won't be missed. The patient will receive another. No harm, no foul.

But taking something that didn't belong to her was wrong.

On the other hand, the United World Order failing to provide Ruby with her needed medication was wrong. This would right that wrong.

The hospital had plenty. Ruby could die without the medication.

1

Neither her parents' account nor hers held sufficient credits to purchase the medication. Light-headed, her chest tightened. The Order had forced her into this corner. Quickly glancing left and right, she extended her hand toward the cup. A crashing noise made her freeze mid-reach.

"Crites!" Pretty boy Declan Costas, a fellow physician student, collected his electronic notebook from the tile floor. Absorbed in inspecting the damage, he failed to notice her.

She ducked quickly around the corner and melted into the wall. Her hands trembled. She'd barely escaped being caught red-handed. Peeking around the corner, she spied Nurse Iris, who was scanning a paper cup from the cart. Her stomach flipped. Had she lost the opportunity?

As soon as Iris disappeared into the patient's room, Rory sprinted silently to the cart.

If Iris dispatched the capsule, it would rescue her from her plan. But Ruby's life depended on it. She released a sigh as she caught sight of the precious capsule.

She should take it. No one would know.

Except for her. She was not a thief. And yet, in one smooth motion, she seized and pocketed the paper cup and capsule. The rubber soles of her shoes squeaked against the tile as she made her getaway.

"Good morning, Dr. Rydell." Iris popped out from the patient's room.

"Crites!" She almost lost her footing but steadied herself against the wall. Had Iris witnessed her transgression? The overhead lights intensified. Her cheeks burned.

The hospital staff referred to physician students as doctors, even though, technically, they were not. The supervising physicians called them idiots, conveying their love/hate relationship with mostly hate. Probably because they disapproved of the training program developed by the United World Order and decided to take it out on the students. The Order-overhauled program consisted of three years of intensive classroom studies, followed by eight years of pairing students with a supervising physician. The Order believed on-the-job training was the best teacher. But physicians preferred practicing medicine, not teaching.

"I'm sorry, I didn't mean to startle you," Iris apologized. "You look like you saw a ghost. Are you all right?"

"Yes." *No.* To hide her quivering hands, Rory clasped them behind her back. Maybe the small talk indicated Iris saw nothing. "I ... I was deep in thought. You surprised me." Did she sound believable? Should she confess? If she did, Ruby would receive no medication, and she might face arrest, constituting a worst-case scenario. Then, her parents would lose both their daughters.

Iris—a head taller than Rory—filled out her navy scrubs nicely. Turning her attention back to the task at hand, she selected the next medicine cup, scanned the label, and struck a key on the electronic pad.

"Your eyelashes are beautiful, so long and thick," Rory said. A little flattery couldn't hurt.

It was difficult to tell under Iris's dark complexion, but she appeared to blush.

"Thank you. Have a nice day." She smiled and headed to the next patient's room.

"You too." If Iris planned to report her, she probably wouldn't mention anything about having a nice day. Exhaling, Rory hightailed it down the hall. The longer the time lapse before Iris noticed the missing med, the better.

Alone in the hall, she removed the contraband from her pocket and stared at the crumpled cup. She couldn't take it back. A returned crushed cup would be more suspicious than a missing one. What had she been thinking? She would never get away with it. She ducked into the supply room and rested against the wall to clear her head.

What if the intended patient skipped the dose and died? Her stomach dropped. So much for do no harm. But no, Iris would make sure the patient received the medication.

Protocols, designed to catch medication errors, should raise a red flag. A quick check of the patient chart would reveal if the medication had been delivered.

The supply room was empty. She removed the capsule. The label on the cup caught her eye. *Zithromax. What the crites?* The purple capsule with a white band was definitely Aztavix, not a dark pink Zithromax tablet. Had the pharmacy dispensed the wrong med? Based on the room number, Chad Taylor should be a Dr. Bourland patient, but a patient by that name wasn't on the admissions schedule.

By taking the capsule, she'd prevented the patient from receiving the wrong medication. This was a welcome turn of events.

If Iris would have detected the error and returned the medication to the pharmacy, protocol dictated the disposal of erroneously dispensed medication. Had Rory not stolen the capsule, no one would have benefitted from it. Perhaps karma created the scenario to provide medication for Ruby. Her guilt melted.

With a smile, she crushed the cup into a tiny ball and tossed it into the hazardous waste container. No one casually noticed anything in there, and certainly, no one sifted through its contents.

What if hidden cameras existed in the corridors and one recorded her crime? Her stomach churned. She wasn't tough enough to survive prison. A death sentence sounded preferable to the abuse inflicted by other prisoners that vividly played in her head.

She had prevented the Aztavix from being wasted. It was the wrong medication. It would have been thrown away.

But if a recording had captured her stealing, the Order wouldn't care if the medication was filled in error. She chewed her lip. She pushed her shoulders back and made her way to her workstation.

Her fingers fumbled on the keyboard of her electronic notebook. After a deep breath, she donned a calm façade to avoid attracting attention. She pulled up Chad Taylor's chart and read: sixteen-year-old male, Nabil Ahmid attending physician, diagnosis of fractured wrist. The patient was admitted after surgery by Dr. Ahmid, an orthopedic physician. Fracture occurred when the patient slipped on a wet floor at home.

Why wasn't the patient occupying a room in the orthopedic wing? And why Zithromax? It wasn't the prescription of choice to treat infections related to broken bones. Something wasn't adding up.

"What do we have going this morning?"

Startled, she almost tipped her chair. "You shouldn't sneak up on a person like that. What are you practicing to be, a ninja?" She grabbed the counter to steady herself.

"Sneaking? Who's sneaking? Why are you so jumpy?" Dr. Chase Bourland, her supervising physician, pulled his e-notebook from his case and set it on the counter. The premature gray peppering his brown hair and beard gave him a distinguished look. He was a brilliant doctor and one of the few people who appreciated her dry wit.

"Sorry, I'm sleep deprived. You know, studying late." She stretched her arms above her head and faked a huge yawn for effect. In danger of hyperventilating, she slowed her breathing.

"That explains the dark circles under your eyes."

Immediately, she looked at her reflection in the window. "They're not that bad."

A smile spread across his face. "Nothing a little sleep won't solve. You already know more than the sum of the idiots they call students in your class. Ease up. Get some rest."

"There are so many things I don't know. What if a patient presents with a condition that I haven't studied yet?"

"You'll do what we all do, research the patient's symptoms. Many cases don't follow textbook examples. Possessing a good foundation is the key. You build from there. You will never know everything." He entered his credentials in his e-notebook.

She sighed. "I know. I'm trying to be as prepared as possible." Her exhaustive study habits had less to do with perfect diagnosis and more to do with finding a cure for Longus Influenza, LI. If only she could find a way to free Ruby from the disease.

He peered over the top of his black-rimmed glasses. "Your dedication and study habits make you stand head and shoulders above the other students, which is why I selected you to mentor. You're the most likely student to assess a patient correctly and offer an appropriate treatment plan. But sleep deprivation clouds the mind. A clouded mind makes mistakes, which, in our profession, can be fatal. If you kill a patient, it will make me, your supervising physician, look bad. Get a good night's sleep tonight. You need to make me look good."

Rory saluted. "Yes, sir, you're right. I'm sorry. I will get plenty of sleep tonight."

"Sir? I'm not old enough to be a sir."

"Got it ... sir."

He threw a pen in her direction. It skipped off the counter and fell onto the floor.

His levity indicated he'd heard nothing about missing medication, a good sign. She tossed the pen back and then got down to business.

After they'd reviewed patient lab results and chart updates, Dr. Bourland casually mentioned, "I hear Costas dropped his e-notebook this morning and requisitioned another one."

Rory grabbed on to his statement. "Really? Where was he when he dropped it?"

"I don't know." He smiled like he'd discovered a secret. "Is something going on between you and Costas?"

"No, I'm engaged." Her mind churned quickly. In the event the pill was missed, Costas could become a suspect if he could be placed in the vicinity at the time the capsule disappeared. Unfortunately, she couldn't sacrifice Costas for her crime, even though he was a jerk.

Dr. Bourland stared at Rory.

"What?"

"Earth to Rory. I'm speaking to you. You're in another world."

"Sorry, what did you say?" She focused her full attention on him.

"Let's make rounds."

Narrowing her eyes, she said, "Seriously? You make a world case about me not listening, and all you said was 'Let's make rounds'?"

He pointed at her. "Hey, focus."

They gathered their e-notebooks and forged down the hall.

"I was expecting some kind of epiphany at the least."

"Everything I say is an epiphany."

Rory rolled her eyes.

Several hours later, after they had finished rounds, Dr. Bourland assessed her performance. "Good job explaining Jeff Connor's condition. Especially the part about how he was lucky to have me as his doctor."

With a faux surprised face, Rory said, "Oh, you thought I was serious? .... I mean, you're welcome. I meant every word."

"You're such a wise guy."

"Who, me?"

They passed Chad Taylor's room. She played dumb and asked, "Was a patient just admitted? The patient in this room isn't on our schedule. Should we check on him or her?"

"Very observant. Dr. Ahmid is borrowing the room for an ortho patient. Apparently, the ortho wing is full. I hear the patient is the son of Proconsul Taylor. Be glad he's not our patient. Those consuls are a pain in the butt." He locked his e-notebook in the top drawer of the counter. "See you after lunch. We have a full schedule this afternoon. I hope you wore your running shoes."

She nodded and plopped onto her chair.

Someone decided, since they serve the people, consul members and their families deserved free health care. That someone was the consul members themselves. But they didn't serve her. They served their own interests. If anyone deserved free health care, it would be health-care workers

7

and their families. That would never happen since healthcare workers didn't make laws.

To save her credits, Rory skipped lunch. A quick scan of the area revealed no one was around. She pulled up Taylor's chart. Per the chart, Iris administered the Zithromax at 8:36 a.m. That was two hours after Rory had taken the erroneously dispensed Aztavix. Rory methodically calculated Iris's steps. After she administered and charted the morning meds, she would have run a medication list. A comparison of the list to the charts would have alerted her that Chad hadn't received a Zithromax. After informing the pharmacy of the missing med, she would have received, administered, and charted it. All was well that ended well.

Except, the pharmacy incorrectly filling the Zithromax prescription with an Aztavix was peculiar. The two meds were not similar. What was she missing?

With curiosity in overdrive, Rory headed to Taylor's room. She plastered on a smile and tapped on the closed door before she entered. Okay, showtime.

Chapter 2

Rory visually appraised the patient. His right wrist was bandaged, consistent with wrist surgery. His face appeared flushed. Either he'd recently exerted himself or had a fever. Probably he was feverish. Reclined in bed, Chad read from a textbook that rested on the edge of the rolling tray.

"Hi, I'm Rory Rydell, a physician student. I treat patients in this wing, but I didn't see you on my schedule."

He glanced at her. "Dr. Ahmid's my doctor."

"Ahmid's an orthopedic doctor. He operated on your wrist?"

Chad nodded.

"What happened? Bet you have a good story." She smiled.

He shook his head and continued reading.

Just her luck, a tight-lipped patient.

"Rydell, what are you doing here?" Dr. Ahmid's booming voice made her jump.

What brought the doctor here during lunchtime? Taylor rated as one special patient. "Dr. Ahmid, I was trying to understand why this patient wasn't on our schedule."

"Ah yes, Rory Rydell, star physician student. One who questions everything." A glare from the overhead lights bounced off his bald head.

She smiled at his compliment.

"You don't need to worry yourself. We're borrowing the room for my patient. You're dismissed." He flicked his beefy hand toward the door.

9

Of course. The compliment was passive aggressive. "Got it. Is his infection from the fracture?"

The doctor attempted to bore a hole through her with his eyes. "Do you think I'm incompetent and need to consult a student?"

A little eye-boring never scared her. "No, I have nothing but the utmost respect for you." She didn't, but she could play the game. "I'm just hoping to soak up some of your vast knowledge."

"I have my own student to whom I impart my vast knowledge. I don't have time to teach every student in the program. I suggest you be a sponge for Dr. Bourland's knowledge. That's all." He returned to his e-notebook.

"I'll just go, then." She pointed behind her. "Chad, I hope you feel better soon."

"Thanks," he replied flatly.

"Rydell."

She halted and glanced in the doctor's direction.

"The family requests strict privacy. Do not mention this patient to anyone. You do not know who he is or anything about him. If I hear you have mentioned him, I will make sure you are out of the program."

A large, barrel-chested man, he projected an imposing figure. While she wasn't intimidated by his size or sharp glare, his words about ousting her from the program troubled her. He probably couldn't arrange her removal, but he certainly could make her life miserable.

"Oh, and do not go into his chart."

"Okay, but I pulled it up earlier." The information staff could easily inform him of dates and times when she had accessed the chart, so she fessed up.

"Why?"

"To figure out why he wasn't on our schedule."

"Then you saw he's my patient."

"I thought it was a mistake, a wrong patient name or information. I was sorting it out." How many lies had she told? She had lost count.

The doctor rubbed his bald head. "Have you ever encountered wrong information before?"

"No. Are you saying no one has ever entered the wrong patient?"

"Not to my knowledge." His eyes lasered in on her.

"There's always a first time."

"But this wasn't it. You're an overachieving student, who just wasted a lot of time on nothing." His condescension rubbed her the wrong way.

"Sorry." She wasn't sorry.

"Let me give you a piece of advice. Most things are meant to be accepted at face value. Stop wasting your time questioning everything. Learn how to play the game."

With her eyes trained on him, Rory pretended to take his rant to heart. He was spouting bunk. "Chad, you are in good hands. I am sure Dr. Ahmid will have you feeling great in no time." She turned to leave.

"Remember, mention nothing."

"What patient?" she called over her shoulder, then closed the door behind her.

She wouldn't be able to pull up his chart now without risking expulsion from the program. What was Ahmid hiding? Flying below the radar would be safest for her career, but the puzzle dangled before her like an irresistible lure.

Groaning, Rory dropped onto her chair. Her eye caught the screen monitoring Chad's room. A well-dressed man and woman spoke with Dr. Ahmid—Chad's parents. From her top drawer, she grabbed her earbuds and jacked in. The conversation piqued her interest. Chad suffered from Longus Influenza. Aztavix currently relieved his symptoms only a few days at a time. His fall resulted from weakness related to LI.

The Order prohibited the pharmacy from dispensing Aztavix when the medication relieved the patient's symptoms for less than a week between doses. They forbade wasting resources on terminal patients.

Dr. Ahmid must have prescribed Zithromax on record to hide the frequency of the Aztavix doses. A pharmacist had to have conspired with the doctor and performed a sleight of hand. Ahmid, a friend of the Taylors, informed them he had heard of a rumored two-week daily Aztavix regimen that allegedly reset the body's response to the medication.

Now it made sense. To avoid suspicion from the other orthopedic docs, Dr. Ahmid had hidden Chad in Dr. Bourland's wing. The fewer hospital personnel aware of his presence, the fewer questions.

Proconsul Taylor promised to reward the doctor for his cooperation. The doctor feigned humility and insisted the proconsul owed him nothing. He casually mentioned that his son was scheduled for the occupation exam in a few months and hoped to test into the physician training program. The proconsul told him to consider it done. Dr. Ahmid's hostility toward her surprise visit was strictly an act of self-preservation.

Good. It had all worked out, well as long as she wasn't caught and imprisoned or expelled. Chad's parents didn't pay for the capsule, and he shouldn't have received it anyway.

But the fear in Chad's eyes tugged at her. He was just a kid. He didn't want to die. His parents didn't want him to die. The stress showed. They looked like the walking dead. Guilty of breaking the rules herself, she couldn't fault their actions.

"Who are you watching?"

She jumped at Dr. Bourland's voice and pulled the earbud from the jack. "What's up with you today, sneaking around all the time?"

"What's up with you is the question. Is there a problem with a patient?"

"No, I was just checking in on the patients while I was waiting on you." She rubbed her forehead.

"I ran into Dr. Ahmid. He told me in no uncertain terms to make sure you stay away from his patient in our wing."

She rolled her eyes. "Yes, he made that crystal clear. Which means I can't discuss this with you, or he'll kick me out of the program. The kid looked scared." She shrugged and pointed to the monitor. "I just tried to calm him. Then, Ahmid came in and got all excited. You know the rest."

"I told you, proconsuls are a pain. Ahmid's a jerk. I suggest you stay away from him and his patient."

"Agreed."

"Let's see *our* patients."

The busy afternoon kept her mind occupied. The morning's misadventures faded into the background. Luckily, no rumors of missing Aztavix circulated, at least not within her hearing. Could she really be getting away with it? The patient received his medication, and Ruby would get hers, a win-win.

The gray metal lockers blurred into the gray of the walls and floor, which made it difficult to ascertain where one ended and the other began. Normally, Rory waited until most of the students left the locker room before she collected her things. The day had taken its toll. Forget waiting. She crept into the room.

"Can you believe how cold it is?" asked fellow student, Willow, who was slender like her name implied. "They say it's been over fifty years since it's been this cold."

"But it's only supposed to last a few days. My grandfather remembers that time you're talking about. The freezing temps lasted for a whole week. His home was so cold that he left ice sitting out in his kitchen, and it didn't even melt." Costas pulled his scrub top off over his blond head.

"Yeah, they say the below freezing temps caused the power to fail, leaving people without heat. Water froze in the pipes, so they didn't have heat or water. A few people died, but not that many, all things considered," Randolph added. "It was the winter of 2021 when this area was called Texas."

Amethyst sucked in her breath. "You're not supposed to talk about things that happened before the Order."

"They're just talking about the weather. What's the harm in that?" Aryan asked. "It was probably exaggerated anyway. You know how the story gets worse every time it's repeated."

"I don't think the Order would appreciate it. Anyway, I'm glad it's cold because I get to wear my new coat." Amethyst swung a white wool coat for all to see.

The coat looked thick and warm. Rory would give one of her kidneys for such a nice coat. Her own was ugly, thin, and most importantly not warm.

Several students discussed their evening plans. They excluded her. Even if she would have had enough credits, she wouldn't have accompanied them. She entered her five-digit code into the electronic keypad and cringed at the sound of metal against metal when she lifted the handle. Maybe no one heard it above the chatter.

Bare-chested, tanned, and toned, Costas glanced her way. "Afraid I won't be able to control myself if I see you in your underwear, Rydell?" He raised his eyebrows and grinned as he pulled on his beige sweater. "Or maybe you aren't wearing any?"

The students laughed as Rory's face burned. *Slug.* Maybe she would allow him to be mistakenly arrested for stealing the Aztavix, after all. They thought she was embarrassed to change in their company because she was a prude. In truth, she was hiding her protruding ribs and less-than-pretty underwear. Better that they believe she was puritanical and antisocial. The lie was less painful than the truth.

Costas couldn't let her slip in and out unnoticed. He had to humiliate her in front of everyone. She should ignore him and leave, but her mouth opened, and words catapulted. "If you concentrated on tasks at hand, instead of fixating on the underwear your colleague wears, or lack thereof, you wouldn't have dropped your e-notebook this morning." Touché.

Costas smiled sarcastically. "Good one." He waved a lone middle finger.

His smile and middle finger sent mixed messages.

"Oooh, Costas, she lunged for your jugular!" Aryan mocked.

Costas waved a middle finger in Aryan's direction.

"Burned by Bourland's butt-kisser." Randolph rubbed his hand across his nose.

The students snickered.

Just because she took her responsibilities seriously didn't make her a brown-noser. She loaded dagger eyes, aimed, and fired.

"Better watch out. She's giving you the evil eye." Aryan pointed to Randolph.

"What is she talking about?" Amethyst sidled close to Costas, clearly worried about the pretty boy.

"Nothing." Costas busied himself in his locker.

The hint soared over Amethyst's head. Costas wasn't into her. Perhaps he was brighter than he looked. Amethyst, on the other hand, was not.

"Don't pay attention to her." Amethyst leaned into him. "She's just jealous."

Rory whipped her head around. "Jealous? Of you?"

"Yeah, you're jealous of me and everyone in here." Amethyst circled her finger to include everyone in the room.

"Sure, if it makes you feel better, go with it." Rory collected her pitiful coat, scarf, and gloves and slammed the locker.

Amethyst was an idiot, a side effect of genetics giving her breasts larger than her brain. It was a travesty that she was assigned to the program. Obviously, her parents had done someone a favor like Dr. Ahmid was doing for his son.

"You're jealous because you're not attractive, and you have no fashion sense," Amethyst returned hostile fire.

The verbal strike hit the truth dead center and created a gaping wound. Rory walked toward the door as if Amethyst had never spoken, as if the words did not scald.

"Amethyst, that's enough," Willow said quietly.

Amethyst pointed at Rory. "She started it. And does anyone ever see her eat? She's like dyslexic."

Rory turned calmly and replied, "Dyslexia is a learning disorder. You mean anorexic. Use the correct word when you insult me." She shook her head and mumbled just loud enough to be heard, "Her ignorance is going to kill a patient."

Amethyst's face reddened, and her eyes smoldered with hate.

Guffaws followed her from the room. Let them laugh. She couldn't care less what a bunch of pretty pea-brains thought.

In a sense, she suffered from anorexia—social class anorexia. Gaining weight wouldn't be a problem, if she could afford food. She hid her lack of finances, so they wouldn't pity her. Who was she kidding? They'd never pity her. To pity, they had to care. They didn't care.

Hatred bubbled within. Life under the United World Order was unfair. Having to deal with vapid airheads like Amethyst was unfair. Since her life was crappy, she deserved to be beautiful, and if not beautiful, at least attractive. Maybe then someone would want to spend time with her. No matter how hard she'd tried, she never had friends. Even teachers disliked her. When her career test scores placed her in the physician program, she should have finally experienced peer respect and acceptance. But that balloon of hope burst quickly. The other students in the program hailed from higher societal classes and avoided her like a contagious, disgusting virus. Who needed them? Not her. She'd survived with no friends before they came along and would long after they were gone. The real question was, did she want to survive?

Hunger gnawed at the pit of her stomach as she passed a patient's uneaten food, returned to the food cart. What a waste. People starved while perfectly good food was discarded. If her family didn't need to use their credits on medication, she would have enough food to fill out her body and possibly look pretty. She probably needed makeup too, but then again, maybe no amount of makeup could make her attractive. Her eyes and mouth were small, but she did have beautiful blue eyes. No matter how many times she said that she didn't care what the pretty ones thought, the truth was far different, if only they would have a reason to be jealous of her.

Just like every day, she trudged through the metal detector. But today, the security guard stepped in front of her and asked, "What's in your pocket?"

"Wh-What?"

He repeated, slower as if she was stupid, "What's in your pocket?"

Her heart leaped into her throat. Had a hidden surveillance camera captured her when she stuffed the capsule into her pocket? If it had, the jig was up. But she wasn't rolling over and admitting anything. He would have to work for it. "Nothing."

"Take off your lab coat." The guard's wrinkled uniform strained at the button around his midsection. A few grease spots shined next to his name tag, Theodus Maneson.

She slipped off her coat and held it at arm's length. She donned an annoyed expression while her temperature rose uncomfortably.

The guard shoved his chubby hand into one pocket and then the next but came up empty.

Her heartbeat echoed in her ears. She managed a poker face, but if he looked into her eyes, sheer terror would betray her.

A line formed. People grumbled.

She grabbed her lab coat, but he gripped it firmly. The stench of sweat attacked her nose. The guard rarely laundered his uniform, or he bathed infrequently.

"I think I should search you to make sure you aren't hiding something," he growled while he held her lab coat tightly.

The foul taste of bile rose in her mouth. This would not end well. If he searched her, he would question the Aztavix stuffed into her bra. He could simply check her Treasury account to prove she hadn't purchased it. Why had she stolen the capsule?

In desperation, Rory fired dagger eyes and jerked at her coat. Something was off. With his eyes locked on her breasts, the guard never saw the daggers. He didn't suspect she stole anything. He just wanted to see her boobs.

This she could handle. She waved a hand across her chest, then pointed to her eyes. "Hey, nothing to see there. Eyes up here." He leered and reached toward her. Her adrenaline surged. "Don't touch me, you pervert!"

"Wouldn't you like to know just what a pervert I am?"

Shuddering, she said, "No, but I do want to speak to your supervisor."

"Too bad—" His attention was drawn behind her.

"Why are you harassing my student?" The familiar voice of Dr. Bourland sounded like music to her ears.

"Just doing my job," the guard snarled.

"Your job is harassing hospital employees, Mason?" Dr. Bourland pushed her past the guard.

"Maneson, it's Maneson." Then in a low voice, he said, "Next time, blue eyes."

"There won't be a next time." Dr. Bourland locked eyes with him.

The guard cursed under his breath and turned to the hospital employees who were lined up behind the metal detector. "Come on, move it."

When they were out of earshot, Rory turned to Dr. Bourland and awkwardly hugged him. "Thank you. You're a badass."

He looked away and shrugged. "Don't act so surprised."

"This is not a surprised face." She circled her face with a finger. "This face says that I have always known you were bad."

"You're full of crap."

"I'm insulted. All kidding aside. You are my hero. That guy creeps me out."

"He's definitely creepy. I'll report him tomorrow. Go home. Don't study all night."

"Yes, sir."

"Ruining a creep's plan makes my day." The doctor swaggered toward the exit.

"Thanks again." She released a long breath. The Aztavix was safe, and she hadn't been arrested, but Maneson would harass her at every opportunity. She would have to check the exits for forever and avoid his station. Why did life have to be so exhausting?

She layered her flimsy flannel coat over her lab coat, wrapped her scarf around her head and neck, and slipped on her thin gloves. As she abandoned the warmth of the building, a blast of frigid air slapped the terror of the security guard from her mind.

Chapter 3

The short walk from the hospital to the trans station was excruciatingly long in the extreme cold. Her breath came out in icy puffs as she walked. Members of the janitorial crew, maintenance workers, and Rory waited for the train to the labor sector.

Onboard the train, she collapsed onto a ripped seat in an unoccupied area. A shield of darkness hid the bleak landscape from view as she stared out the window. So far, so good. She'd get the capsule home to Ruby in less than an hour.

Longus Influenza was a chronic flu. In young people, the body failed to produce antibodies to fight the virus. Aztavix suppressed the virus for a time. When initially diagnosed with LI, patient symptoms were typically relieved by the medication for forty to forty-five days. Over time, the number of days the medication relieved symptoms shortened. First diagnosed six years prior, the virus had infected adolescents predominantly between the ages of four and sixteen. Adults' immunity to the virus baffled scientists. Adolescents who presented with LI typically already had a weakened immune system due to an underlying condition.

Ruby contracted the infection three years ago. Mom had been forced to stay home with her. She lost her teaching credits and academic housing. Their family was transferred from a three-bedroom apartment to a two-bedroom in the labor sector. Her mom said they should be thankful to be alive and have each other. But their life constantly teetered on the brink of disaster.

Aztavix currently provided Ruby relief for about thirty days. The purchase of the medication strained their finances, and it would be another week or so before they accumulated sufficient credits to acquire one. Based on Ruby's symptoms, pneumonia would likely set in before then. Rory had never stolen anything before, but fate stepped up. She bit her lip. Fate wouldn't be considered a valid defense in court.

This had worked out better than using an arranger, someone who connected citizens in need of credits to those willing to exchange credits for services, usually sexual in nature. Rory had almost contacted one, but she couldn't pull the trigger. Her mom said sex should be saved for someone she loved. If love wasn't involved, did that make it wrong? But love would have been involved. She loved her sister and needed to provide her medication.

Rather than help, the Order preferred the elimination of those unable to be productive. Ruby's only hope to receive medication on a regular basis depended on the credits Rory would earn after becoming a doctor. The weight of the world rested on her shoulders.

Dr. Ahmid had also risked his career to secure a place for his son in the physician training program. Which pharmacist had worked with him? Maybe the pharmacist would bend the rules for Ruby too. It would be a miracle if Dr. Ahmid's regimen actually relieved Chad's symptoms.

But what if it didn't? What if Ruby died anyway? Was there any type of existence after death? The Order subscribed to the theory that people came from nothing and returned to nothing. They forbade discussion of gods, except to say they don't exist. If gods were fictional, what was the harm in discussing them? But forbidding and enforcing were two different things. Surprisingly, even with the threat of execution, people whispered about various gods and heavens and hells. Not that anyone discussed anything with her, but she overheard things. As far back as elementary school, students considered her invisible. If she pretended to read, they thought she couldn't hear, even when she sat beside them, the idiots.

Once, Rory had asked her parents about a discussion she had overheard. Her dad went berserk. He looked on the verge of hitting her. She never asked again but tucked the eavesdropped deity conversations into the recesses of her mind. Too bad no god existed to smite bad people. Too bad there wasn't a hell for the leaders of the Order, the pretty ones, and that security guard. Since she was a thief, aka a bad person, it would behoove her to be careful what she wished for. Maybe it was better there was no god. Then again, if righteousness prevailed, she wouldn't have been forced to steal.

If there is a good god out there, please reveal yourself. Her heart sank when no response presented itself. *Just like I thought.*

With her head against the back of the seat, she closed her eyes. The clickety-clack of the train wheels against the track lulled her to sleep.

The trans braked and jolted her awake. Rory rose and traipsed off the train in a zombie-like state. It was a good thing she hadn't slept through her stop. The frigid wind whipped outside the station. She halted and blinked. Nothing looked familiar. The sign above the station read Station 35, the trans station immediately before her stop. She ran back inside and arrived just in time to watch the trans pull away.

"Argh!" The station stood empty, except for her. She kicked a column and bruised her toes.

The next scheduled train was not for an hour. Her breath rose as frosty fog. The Cinders was only a thirty-to-forty-minute walk. She would be home and warm long before the next trans pulled into the station. Plus, walking would generate heat. Only an idiot would get off at the wrong station on a night like this. She shoved her hands into her coat pockets.

The clouds blanketed the moon and stars and smothered any celestial illumination. One in three streetlights worked, producing a dim glow. Their dismal light aligned with her dark mood. The few scattered bare trees resembled skeletons. It was difficult to ascertain if they were dead or alive. The sparse, brittle, brown grass was definitely dead. Rory tucked her head and forged onward as the wind clawed at her face.

The air smelled of snow. Great, that was all she needed. The icy wind penetrated her clothing and slashed her skin as she maneuvered the deserted streets. Of course, the streets were deserted. Who else would be crazy enough to be out in this weather?

What if the freezing temps lasted for an extended time? Would the infrastructure collapse like it had fifty years ago? She shuddered. Her family already had to bundle up inside their apartment when the temperature dipped. Would they be as resilient as the Texans who'd survived the freezing temperatures without power fifty years before? Texan had a nice ring to it.

A rumble broke the silence and announced the approach of a vehicle. The driver had to be an outsider because residents of the labor sector were not assigned cars. A black military jeep slowed alongside her.

The driver leaned across the seat as the passenger window lowered. "Where are you headed?"

"The Cinders," Rory answered automatically. That was stupid. She increased her pace. Her mind raced with paranoia.

"You shouldn't be walking in this weather. I can give you a ride."

Some men in authority took advantage of women. What a lucky day. Every pervert in the district wanted to strip-search her.

"Thank you, but I'm enjoying the walk." If only he'd just drive on.

"Why didn't you stay on the trans instead of getting off here?"

An excellent question. "I'm walking to clear my head." That sounded stupider than the real reason. However, he would expect her to accept a ride if she admitted she had gotten off at the wrong stop.

"Are you suicidal? You'll be lucky if you don't come down with frostbite by the time you get there. If you make it at all."

Why did he care? She stared straight ahead. "You are kind, but my parents warned me about accepting rides from strangers."

"My name is Dawson Fortis. Tell me your name, and we won't be strangers."

Nice try, but she wasn't born yesterday. In a saccharine sweet voice, she said, "Mr. Fortis, the cold is good for circulation. Have a nice evening." He probably thought she was crazy and rightfully so.

"Your parents should have warned you it's stupid to walk home in weather like this. Don't be an idiot."

Perhaps the stress of the day or the intense cold caused her to snap. Rory looked directly at the officer and struggled to speak above the chattering of her teeth. "I'm not breaking any laws. I'm minding my own business. Now why don't you mind yours?"

"It's ten below. Anyone walking in this weather is stupid or doing something illegal."

"Let's go with stupid. Last I heard, stupid's not illegal." Yeah, stupid summed it up nicely.

"You are a blooming idiot. Well, that's the thanks I get for being a nice guy. Go ahead and die of pneumonia. See if I care." The officer rolled up his window. His tires threw gravel as he screeched away.

"Slug!" she yelled after him.

She watched the red taillights fade in the distance. His assessment was accurate. The cold had to have affected her cognition. Provoking an officer was foolish. He could easily trump up charges against her. She never visited this neighborhood, so if it was his patrol area, at least she wouldn't run into him by chance. But she'd mentioned the Cinders was her destination. No matter. With the scarf wrapped around her nose and mouth, he'd seen only her eyes. He shouldn't be able to recognize her if they met again.

The wind howled a ferocious warning through the branches of the leafless trees. Foolishly, she ignored the warning, dipped her head, and trudged forward. In an effort to create warmth, she jogged. When she inhaled the cold air, a burning sensation circulated through her respiratory system.

A wet snow fell, which added to her discomfort. How could the snow be wet with the temperature below freezing? It should be frozen solid.

The precipitation dampened her clothing. Her eyeballs felt like ice cubes. Could exposure to freezing temperatures harm vision? She kept blinking just in case.

She would never again complain about sweltering summer days, assuming she ever experienced them again. Shivering made running awkward. She settled for a brisk walk. The decision to walk home might have been a fatal mistake.

The precipitation had formed an invisible layer of ice on the sidewalk. Her feet flew out from under her. She landed hard on her glutes. It took a few moments to recover. Unable to generate traction, she couldn't stand. She would freeze to death, right there. As a last-ditch effort, she crawled on her hands and knees to the ground beside the sidewalk. The uneven surface provided some grip. Once on her feet, she avoided the pavement as she continued to walk.

Her extremities numbed as her blood centralized to her core to protect vital organs. Shivering was good. It was not good when shivering ceased. Movement was crucial. No one ever froze to death while in motion. They lost fingers and toes but didn't die.

Headlights approached. Should she wave the vehicle down? It was a military jeep. Had he decided to arrest her for being stupid or for provoking him? Jail was warm, better than freezing to death. Or was he waiting to rape her after she succumbed to the cold? Trading sex for warmth didn't sound terrible at the moment. She attempted to wave him down, but her arms wouldn't move. Her heart sank as the jeep passed. She had ticked him off. He no longer fancied arresting her. He wanted to watch her die. He *was* a slug.

She was going to die from hypothermia. Stealing the Aztavix, the gutsiest move of her life, would be voided by the stupidest. The military jeep passed her again. Would what's-his-name try to revive her? How long would it take until her family was notified that she had died? How did death feel? Probably better than the intense pain that stabbed her.

Death sounded nice. Motion required enormous effort. If she lay down, she could slip into nothingness. An empty void trumped this life. Dying this close to home would be poetic justice, payment for her crime.

She swallowed a lump in her throat. She hadn't told her family she loved them before she left this morning. What had been her last words to them? Ruby and her mom knew she loved them. But her dad probably had his doubts. Her fiancé, Darius, would find someone else. It wasn't like she was that great of a catch anyway. Without her credits, her parents wouldn't be able to afford Ruby's medication, and she would die. Rory blew out a defeated breath. Would they blame her? It would be her fault. Her mom would be inconsolable after the loss of both daughters, but they shouldn't have brought children into this world. What had they been thinking?

She should lie down for just a moment.

Her eyes popped open. Why was she lying on the frozen ground? Where was she? Her teeth chattered. Shivering, she pushed to her hands and knees, then stood. To get her bearings, she turned in a circle. At the sight of station 36, she breathed a sigh. Right, she had been walking home and needed to deliver Ruby's medication.

She was close, but her feet were heavy like she wore lead boots. She had to keep going. Ruby needed the Aztavix.

Looking toward heaven, she called out, "If you exist, help me make it home, and I'll believe!"

Determination forced her feet forward. One step and then one more. The unremarkable cinder block apartments appeared like a mirage. She could make it.

Warmth radiated through her core. A warning blared in her subconscious—warm was bad. Wrong. Freezing cold was bad.

With numb fingers, Rory fumbled to retrieve the key from her coat pocket. Her fingers couldn't grasp it or form a fist to knock. Her gloves muffled the sound of her hand slapping the door. She fell against the door with a thud and then slid to the concrete. Intense peacefulness washed over her as her eyes closed, and she slipped into darkness.

Chapter 4

"We should have told her. Now it's too late!" The voice belonged to Rory's mother, Randa Rydell.

What was she talking about? And why did her voice sound disconsolate?

"There was nothing to tell," her father, Rydge Rydell, responded.

Rory's eyes blinked open as she squinted against a bright light that surrounded her.

"Yes, there was. We failed her." Her mother's wails drifted from somewhere below.

Rory looked down. Her father embraced her mother. She collapsed in his arms. Ruby's frail body was stretched on top of someone. Rory peered closer. It was … her? She had been disrobed, and her skin was blue. How could she see herself down there when she was here? Where was here anyway?

You must return. Listen for my call and then follow me.

Who said that? She whirled in search of the masculine voice's source. A dazzling light masked someone. She raised her hand to shield against the glare. Her eyes began to adjust. Rory trembled. The form of an extremely tall man was barely visible. A sparkling green hue encircled his head. The man wasn't behind the light. It radiated from his face. The light dimmed. Severe pain ripped through her chest. Everything darkened. "No," she moaned. Sharp pain pierced her skin like she was a human pincushion. Her eyes fluttered open. "Argh!"

Ruby jumped up, and her parents' heads spun toward Rory. Their jaws dropped.

What happened? The pain allowed only a groan to escape her lips. Where had she been? Who was that man? The intense pain hijacked her thoughts.

"Thank you, thank you, thank you." With tears of joy, her mom ran to her. "It's a miracle."

"No, it's not," Dad barked gruffly.

"You know it is." Mom brushed her dark blond hair from her eyes.

"What happened?" Rory struggled to speak.

"I heard a noise at the door, and when I opened it, you fell into the apartment. I couldn't feel a pulse. I thought you were dead." Mom's voice broke on the last word.

Dad put an arm around Mom. "We stripped off your wet clothing and rubbed your arms, legs, and feet, trying to warm you."

"I figured my fever should be good for something, so I laid down on top of you, and it brought you back." Ruby's skin was flushed, and her strawberry blond hair was matted to her forehead.

Dad draped blankets over Rory. Mom brought a chipped, plastic bowl filled with warm chicken soup.

Ruby helped Rory to a sitting position and tucked the blanket around her.

Propped between Ruby and her dad, she swallowed a spoonful of the warm broth. The liquid soothed her aching throat.

Mom said she hadn't had a pulse. Had it been too faint to detect, or had she died? The pain-free place with the glowing man had to have been a hallucination. No such place really existed. A fierce pain stabbed her heart.

Ruby caressed Rory's frozen right hand in her feverish ones. Rory's fingers erupted in sharp pain. She held up her left hand. Her fingers were swollen and blue-gray. Would she lose them? That would end her medical career.

"What's this?" Mom freed the plastic bag that peeked from inside Rory's bra. She gasped as she examined the contents. "How did you get it? We were weeks away from accumulating enough credits."

"I had enough." Her words formed slowly. Her throat burned, and her raspy voice was barely audible. She was a thief, so liar wasn't difficult.

"What if Treasury made a mistake? What will happen when they figure it out, and she doesn't have enough credits to take back?" Dad rubbed his hands through his unruly brown hair.

"If Treasury made a mistake, they can't take it out on Rory." Mom was always the optimist. "We'll worry about it if it happens." She offered the capsule and a glass of water to Ruby, then turned back to Rory. "I don't understand how you got this frozen walking from the station."

"Wrong stop," Rory croaked.

"You got off at the wrong stop?"

Rory nodded slowly.

"You should have waited for the next trans. Why did you walk?" Mom admonished her through tears.

Rory's head pounded, and her throat ached. Why did they insist on talking?

"You walked home because you used almost all your credits on the Aztavix, and you didn't have enough to ride to our stop. Isn't that right?" Ruby accused.

Rory shook her head.

"Liar. You're so cold, but it feels good." Ruby snuggled against Rory. Her feverish body radiated warmth against Rory's cold skin. "Thanks for getting the pill, but it won't help me if you kill yourself."

Rory continued to study her fingers as she blocked everyone out. They had turned blue and red, and the swelling had gone down. She flexed them. On a scale from one to ten, they stung at an eleven. But they looked better, so maybe she wouldn't suffer irreparable damage.

Her mother delivered a cup of a homemade herbal concoction to prevent colds and flu. "Sip this. We don't need you getting sick."

Rory sipped the home remedy. It had better work. Scheduled at the hospital the next day, she couldn't afford to stay home sick.

"That's right. I'm the sick one," Ruby chimed in. "You have to find something else to be. Sick is taken."

Although not tasty, the liquid warmed her slightly. She wrapped her fingers around the mug and held it against her cheek.

The small, purple capsule kicked in and lowered Ruby's body temperature to normal as Rory's temperature rose from frozen to cold. They both dozed on the sofa off and on.

Eventually, Mom roused Ruby to go to bed.

"Let her stay. She's warming me," Rory mumbled.

Her mom looked haggard. "I still can't believe you walked home in this weather. I thought we lost you."

"I'm sorry."

Mom wiped her eyes. "If she starts feeling warm, or you feel worse, call me."

"Promise. Mom?"

She looked at Rory.

"I heard you tell Dad you should have told me something. What were you talking about?"

She looked toward the bedroom where Dad had retired, clearly uncomfortable. Her whole body sagged before she shrugged. "I'm not sure what you're talking about."

"You said you should have told me something, and now it was too late."

"Maybe you imagined it." Mom hurried toward her bedroom.

Had she imagined it? Could she trust her mind? Was the shining man and the image of her lifeless body just her mind playing tricks?

Ruby craned her neck to look at her sister. "Are you awake?"

"Uh-huh."

"You can't pull another stunt like you did tonight."

"Hmm?"

"Walking home to save your credits and almost freezing to death."

"I got off at the wrong stop."

"Yeah, whatever. I'm going to die, and it will kill them if they lose both of us."

The words punched Rory in the gut. "We're all going to die, but not in the near future." She hugged Ruby. A lump in her throat made it difficult to swallow.

"I'm not stupid. There's no cure for LI. The pill isn't making me feel better for as long as it used to. Sometime, it will stop helping at all."

"There is no cure right now. At one time, there were no antibiotics, but then a scientist developed them. A cure for LI is coming."

Ruby released a tired sigh. "It probably won't be soon enough for me. It's okay, don't be sad. It's not like being sick is such a great life. Mom had to quit her job. Everybody uses all their credits to buy my pills. Everything will be easier when I'm gone."

Rory propped herself on her elbow and stroked Ruby's hair. "Don't say that. Our life is fine. Think positively. The mind's a powerful thing. Believe you're getting better."

"I used to, you know, believe I would beat Longus. Now I'm too tired. It's okay because I don't think this is all there is." Her face lit up. "I think there's something after we die, something better."

Ruby looked and spoke as if she knew a secret. Maybe she did. Should Rory share her experience? What *had* she experienced? If she shared, it might make Ruby give up and embrace death. She couldn't take that chance. "What makes you believe in an afterlife?"

"I don't know." Ruby shrugged. "I just feel it. Do you ever feel tingly when you think certain thoughts?"

"Do you?"

Ruby's deep blue eyes stared into space. "Yes. Sometimes when I think about dying, I see a beautiful place where there's no pain. Then I feel tingly all over. I think the feeling tells me the thought is true. You've probably felt it. You just weren't paying attention."

The feeling could be a physical euphoric response to the hope that the thought was true.

"The Order says there's nothing after we die, but I think they're wrong. What do you think?"

"They're wrong about most things, so makes sense they'd be wrong about this."

Snuggling closer, Ruby said, "Don't be sad if I die before a cure is found. I'll be in that great place. I'll be better off than you." Yawning, she closed her eyes.

Rory nudged her. "Well, I will be sad if you die, so don't." Sick people died when they gave up hope. She needed Ruby to fight. A fifteen-year-old shouldn't be comforting others and making peace with death.

Ruby believed there was something after death. The Order promoted death was all she wrote. The end. Period. Her experience definitely raised questions. She could share it with her family, but they would think she was crazy. Was she?

A chill lingered as she lay on the drooping sofa under multiple blankets. The pain decreased from an eleven to an eight or a nine. Her thoughts tumbled. Someone as good as Ruby shouldn't have to die. The Order didn't allow sufficient credits to provide necessities. They were the reason she had to steal in the first place. Stealing was wrong, according to the United World Order. Yet poverty was not? Life wasn't just unfair, it was cruel.

Each time she drifted off the mysterious voice whispered. *You must return. Listen for my call and then follow me.* Between the pain and the voice, she couldn't sleep. While the voice haunted her, Ruby snoozed beside her fever-free, thanks to the stolen Aztavix.

What about when she impulsively cried out to God? He hadn't really saved her. She would have made it anyway. But then, whose voice had she heard, probably her dad? Who was supposed to call? She would ask him tomorrow.

Chapter 5

Slumped at her workstation, Rory's throat burned, and an odd warmth filled her inner ears, even though she had no fever. She was the opposite of feverish actually. She was chilled to the bone. Her muscles ached. If only she could curl up under a blanket and sleep. However, to avoid losing attendance points, she was present and accounted for.

It took all her willpower to stay out of Chad Taylor's chart as she watched the monitor for his room. Chad appeared to be asleep. He might look better than yesterday. It was hard to tell over the screen. She needed him to improve, to offer hope for Ruby.

"Rydell, you look like death warmed over." Dr. Bourland set his coffee on the counter, walked around, and took the seat across from her.

She pointed at him and quipped, "You're good."

"Didn't I tell you to get some rest last night?"

"You did." Should she share any of her escapades from the previous night? Probably not. She sat and returned his stare. Her deep-chested cough broke the silence. "I believe I experienced hypothermia last night, so death warmed over." She returned to her e-notebook as if she'd merely commented on the weather.

After a moment, he said, "You're serious." He opened a drawer, retrieved a thermometer, and scanned her forehead. "Go to the exam room."

Despite her protest, he ushered her into the room. Her face flushed as he examined her bony fingers, hands, toes, and feet. Luckily, he didn't comment on her malnourished state.

She briefly described the prior night's events.

After he thoroughly examined her exposed skin, he asked, "Did you feel a sensation of warmth at any time?"

"Right before I collapsed at the apartment door. I felt warm and tired and then the strangest …"

"What?" He listened to her lungs with his stethoscope.

"Um … I saw myself." She had said too much.

He wrapped his stethoscope around his neck and looked her in the eye. "What do you mean, you saw yourself?"

Her stomach cramped. Dr. Bourland would have to report her. She fidgeted. "Nothing, forget it."

"You can't say you saw yourself and then tell me to forget it. What did you see?"

Her eyes darted around the room. "Um, I heard my parents speaking, then I was surrounded by a bright light. I looked down and saw my mom, my dad, Ruby, and … me."

"Continue."

"I, well, my body was lying on the sofa, and Ruby was stretched across me. I didn't feel anything."

His lack of facial expression unnerved her. Could he read her thoughts as he stared into her eyes?

"What did you look like?"

"Like me, except my skin was blue, and I wasn't moving. My chest didn't rise. I wasn't breathing." She needed to stop sharing.

"Did you feel cold, warm?"

"I felt nothing, no pain."

He stroked his beard. "Interesting. What else do you remember?"

If she could rewind and erase the conversation, she would. She clenched her hands. "My parents were crying. I felt intense pain, like pins pricking my entire body. Then I was back."

"What do you mean, you were back?"

"Back in my body." *Please stop with the questions.*

"You no longer saw yourself?"

"Right, I saw through my eyes."

"Did you see anything else? People who died before?"

She shook her head.

"Did you hear any voices other than your family?"

"No." Perspiration erupted on her forehead. Was he simply curious, or was he testing her?

"Are you sure?"

Did he suspect her of lying? "I'm sure."

"Would you tell me if you experienced something else?"

Now he was baiting her. She put on an innocent look. "I don't understand."

"Never mind. What else do you remember?"

"Just the pain after I returned to my body."

The doctor stared for what seemed like ages. Finally, he broke the silence. "What do you think you experienced?"

What was the intent of his question? His face was a blank slate. "I believe I experienced hypothermia."

"Hypothermia is likely based on the temperature, the length of exposure, your limited body fat, and inadequate clothing. Why do you think you saw yourself?"

"I don't know. It makes no sense." She seized the opportunity to turn the tables. "What is your opinion?"

"During the end stages of hypothermia, people feel warm and often hallucinate. You experienced the warmth. In your subconscious, you heard your parents speaking. Obviously, you hallucinated when you saw the bright lights and yourself. It was a neurological event, perhaps caused by a lack of oxygen to the brain when your organs slowed. You may have been near death."

"Obviously." After a moment, she asked, "When you hallucinate, do you see yourself, or do you just see everyone else?"

"What do you mean?"

Rory's eyes darted around the room. "When I dream, I never see myself. It's like I'm seeing through my eyes. I see others, but I don't see myself. Are hallucinations like that or different?"

Dr. Bourland studied her intently. "What are you saying?"

"I'm not saying. I'm asking."

"Semantics."

"No, it's not the same. Saying implies I know or believe I know something, and I'm stating it. Asking means I don't know, and I'm searching for the answer. I'm asking if dreams and hallucinations are different or the same? I don't know if everyone dreams the same way, but when I dream, I don't see myself."

Dr. Bourland considered her question. "The mind is complicated. If it wasn't a hallucination when you saw yourself, what do you think it was?"

Rory shrugged. "I don't know. That's why I'm asking you."

"What is there besides a hallucination? Vision? Out-of-body experience?"

"You think I had an out-of-body experience? I'm not exactly sure what that is." He had been putting her on the spot, so she returned the favor.

The doctor's face paled, and he stuttered, "I-I didn't say that. I asked a question."

"You know, it had to be a hallucination. Nothing else makes sense. There are no such things as visions or out-of-body experiences. It's the only possible explanation. Whew, I'm glad we cleared this up." It was definitely an out-of-body experience.

The doctor sighed. "Yes, we cleared it up. Your body temperature is low. You should have stayed home and rested today."

"I don't want to lose points."

"You have the highest score in the program and will continue to, even if you lose a few points. Go home."

"You sound like my mother. Like I told her, what better place to be than at a hospital when you're ill?" She smiled.

"Physicians make mistakes when they lose focus. Your exhaustion almost took your life last night. You don't want to kill a patient due to fatigue."

Rory put on her most professional face. "I am fine. If I start feeling worse, I'll go home. I swear." She held up her pinky finger.

He rubbed his beard and gave in. "You are so obstinate. Although, I suppose it's good I examined you."

"Agreed."

"You agree you're obstinate, or it's good you were examined?"

"Either or." She raised the crook of her elbow to her mouth as a rumbling cough escaped.

"That sounds nasty. I'm ordering a chest scan." He entered the order into his e-notebook. "Get dressed and go to radiology. If the scan shows fluid in your lungs, you're going home. No arguments."

With a heavy chest, Rory dressed and slouched to radiology.

An out-of-body experience didn't mean there was a god. She had experienced a neurological event. There were no gods. Too bad. A god would have been great as long as it was a good one.

Not busy, radiology was able to get her in and out quickly. The sweet fragrance of herbal tea greeted her on her return to her workstation.

"The tea will help raise your body temp," Dr. Bourland said.

"Thank you." It was a pity offering, but she accepted it anyway. The heat radiating from the cup warmed her hands.

Dr. Bourland reviewed her scans. Was he still thinking of their conversation? He probably thought she was crazy or a traitor or a crazy traitor.

"Amazingly, your scans are clear. You just have a cold. Rub this ointment on your hands and feet. Get plenty of rest, push fluids, and when your temperature returns to normal, you should feel fine. In the meantime, I have just the assignment. Monitor the patient in room 377 and report any changes in his status. I predict he'll expire within the next few hours. Looks like this will be the first patient you lose."

Expire? What was he, a bottle of milk? Would Dr. Bourland have said she expired if she had succumbed to hypothermia? Expire wasn't the right word to refer to a formerly living human. Was die a better word? Maybe not. She scanned the patient's chart. "His name is 76924?"

"He's from Gibbons Maximum Security Facility. They only gave us his number."

"I thought the prison provided medical services to inmates."

"Normally, but they don't provide morphine drips. Lucky us, we're the closest hospital to the facility."

"He's in a coma, receiving a high dose of morphine, and no nutrition. The only change will be when he di—uh, I mean, expires. I don't understand why he needs close observation." Then it hit her. "He doesn't. He's going to expire, so if I make a mistake that expedites his expiration date, no big deal, he's dying anyway."

"I can't pull anything over on you. Now go." He returned to his e-notebook.

Physically, she wasn't up to a rigorous day. Babysitting a comatose patient was the next best thing to resting at home, actually better. She didn't lose points, and she wasn't constantly nagged by her mom. With her e-notebook and cup of tea in hand, Rory trudged down the hall.

Room 377 was furnished exactly like all the patient rooms on the floor: hospital bed, monitoring equipment, metal dresser, rolling tray, vinyl recliner, and two vinyl chairs. The gray walls were bare, except for the dry-erase board to post patient notes. The board in room 377 was void of notes. She checked the monitor. How were his vitals so strong? On the prescribed morphine dose, he should be dead. Was the bag really morphine? The label on the bag indicated it was.

A gaunt man lay in the bed, perhaps a ghost of a man depicted him most accurately. The roadmap of lines etched in his face narrated the hardships that had assaulted him over his seventy-one years. His white hair and matching beard hung long and unkempt. Why had he been incarcerated at Gibbons? Her stomach cramped. Gibbons could be her residence if they discovered the missing Aztavix. She shook her head and settled into the recliner under a blanket. As she read, her eyelids grew heavy, and the words on the e-notebook blurred.

Her cough awakened her.

Then, a voice called out, "Hey, granddaughter, come closer, so I can get a good look at you."

Granddaughter? The comatose patient was conscious, and he'd spoken. She jumped up, and her legs tangled in the blanket, causing her to fall. After she kicked herself free, she sprinted to his side, breathing heavy.

The patient chuckled and said, "How can it be you?"

"You expected your granddaughter?" Rory shined her penlight in his eyes. His pupils responded.

"I expected a big guy with lots of muscles."

"How can your granddaughter be a big guy?"

"You don't understand."

Slowly, she enunciated each word as she said, "You were in a coma. You are in the hospital. You are disoriented."

"I am not disoriented, and I'm not dense either. God"—her blood froze at the forbidden word, and she glanced at the camera capturing the conversation—"promised before I die that I would meet the leader chosen to lead his people from oppression. I wasn't expecting the leader to be you. God has a sense of humor."

The man was clearly delusional. She carefully phrased her response. "It is treason to say ... that word or speak of rebellion."

"What word? God? God, God, God," the patient chanted.

She whispered, "You can be executed for saying that."

"Look at me. Do you think I'm afraid of dying?"

Good point.

"They've been trying to kill me for longer than you've been alive. They've tried to give me a lethal injection, shoot me, and stab me, but here I am." He mimed each type of execution as he described it. "They have me on enough morphine to kill a horse, but I'm not dead."

The Order couldn't execute him, really? She rolled her eyes.

"It's true. They gave me a lethal injection, but it didn't even make me sleepy. Then they gave me a second one. When I was still alive the next day, they stood me before a firing squad. The rifles misfired and injured the shooters. Commander Duterte was beside himself. He grabbed a knife, ran at me, and died of a heart attack. Coincidence? I don't think so. They didn't either. They were afraid to keep trying to kill me, so they threw me in solitary and left me there."

"Who are you?"

"David Abrams, a Christian minister. Hey, where are you going?"

"To report that you're out of the coma."

"He'll never believe you. You're wasting your time."

Chapter 6

"He can't be conscious." Dr. Bourland pointed to room 377's monitor. "Still comatose."

Rory studied the monitor. "Maybe he's resting."

The doctor backed the feed to the time when she had entered the room. The recording captured her as she entered and checked the patient's vitals, then she left the frame. He fast-forwarded the feed. The patient never opened his eyes, never spoke, and never moved. She reappeared in the frame when she left the room. The feed picked up no conversation.

"I swear he spoke to me, just like I'm speaking to you. I don't understand." She massaged her forehead. Was she losing her mind?

He replayed the footage. "You probably dreamed it. Maybe you're experiencing residual effects from last night."

That was the only thing that made sense. Dr. Bourland probably thought she was crazy.

"Go home. Get some rest."

"No, I'll be fine." She turned around to return to the patient's room.

"Stubborn."

"I heard you."

"I meant for you to."

She trudged back to room 377. The patient's eyes were closed. She poked his shoulder. No response. She whispered, "Mr. Abrams."

The patient's eyes remained closed. She pried his right eye open and shined her penlight at his pupil. It was unresponsive. She settled back in the recliner under the blanket. It was difficult to concentrate on her studies.

"Come here."

Without looking up, Rory said, "You're not real. You're a hallucination."

"I've been called a lot of things, but this is the first time I've been called a hallucination." He chuckled. "Come here. Don't worry. Those cameras won't pick up anything."

Reluctantly, she stood and inched closer, but stayed outside the camera's range. His assurance meant nothing.

"You have been chosen to lead the rebellion."

"Don't say that," she whispered, then silently mouthed, *What rebellion?*

"God's children against the Order."

"I'm supposed to lead children? That's crazy." She shook her head.

"Not children as in a child. God calls his followers children. You're to lead his followers out of oppression."

Rory sucked in her breath as her heart hammered against her chest. He was going to get her arrested, except how could he if he wasn't real? This was a dream. She must have fallen asleep again. Even if she said something incriminating, it would just seem like random mumbling in her sleep.

She spoke in a normal volume in the event someone replayed the recording. "There are no gods. I'm not a rebel. I'm training to be a doctor." She returned to the recliner and intended to ignore the man. Why had she spoken to her hallucination anyway?

"Last night, you asked God to show himself. Then when you walked home, after getting off at the wrong stop, you said you would believe if you made it home."

"That's just what people say when they're desperate. It doesn't prove anything. I would have made it home, even if I hadn't said that." Rory broke out in a sweat. If she wasn't dreaming and someone reported this conversation, she would be in much deeper trouble than for stealing the Aztavix.

"People make deals with God when they are desperate because, innately, they know he's real. Jesus created the perfect storm and allowed you to die to get your attention. He told you to return and wait for his call. Then, he returned your soul to your body." He held his hand to his ear as if he held a phone. "Hello, I'm going to help you with your call."

A tingling sensation shot up her spine and into her brain. How did he know all these things? The name Jesus was familiar. It had been stored in the recesses of her mind. The nice one—he promoted love—but not even he could love the people in charge of the Order. It was rumored he died for those who didn't like him. Could he be the one who spoke to her?

No, this was crazy and dangerous. She must not appear to agree. "The Order says gods don't exist. They say that man created them and that belief in different gods caused all the world's problems. Religious people killed those who believed in different gods. It was a terrifying time. The United World Order rescued the people when they took over and banned belief in gods. Without religion to divide us, we have no reason to hate and kill."

"How is that working? Is hate gone? Do all men love each other?"

No, hate thrived.

"If there truly is no God, why does the Order execute people for discussing him?"

"Talking about a false god might convince rebels to unite. They then would attack and take many lives." She regurgitated the Order's words.

"How is this wonderful one-world system taking care of your sister?"

"What do you know about my sister?" Uneasiness flitted in her chest.

"She has the chronic virus, which requires medication your family can't afford. Why doesn't the Order provide for her?"

The man was a mind reader. How did he know so much about her? Of course, he should. He was her hallucination, so he knew everything she knew.

"Unlike the United World Order, God grants us the choice to believe in him or not. The Order abolished that right."

Everything he said rang of truth. She had to use caution. These kinds of thoughts could get her family killed.

"How does the Order explain the creation of the world?" the man asked.

"Over millions of years, intensely hot dense matter expanded to form the universe, man, animals, plants, land, and water."

"Does that make sense to you?"

"Yes." She flinched from a painful memory. Mr. Durbin, her high school science teacher, had taught the expansion theory. She asked about the composition of the density and how it magically appeared. He said no one knew. She told him that expansion as a way to create planets and stars seemed reasonable, but it didn't make sense when it came to humans, animals, and plants. He ridiculed her and encouraged the other students to do the same. After class, he beat her for defying the Order's curriculum. She stopped voicing her questions. "I'm not listening to you." She returned her attention to her e-notebook and ignored him.

For several minutes, she stared at the words on the screen, but comprehended nothing. She abandoned her studies and quietly asked, "If there is a god, where is he? Why doesn't he show himself? Why doesn't he appear on the home monitors and tell us the rules?" She gave another glance at the cameras. It was probably insane to continue speaking to him, but this could still be a dream. "Why does he allow them to say he doesn't exist? Why did he abandon us?"

"When God created the first man and woman, Adam and Eve, he walked on Earth among them. They chose to sin, to disobey God. Sin created distance between God and man. But still, God has spoken to man throughout history."

"Why did he stop?"

"He hasn't. He spoke to you last night."

Her pulse raced. "No god spoke to me last night."

This man was going to get her arrested, but she couldn't stop listening to him.

"You saw the light of his glory and heard his voice. I am here to help you."

The blood rushed from her head. Could this be real? Could he be telling the truth?

"God gave us his rules in the Bible, but the Order destroyed it. They stole citizens' possessions and assigned them the necessities they deemed appropriate based on status, which they also assigned. Businesses were ripped from families who had owned them for generations. The Order decided which businesses continued under government ownership, and the others were shut down. Imagine how you would feel if a business your family had sweated and toiled over for years was stolen."

"Citizens once owned businesses? How did that work?"

"Businesses were privately owned before the United World Order. It was a great system called capitalism. The system incentivized individuals to work to create wealth. The government served the citizens instead of dictating them."

He went on to describe banks, loans, mortgages, and taxes. He spoke a foreign language. Her brain was overheating with too much information.

Mr. Abrams's eyes took on a greater intensity. "The Order also stole individuals' freedoms. Freedom to choose their profession, employer, or where they lived."

"They don't see themselves as thieves. They see themselves as the great protector. They make choices for citizens because people choose poorly."

"Some do, and that is their right."

She narrowed her eyes at him. "Why should it be?"

"Without the right to make choices, good or bad, we are effectively slaves."

"The Order prohibits slavery."

"How can you be free if you have no freedoms?"

That was a good question. Her eyes darted to the camera. What had it recorded? "You're not real. I'm not listening to you."

The man ignored her objection and continued speaking of the world before the Order. It sounded too wonderful, like a fairy tale.

His story sucked her back in. "If what you say is true, how did the world go from what you describe to this? Why would people surrender their freedoms?"

"They didn't know that's what would happen. Wealthy and cunning, the founders of the United World Order used their money and influence to execute religious terrorist attacks worldwide. They bombed churches, mosques, and temples and killed thousands of innocent people each time. They falsely accused and prosecuted religious groups for the attacks. Many religious leaders who recognized the truth spoke out. One by one, we were falsely prosecuted and convicted."

"That's why you were in Gibbons?"

"Yes. They blew up a mosque in my city and killed 867 innocent men, women, and children." Tears formed as he spoke. "It was horrible. The blast vaporized the victims. There were no survivors. Entire families were wiped out. They planted evidence to implicate me."

"You said before the Order the courts were fair. How were you convicted if you were innocent?"

"The courts were fair until those behind the Order paid off judges, prosecutors, and juries. The judge threw out all the evidence that proved my innocence—witnesses, my alibi, even character references. Those behind the Order controlled the media outlets. They scripted the information broadcast to the people. Anyone who opposed them was arrested with trumped-up charges. Fear prevailed. People are easily manipulated when paralyzed with fear. People locked themselves in their homes, afraid to leave. Terrified citizens begged their government leaders to ban religions. The government obliged, then went a step further, and banned possession of firearms by citizens. This rendered them defenseless. Half the population supported the firearm ban, and the other half were up in arms. Get it? Up in arms." He chuckled at his joke.

"Non-military individuals owned guns?" That sounded unfathomable.

"The weapons ban caused more of an uproar than outlawing religion. People loved their guns more than their God." He shook his head in disappointment. "Some citizens resisted, but their homes were searched and weapons seized. Rumor has it, some took their family and weapons and disappeared to remote areas where they are presumed to live in hiding."

Those rumors still circulated.

"After the confiscation of weapons, a proposal that all nations, including the United States of America, dissolve and form the United World Order gained momentum. The masses supported the redistribution of wealth platform. Poverty would be eliminated by closing the wealth gap, like Robin Hood."

Rory scoffed, "That's a joke. I'm living proof poverty is alive and well."

"They accused individuals who wanted to keep the money they earned of being greedy, but they never applied the same term to those who wanted to take other people's hard-earned money. The masterminds behind the Order never intended to spread the wealth evenly. They merely planned to redistribute it to themselves. They also advocated that a one-world nation would create world peace. I guess they forgot about the civil wars that plagued mankind since the beginning of time. Once people were accustomed to the new world government, the consuls declared people incapable of reaching their full potential. They claimed individuals didn't choose appropriate occupations and places to live. Infrastructure was created to assign our lives away. Businesses were nationalized. Those who protested the radical changes disappeared. The Order's grand miscalculation was they believed laws could change an individual's beliefs."

"Laws can and have changed what people believe. When people who believe in gods die and no god prevents it, it becomes obvious that gods don't exist."

"Casual believers may have lost faith, but those with a firm relationship haven't. Cells of believers exist all over the world. They covertly teach God's word. They're waiting for him to lead them in rebellion. That's where you come in."

A freezing sensation, as if she'd drank a milkshake too quickly, intensified in her brain.

Mr. Abrams winked. "That's the Holy Spirit confirming that I speak the truth."

"What?"

"The feeling in your brain is the Holy Spirit speaking to you."

"How do you know what I'm feeling? And besides, there are no spirits or gods." Poor guy, he was clearly crazy, babbling about spirits.

"Ruby told you about the feeling last night."

That confirmed it. He had to be a figment of her imagination. A search for schizophrenia revealed that a person with the condition may have difficulty distinguishing between reality and fantasy. No cure existed. If it got out that she was hearing voices, she would never be allowed to continue in the physician program.

"People with schizophrenia don't know they hallucinate. They believe the voices are real. You wouldn't suspect having it if you did."

"I recognize it because I'm studying to be a doctor."

"The stolen medication made Ruby's fever and other symptoms go away. Her symptoms are returning as I speak. This is to prove God is real and that I speak the truth." The man closed his eyes and slipped into unconsciousness.

The time was three fifteen.

She shook her head. Ruby was fine. A hallucination couldn't make her sister relapse.

Luckily, Dr. Bourland was gone when she stopped by her desk after her shift. Rory fast-forwarded the day's recording from room 377. According to the feed, the patient's eyes never opened, he never spoke, and she never answered. What was going on? Was she going crazy?

Chapter 7

"Her symptoms returned around three this afternoon." Rory's mom looked as though she'd been hit by a trans. "She's worse than ever. We've always known the Aztavix's effectiveness decreased over time. I just didn't think it would happen this suddenly."

"No!" Rory's legs buckled. She sat down hard and pinched her hand to make sure she wasn't dreaming. It hurt. This was the exact scenario the man in room 377 described, but he wasn't real. She'd replayed the recording. He never spoke. The conversation had been imagined. How had her imagination known that Ruby would get worse so quickly? She pinched herself again to focus. Her delusional state would have to wait. Ruby needed her help. "We need to purchase another Aztavix. How many credits do we have?"

Her mom wiped her brow. "Your dad and I are weeks away, and you used yours yesterday. Even if we had enough, the pharmacy won't let us purchase another one. It's too soon."

The good news was that there was no record of yesterday's capsule. The bad news was that she didn't have enough credits to purchase one yesterday, and she still didn't. "I'll tell the pharmacy I lost it. I just have to get the credits."

"It doesn't matter. It didn't even work for twenty-four hours," Mom moaned.

"Maybe not. Maybe the freezing temperature compromised it. It's my fault for getting off at the wrong stop." What if she'd killed Ruby by exiting the trans at

51

Station 35? If she'd just accepted the ride from that officer, the Aztavix probably wouldn't have lost its potency.

A knock at the door announced her fiancé's arrival. When she opened the door, Darius Prodit stood in the doorway with his disheveled brown hair framing his boyish face. One look at Rory erased his mischievous grin. "What's wrong?"

She threw herself into his arms. Darius wrapped her in a tight hug. Her words tumbled out as she explained Ruby's deteriorating condition. He held her at arm's length, his eyes brimming with compassion. He wiped her tear with his thumb. Strength radiated from his touch. Of course, he was the answer. Her heart pounded as she grabbed both his hands and gazed deeply into his eyes. "Do you have enough credits to purchase an Aztavix? I'll pay you back as soon as I can, maybe in a few weeks."

He shifted and stared at the ground. "You know the Order says treatment is supposed to stop when the pill stops working."

"I told you the cold weather affected it. She just needs one that wasn't subjected to the cold." Rory dropped his hands and backed up a step.

"They don't want anybody to be a drain on society. You know that's the way it works. The strong survive and the weak, well, the weak ... you know ..." He looked away.

"Say it. The weak die. But that's not exactly true, is it? The weak and *poor* die. The Order says they provide for our needs. Apparently, medication for the lower classes is unnecessary. If she was the daughter of a consul, she would receive all the medication she needs or wants because they don't pay for it. They consider people like my family a drain on society."

Darius embraced her and said matter-of-factly, "You know how it works. The more productive citizens get more credits, a better place to live, and better everything. It's because your mother had to quit her job to take care of Ruby that you're in this predicament. Well, and because your dad's a sanitation worker. It'll be better when you're a doctor."

She broke free of his embrace. Her blood boiled every time he implied the Order's rules made sense. She normally bottled those feelings, but this time, the bottle exploded. It took all her restraint to refrain from slapping him. She spoke through gritted teeth. "My father shouldn't be a sanitation worker."

He held his hands up in surrender. "I didn't say he should be, but his test results did."

"You can't believe that. Darius, you're smarter than this. How can you fall for their propaganda?"

"He's your dad, you love him, but you've got to admit he doesn't have much drive."

She shoved her finger into his chest. "He has picked up garbage in rain or shine for over twenty years. How motivated do you think you'd be? They say the occupation placements are based on testing, but that's a load of crap. My father is more intelligent than most of the people in the physician program. I'm certain they aren't smart enough to pass the qualifying test, yet there they are. Even if the testing is legit, being good at an occupation takes more than answering questions correctly. It's about interests and passions. Our occupations shouldn't be dictated. I'm sick of them controlling every aspect of my life. We have no freedoms. We're basically slaves."

His face paled, and his eyes grew large. He looked around like he thought someone in the apartment might report her traitorous talk. "The tests are good. They picked right for us."

"You love your job, but I want to be a researcher. I want to discover a cure for LI. Since they've been assigning occupations, there have been no innovations. Prior to the Order, there were constant medical and technological advances. But advancements cease when people aren't allowed to pursue their passions."

"Most everything's already been invented. What do you want? To drive spaceships? Or maybe you want to live on the moon?"

His patronizing tone grated on her last nerve. "Plenty of improvements in medicine, transportation, and communication would happen, if people were allowed to pursue their dreams."

"This isn't about our jobs. It's about accepting what's going to happen to Ruby. You know LI will kill her. That's what happens when you have LI. You've done everything you could." He grasped her shoulders.

She clenched her jaw. "Medication is available and being denied because we can't afford it. You make it sound so casual, saying this is the natural order. This is *my sister* we're talking about."

"She's very sick. She's going to die. It's just a matter of time."

Rory shrugged his hands off. "We're all going to die. It's just a matter of time."

If looks could kill, Darius would be lying on a slab in the morgue.

He rubbed his hands across his face. "I'm sorry. I'm not saying this right. You know there's no cure."

"There is no cure *yet*. There will be."

"There probably won't be one in time for Ruby. So, your family will use all your credits on her pills while you barely have enough food, and she dies anyway." He reached for her hand. "I know you love her, and you don't want her to suffer. It's time to let her go."

Why didn't he just stab her through the heart? She jerked her hand away. "Correction, it's time I let you go. You should leave." Tears streamed as she turned her back to him. How could he be so callous?

He released a huge sigh. "You're upset. You're saying things you don't mean."

"Oh, I mean everything I'm saying."

"Rory, I know you don't want her to suffer." His eyes darted around the room. "The things you said tonight, well, you need to be careful who's around when you say things."

She pointed to the door. "Leave."

"I'm sorry. I hope Ruby gets better." He reached for her, but she backed away.

The hurt reflected in his face, but she didn't care. Pain pierced her heart.

At the door, he turned and said, "I'll see you tomorrow."

She slammed the door behind him. Was it possible to hate someone she loved? Yes, when he implied Ruby didn't deserve to live. Anger, fear, and betrayal swirled into a heartbreaking cocktail. She swiped at her tears. Did she even know Darius?

Mom bathed Ruby in cool water in an effort to lower her fever.

Rory ate a bowl of soup in silence. The meal was meager because they'd spent most of their credits on medication. What kind of person would she be if she let her sister die so she would have more to eat? Why wouldn't Darius give up any of his precious credits for her sister? How could he be the same guy who made her walk on air when he first noticed her in high school? Attractive and popular, his interest in her never made sense. Assigned to a courier position, he delivered documents to Order officials and the military. He loved his job. At the moment, she couldn't stand to see him again, much less marry him.

She rotated the engagement band on her finger. How much could she get if she sold it? Maybe enough to cover the capsule if they used all their credits too. Tomorrow after shift, she would stop by Walton Street and see what an arranger would offer.

After her mom settled Ruby in bed, she asked Rory if she was okay.

Discussing Darius was off the table, so she said she was fine.

Her mom retired for the night, but Rory stayed up with her turbulent thoughts. Citizens should be allowed to make their own decisions, right or wrong. Maybe her hallucinations were her repressed musings rising to the surface. But how could her repressed thoughts predict Ruby's relapse?

The words in her textbook ran through her mind without pausing. Deeper thoughts collided in her head crashing off each other. She gave up trying to study and changed into her nightgown. After she crawled into bed, she stroked Ruby's feverish cheek. Ruby looked sweet and innocent. Why couldn't only evil people contract LI? Why did the good suffer?

The entire evening seemed unreal. Had Ruby's symptoms truly returned? Had Darius refused to use his credits? Had he even been there? With the stress of Ruby's illness, her mom wasn't strong enough to deal with Rory's experiences. She would have to keep everything to herself.

The sensation of heat as she stroked Ruby's cheek meant she wasn't hallucinating at the moment. She covered her eyes with her arm. A talking comatose patient, conversations not picked up on camera, and an accurate prediction simply added up to a bunch of weird hallucinations and one strange coincidence. She was no leader and certainly no rebel. Now that idea was crazy.

Chapter 8

Exhausted from another night without sleep, Rory stifled a yawn while checking her schedule. Mr. Abrams wasn't listed. Did he die? She pulled up his chart. His vital signs were strong, too strong. How was that possible?

"Rydell, has your comatose patient spoken anymore?" Dr. Bourland asked.

She shot dagger eyes at him.

He pointed. "That look should be banned by the Order as a lethal weapon."

"I'm sorry." She rubbed her forehead.

"Glad to see you're back to normal. It's bizarre that patient is still breathing." He grabbed his e-notebook and logged in.

"You can say that again."

"It's bizarre—"

She fired another lethal look.

The doctor smiled.

The morning was busy as they completed their rounds and charted. As soon as Dr. Bourland left for lunch, Rory popped in on Mr. Abrams. His eyes fluttered open upon her entrance.

"You couldn't stay away?" The man grinned.

"Ruby deteriorated last night."

His smile fell. "It's a sign, so you will believe."

"God's going to kill her so that I'll believe? I don't want to serve a god who kills my sister. It's not like I can lead anything, anyway." She sank onto the chair beside the bed.

"God will heal her before the end of this day as a further sign. She will be healed of the virus, not just the symptoms."

Her heart fluttered, and her brain tingled, but the man's words were ludicrous.

"You don't believe me?"

"I want to believe everything you say ... well, not everything. I want to believe Ruby will be healed, but I don't really want to believe I'm supposed to lead a rebellion." She leaned closer and reached out a hand to touch him. The skin on his arm was rough, weathered, and real. "How are you still alive?"

"When my purpose is fulfilled, I will join my wife." He stared wistfully into space.

"Join her where?"

"In heaven."

"She's dead?"

"Child, she's more alive than you or me. Cancer took her shortly before the bombings started. By the time she was diagnosed, the cancer had metastasized. She went quickly. Thankfully, she didn't suffer long. I was devastated. She was beautiful inside and out. I didn't want to live without her." His eyes revealed his intense love.

"Did you pray for God to heal her? If you did, why didn't he?"

"As humans, we look at death as bad, as the end of life. If you believe in Jesus Christ as Savior, life begins when you die." His face creased with laugh lines as he smiled.

She stared blankly.

"She lives in heaven, in paradise. To your point, God certainly could have healed her. I believe he spared her from witnessing the debauchery of the United World Order. And it was easier for me to accept my path. Without her, I didn't care if they executed me." He blinked his misty eyes. "They publicly announced my execution and gave my daughter a jar of ashes. Then they threw me in solitary. Solitary was worse than you can imagine."

"I think if I was in prison, I'd prefer solitary." It was a topic of interest as of late.

"Make no mistake, solitary is torture." With a haunted look, he continued, "At first, I was relieved, but it turns out being cut off from all human contact, sound, and touch is the worst form of torture. What's the longest you've been alone? Totally alone with complete silence."

She shrugged. "I'm not sure, a few hours, probably three or four."

"A few hours is a nice reprieve—twenty years is torture."

Sometimes, a life where she never saw or spoke to anyone other than her family sounded preferrable. Some family members were optional. Would she miss human interaction? Probably not.

"The lights shined all the time. I didn't know when one day ended or another began. I couldn't sleep, and I hallucinated. Sometimes they were pleasant, other times terrible. I couldn't distinguish between hallucinations and reality." He shuddered at the memory. "The pain was unbearable. I was angry at God. I thought he had abandoned me."

"Sounds like a fair assessment."

Passion lit his crystal blue eyes. "No, it was me who abandoned him. I felt sorry for myself, so I stopped talking to him. I missed people, companionship. I missed sound, hearing voices. I missed darkness. On the verge of madness, I asked God why he didn't let the Order kill me. Then I heard his voice. He said I wasn't alone. He was beside me and would never leave me. He reminded me that I wouldn't die until I met the leader of his rebellion. I would impart knowledge to him, er, you. I argued that I couldn't survive the loneliness. He said together we would, and we have. I slept for the first time in I don't know how long. I decided to change my attitude. I praised him for everything."

"You thanked him? For what? Letting you rot in prison?"

"Yes, I thanked him that I was worthy to suffer imprisonment for his sake."

Rory couldn't stop her eye roll. "Seriously?"

"Should you find yourself in a similar situation, remember that daily talks with him kept me sane."

Her eyebrows shot up. Sane was questionable.

"I had no sense of time, so it's hard to say, but I think God allowed me to sleep for days, maybe months, at a time. I expected to meet God's leader in weeks or perhaps a year or two. I never dreamed it would take over twenty years."

"Why did they send you to the hospital now? If what you say is true, you displayed symptoms of a coma for years."

"My words are true. I am here now because you are. God promised I would meet and instruct you."

She shook her head. "No, your god promised you would meet the leader, not me. If you are real and not my mental creation, surely you can see that I am not and can never be a revolutionary leader. Look at me. You're supposed to meet someone else."

"You might as well stop denying it and accept it. God often uses the least likely person. He used David, a young man, to defeat a giant warrior with a slingshot. In this situation, if God chose a valiant, charismatic leader, the people would attribute the downfall of the Order to the leader instead of God. He needs a leader who depends on him, one who recognizes her inadequacy. He needs someone *exactly* like you."

She shook her head. "You're delirious. I don't even know this god you speak of."

"That's why I'm here, to introduce you. I'll instruct you until my time is up. Then another will take over. What year is this?"

"2078."

"I was in solitary for twenty-four years."

"Why is God doing something now? Why wait over twenty years?"

A haunted look crossed his features. "In his infinite wisdom, he knew his people had to be stripped of their comforts to humble them in order to find their way back. History repeats itself. You'd think we'd learn, but we don't.

Throughout history, people don't value freedom until they lose it. Now that we're broken, we're ready to fight. This is where you come in."

"Why me?"

"Your role was planned before your birth. God will guide you. Don't fear what people do to you. He will protect you."

"Well, I am afraid of what people will do to me, particularly the Order people. I can't do this. It should be you. You believe. God talks to you. I don't even know if I believe." Rory had a hard time catching her breath.

With a far-away gaze, Mr. Abrams said, "I tried to warn people. They ignored me. The time wasn't right. God will heal your sister as a sign that you are to lead his people."

"I'm still waiting to see that happen." She blinked back tears.

"You will witness her healing before the day ends."

She looked at her feet. "I'm not a rebel."

"It won't be you. It will be God. You're stronger than you think. You rebelled when you stole the medication and when you questioned the Order's creation theory."

"After they beat me, I stopped questioning."

"On the trans car, you asked God to show himself because you believed."

Might as well play along with her hallucination. Maybe leading a delusional life with a healed sister and a pretend revolution wouldn't be so bad. "So, what am I supposed to do?"

"I'll teach you about God."

She rubbed her forehead. "How will learning about God help me lead a rebellion?"

"God gave us instructions in the Bible. When you study those directions, you develop a relationship with him. The devil will speak to you using words similar to God's, but he twists them to throw you off."

"Who's the devil?"

"An angel who rebelled against God. It is imperative to be well versed in the Bible to know whether it is God or the devil who speaks to you."

The man's logic made sense for an imaginary revolution. "Wouldn't choosing a leader who already possessed this knowledge be more efficient?"

"God chose you. He knows what he's doing."

That was debatable.

While she listened, Mr. Abrams summarized from the creation of the world through Noah building an ark to save his family, along with two of every animal. The rest of mankind was destroyed in a great flood.

"So, two of every animal—elephants, tigers, lions, bunnies, and all animals—went on this boat with eight people, and there were no casualties?"

"Correct."

Her eyes rolled before she could stop them. She glanced at the clock. She had exceeded her lunch hour. After a quick goodbye, she walked briskly down the hall. Luckily, she beat Dr. Bourland to their station.

The remainder of the day was spent on patients with scheduled appointments. Overbooked, she was unable to drop back by room 377 to see the patient that all the doctors had given up on.

At the end of the day, Rory tramped to the trans station. She plopped onto her usual seat in an unoccupied section. With the side of her head resting against the window, she stared but didn't see. Absentmindedly, she twisted the engagement band on her finger. Mr. Abrams had promised Ruby would be healed. Before she haggled with the arrangers, she would check on her sister. If a healed Ruby greeted her at the door, the trip wouldn't be needed. But precious time would be wasted if Ruby was confined to bed as sick or sicker. She banged her head against the glass as hope and hopelessness duked it out.

Chapter 9

Her mom's face said it all when Rory burst through the door, but she asked anyway. "Has there been any change?"

Her mom shook her head. "She slept all day. I tried to wake her to eat but couldn't rouse her."

Unable to contain her emotions any longer, Rory burst into tears. There was no god. Mr. Abrams was a figment created to produce a miracle for Ruby.

"I'm afraid this is the end." Her mom buried her face in Rory's shoulder.

Rory held her mom but lacked any comfort to share. Why didn't she go to Walton Street? It was too late now.

Mindlessly, they prepared dinner in silence. Rory chopped an onion and some celery to add to boiling water and rice while her mom removed the bread from the oven.

Like zombies, she and her parents sat at the gray metal and Formica table. The rice soup cooled as grief strangled their appetites.

The mattress creaked from their bedroom. Had Ruby finally awakened? Rory placed her spoon on the table. She should check on her. It might be her last chance to say goodbye. A lump blocked her throat. How could she face her sister after failing her?

Bare feet slapped against the cement floor. Rory spun around, and her mouth dropped open.

Ruby bounced into the room clad in gray pajamas. "I'm starving. What's to eat?"

Mom grabbed Ruby's arm and pulled her over, placing a hand to her cheek. "Your fever broke." She threw her arms around her daughter.

"Yeah, I feel good. I mean really good. I can't remember ever feeling this good." Ruby pulled free and grabbed a slice of bread.

Rory stared at her sister. Eyes bright. An impish smile on her lips. Ruby never looked better. It was a true miracle.

But then, Rory's palms erupted in sweat. God existed. He'd healed Ruby. He fulfilled his promise. Now she had to step up and make good on her end. She chewed her lip.

Her eyes darted from her parents to Ruby. When was the last time they looked this happy? Should she tell them God healed Ruby, not the meds? Should she tell them about Mr. Abrams? No, she couldn't ruin the moment.

Ruby took a seat at the table, and her mom placed her own bowl of soup in front of Ruby.

Between spoonfuls of soup, Ruby said, "I had the strangest dream. I was burning up. I heard voices. I didn't know where they came from, but they told me to 'touch his garment.' Then, I saw feet wearing sandals, and a white robe floated above them. The robe was so white it glowed. I stretched out my hand, but I was too far away. I crawled, holding my hand out like this." She demonstrated with her hand outstretched. "I barely touched the robe with my finger. But as soon as I touched it, I woke up, and I felt great!"

Her parents exchanged peculiar glances. Mom opened her mouth to speak but stopped when Dad shot her a deadly look and shook his head no. Rory inherited her dagger-eye skill from him. Mom could barely contain herself.

Had Ruby's dream really been a dream? Or was it an encounter?

A knock at the door interrupted their moment. When Rory answered it, her heart turned cold at the sight of Darius. He looked nice in his blue button-down shirt tucked into khaki slacks, but she scowled.

Darius smiled and held up his account card. "Grab your coat. Let's go pick up that pill."

Just like that, her anger thawed. Rory gave him a tight hug and murmured through tears, "She doesn't need it."

"I-I'm so sorry. I—" Ruby ran to the door, and his jaw dropped. It took a moment for him to close his mouth, then another moment before he spoke. "When Rory said you didn't need it, I thought ... I thought ..."

"You thought what?" Ruby asked innocently.

He ran a hand through his hair.

"You thought I meant she died? No, I mean she's better!" Rory shoved him.

He released a sigh. "That's great. I don't know if I could've lived with myself if she had, you know ... Rory, I love you so much." He grasped her hands.

"I love you too." She threw her arms around him, and butterflies swarmed her stomach as they kissed. Funny how she detested him a few minutes ago, and now she was crazy in love.

"Come, eat with us." Ruby pulled Darius from Rory's embrace.

"I already ate, but you go ahead." Sensitive to their struggle to afford food, he always ate before he visited. "My mom made oatmeal raisin cookies and sent some." He pulled a bag from his coat pocket and handed it to Ruby.

"I love her cookies." Ruby snatched the bag, opened it, and took a big whiff. "The cinnamon smells so good. This is turning out to be the best day ever."

"Eat dinner first." Mom reminded her.

Ruby sighed, closed the bag, and carefully placed it by her bowl of soup.

Before Ruby contracted the virus, they had enough credits to splurge on treats like cookies. The night felt like old times, actually like better times. Except when Rory thought about the revolt. She gazed at Darius, and her stomach flipped. He was a staunch Order supporter. There was no way she could lead anything against the Order while engaged to him. She released a long sigh.

All eyes zoomed in on her.

65

Her face warmed. "I'm just relieved Ruby's better."

"We're all surprised by Ruby's recovery. I thought today was the end," her mom said. "But then she came out of the bedroom as if she'd never been sick."

"What happened?" Darius asked.

"Can't explain it." Dad shrugged. "Maybe a delayed reaction to the pill."

Happy conversation filled the room. Rory smiled and nodded along, but her thoughts raced.

After Rory finished eating, Darius pulled her to the corner of the living room. They sat on chairs with cracked, gray plastic seat cushions. He held her left hand in both of his and announced, "I'm up for a promotion."

"That's great. You deserve it."

"Thanks. They're sending me to training."

"Where?"

"The West Coast facility. It's supposed to be really nice there. It's for eight weeks, and we're not allowed to communicate with anyone outside the facility."

"Eight weeks is a long training. I'll miss you."

"It's not that long. It'll go by fast. You won't even have much of a chance to miss me." He bounced her hand on his knee.

This would allow her time to figure out what she was supposed to be doing. "It will pass quickly. Are you traveling by train or bus? The train would be faster and more comfortable."

His brown eyes sparkled. "They're flying me. Can you believe it? I get to fly in an airplane, just like the consuls."

"Seriously, you're flying? I don't know anyone who has flown." She lightly slapped his shoulder. "They must have big plans for you." Her stomach tied in knots as she uttered the statement.

"I don't know about that, but my promotion is going to be great for us." He rotated the thin band on her left ring finger. "When I get back, I'll be able to buy you the ring you deserve."

In an effort to hide her rising panic, she pulled her hand away and held it up. "There's nothing wrong with this ring. It's silly to waste credits on a piece of jewelry."

Darius got down on one knee and gazed into her eyes. "It's a symbol of my love for you. This was all I could afford when I proposed, but it'll be different after my promotion. I'll qualify for logistics housing and an increase in credits. We can go ahead and get married as soon as my housing assignment comes through."

"What?" Blindsided by his words, she scrambled to recover. "We agreed we'd marry in a couple of years when I qualify for medical housing."

"Why wait? The logistics sector is nice. We can move to medical when you qualify. I don't want to wait." His brows rose.

Ruby's healing changed everything. It had sparked belief within Rory's heart. That belief in God would make her a traitor in Darius's eyes. Even though she loved him, she couldn't marry him. It wouldn't be fair. "I'm sorry. This has been a crazy day. I'm having trouble concentrating. Remember how upset I was last night? Ruby's better now, but it's a lot to wrap my mind around. We'll talk about our wedding date and where we'll live when you return. But please, don't buy another ring. This is the one you gave me when you proposed. It's the only one I want." She hugged him. How would she be able to break off their relationship without hurting him?

His crushed expression broke her heart.

"You look tired. After you get some rest, you'll change your mind. Rory, I don't want to wait. I'm ready for you to be my wife. I love you so much." He caressed the back of her neck.

She stared at the floor. "I love you too, but I'm afraid living with you will distract me."

"That's for sure. Once we're living together, I'm definitely going to distract you, all the time." With a devilish grin, he nuzzled her ear.

67

"This is what I'm talking about. I can't have these distractions while I'm studying. When do you leave?" Rory took his hand.

"Next Monday." He hugged her. "I better be going. Get some rest. See you tomorrow?"

"Sure."

They walked to the door hand in hand. He placed his palms on each side of her face and tenderly kissed her. After she closed the door behind him, she rested her forehead against it as she braced herself for the impending storm.

Chapter 10

Rory normally slept in on her days off but her jittery nerves didn't allow it this morning. She rose and dressed hastily. The sooner she arrived at the hospital, the quicker she could receive Mr. Abrams's interpretation of Ruby's experience. Since it was not uncommon for her to show up at the hospital on a day off to review patients' cases, no one would question her presence.

When she arrived, she made a beeline to Mr. Abrams's room. The words poured out as she narrated the events of the prior evening. He hung to her every word. As she concluded, she collapsed into the chair beside his bed with a huge sigh.

Mr. Abrams raised a hand toward heaven. "Praise God. He revealed himself when he healed Ruby. Her experience is like the woman in the Bible who suffered with constant bleeding for years. She believed she would be healed if she touched his clothing, and she was."

"Was it a dream or a vision, or did Jesus appear to Ruby in our apartment?"

"Only Christ knows. Does it matter? She was healed by his grace."

"Yes, but it also means I must lead a revolution. Honestly, just thinking about it makes me want to throw up." She chewed on her bottom lip.

He patted her hand. "God is with you. That being said, following God won't necessarily be easy, but it is always worth it. You will be tested and think you're too weak, but you aren't. I am privileged to meet you and play a small role in your journey. I'm a little sad I won't be around to see how God uses you." A tear formed in the corner of his eye.

She swallowed a lump in her throat to ask her most pressing question. "Why was I chosen? I'm not a good person."

"God sees who you can become. None of us are good. But God created us to live in close communion with him. When we do things that are wrong, those sins separate us from God. We feel lost. Something is missing."

His words resonated with her. The emptiness she'd kept trying to fill was God's absence from her life.

"In his mercy, God provided a conduit to reconnect with us. His Son, Jesus Christ, willingly died on the cross to atone—to take the punishment—for our sins. If you repent, you will be forgiven, and your sins will be remembered no more."

"He took the punishment for me? But that isn't fair."

"You're right. Fairness has nothing to do with it. It demonstrates the depth of God's love for us. The good news is that you can cover your sins with Christ's sacrifice. Admit you're a sinner, ask forgiveness of your sins, and surrender your will to him. Tell him you believe Christ died for your sins and was raised from the dead."

"Raised from the dead? Jesus was healed like Ruby?"

"Not exactly. Three days after he died, God brought him back to life just like the Bible said it would happen."

A freezing sensation tingled in her brain as the message of unconditional love started to emerge. "But why did God love us enough to let his Son die?"

"I can't explain it, but when you give yourself to God and experience his perfect love, you will understand. There is no better feeling. He wants to save you. Are you ready to accept his gift of salvation?"

Goosebumps formed on her arms as she closed her eyes. She was ready, but how was this done? Mr. Abrams grasped her hand.

Her eyes popped open. "What do I say?"

"Thank him for giving his Son, then ask for forgiveness."

Would he forgive her? She closed her eyes again and bowed her head. "God, thank you for sending your Son to take the punishment I deserve. I'm sorry I have sinned. I believe you brought Jesus to life again. I was searching for you, even though I didn't know who you were. I don't see how someone like me," she whispered, barely audible, "can help you overthrow the Order." Tears trickled down her cheeks. "Please, tell me what you want me to do. Thank you for forgiving me." She opened her eyes. Her shoulders relaxed as her tension melted. Could it be that easy?

Rory grabbed a tissue from the nightstand and blew her nose.

I don't make mistakes.

Her head whipped toward Mr. Abrams. "Did you say that?"

"Say what?"

"Nothing, never mind." Was God talking to her? Encouraging her that she could do this? She exhaled slowly.

Mr. Abrams sniffled, breaking her from her trance. She handed him a tissue.

He dabbed at his nose. "Accepting Christ is the best decision you'll ever make. I'm so proud of you." He squeezed her hand. "Now that you've accepted Christ, it's time for water baptism."

"What's that?"

"Submersing a believer under water is symbolic of burying the old sinful life and rising to a new spiritual one. We don't have access to a pool of water to dunk you, so we'll improvise. Pour a cup of water and bring it to me." His smile lit up his entire face.

She poured half a cup of water, in case he emptied it over her.

Mr. Abrams dipped two fingers into the water and motioned for her to lean toward him. "Rory Rydell, do you believe Jesus is the Son of God and that he died for your sins?"

"Yes."

"Do you ask forgiveness of your sins and surrender your will to him?"

"Yes, at least I'll try."

With damp fingers, he outlined the symbol of a cross on her forehead. "I baptize you in the name of the Father, the Son, and the Holy Spirit." He lifted his hands toward the ceiling and ordered, "Arise as a new creation in Jesus Christ."

A jolt of energy made her shiver. *A new creation.* Now that had a nice ring to it.

Mr. Abrams raised his head and kissed her cheek. Hope, joy, and love surged in her soul. The burdens that had weighed on her floated away.

"You remind me of my daughter, Ruth." He closed his eyes. "I miss her so much."

"Do you know where she is? If I could contact her, maybe she could visit." Reuniting him with his daughter would repay him for some of the things he'd done for her.

"No, it isn't safe for her to visit." His blue eyes darkened.

"I'll sneak her in. No one will know. What's her last name? Do you have any idea where she lives?"

"Listen to me. Bringing her here would be dangerous for both of you."

Rory opened her mouth to press the issue but closed it at the fear in his eyes. He was right. It would be dangerous. Time to change the subject. "How does God decide who he heals?"

"He heals people to reveal himself, like with Ruby. He heals in response to an individual's faith. Sometimes he doesn't heal, like with my wife, because it was better for her to leave this world. Why do you ask?"

"There's a patient, Chad Taylor. He has LI. The Aztavix isn't relieving his symptoms for very long. He probably has a few months to live unless God heals him. I thought maybe you could pray for him."

"Why don't you pray for him?"

She shrugged. "You've known God longer, and you're a better person, so God is more likely to answer your prayer."

"It doesn't matter how long you've known him. It has to do with faith."

"You've got more of that too."

He held out his hand. "I'll join you in prayer. Does Chad know Christ?"

"I don't really know him, but probably not. His father's a proconsul."

"First, let's pray that Chad and his family find salvation and then for healing."

"This is why *you* should pray. You think about these things." If she couldn't even make a proper prayer request, how was she supposed to lead a revolt?

"You start, and I'll add a few words at the end."

When she closed her eyes, she went blank. After several seconds, she plunged in. "I'm sorry, I'm not familiar with prayer protocol. Will you show yourself to Chad Taylor and his family so they can know you? That's the most important thing. Then if it's not too much trouble, please heal Chad of Longus Influenza. Mr. Abrams says I need faith for my prayers to be answered, so I probably need you to give me some of that. I don't deserve anything, and I'll understand if you don't answer my prayer. Okay, I guess that's it." She opened one eye and sneaked a peek at Mr. Abrams.

He didn't disapprove. He smiled. "Jesus, I agree in prayer with Rory for the salvation of this precious family and the healing of their son. You don't desire for any to perish. I pray for Chad's healing and for his family to recognize the healing comes from you. Thank you for hearing and answering our prayers. We pray that your will be done. Amen."

God's will was a foreign concept. Per Mr. Abrams, it was God's will for his Son to die a painful death for the mistakes of others. If he didn't spare his Son, would he spare her? Not likely.

Chapter 11

Each morning after Rory's profession of faith, she woke with a smile. Life was no longer haphazard. An omnipotent God was in control. At every opportunity, even on her days off, she visited Mr. Abrams and soaked up the biblical knowledge he freely shared. Her soul hungered for God's Word. One day was like a thousand years to God, so it could be many years before she was thrust headlong into her call.

One morning, after finishing early with patients, she glanced up at the bank of monitors. Dr. Ahmid stood in Chad's room along with his parents. She quickly inserted her earbuds.

Dr. Ahmid smiled broadly. "Chad's test results indicate he is negative for LI."

Chad's mother dropped into a chair as both parents stared wide-eyed at the doctor.

"Are you sure?" Proconsul Taylor asked.

Dr. Ahmid scratched his bald head. "I ran the test three times. All three returned negative."

The proconsul shook the doctor's hand vigorously. "We can never thank you enough!"

Mrs. Taylor clung to Chad and sobbed. "It's a miracle."

"The only miracle was Dr. Ahmid arranging the daily Aztavix." He gave his wife a sharp look, then returned his gaze to the doctor. "I know you put your career on the line. Your son will be placed in the physician training program and watch your Treasury account for an increase."

"That's not necessary," the doctor protested.

"Oh, but it is. We are forever in your debt."

They were forever in God's debt. They just didn't know it.

The doctor rubbed his bald head. "Actually, I'm shocked. I had hoped the treatment might buy him some time, but I never expected it to cure him. You cannot report this to anyone. I could lose my license."

"Of course. We'll never breathe a word," the proconsul assured the doctor.

Rory burst into Mr. Abrams's room and announced, "God healed Chad Taylor." She shared all she had overheard.

"Praise God. He answered your prayer." Mr. Abrams beamed.

"It probably was yours, but Chad's mom might believe. She called it a miracle. I don't really care whose prayer it was. I'm just happy for him."

"Most likely, it was a combination. Does this help you believe in the power of prayer?"

"It does. I'm praying for all my patients. I figure it can't hurt."

"That's the spirit." After a pause, he said, "I'll be going home soon. After I'm gone, find Henry Leeman."

No, not yet. There was so much she still didn't know. If she argued, he'd only say it was God's will. Her eyes stung. "Who is he, and where will I find him?"

"He was a good friend and one of the elders of my church. A strong man of faith. I don't know where he is, but God will lead you."

"When was the last time you spoke to this Henry Leeman?"

"Right before I was imprisoned."

She rolled her eyes. "Over twenty years ago? You don't even know if he's still alive."

"I know he is."

"How?"

"God wouldn't tell me to send you to him if he wasn't."

"If God wants me to find him, then he needs to give you his address."

"What fun would that be?" He laughed. "After all the miracles you've seen, you don't think God can lead you to Henry?"

Why couldn't he understand that blind faith allowed no opportunity for planning? Planning was important. But nothing she could say would change his mind. He was so stubborn. She massaged her temples. "Okay, what can you tell me about him?"

"He was a computer programmer, a very good one."

"If he's still a programmer, he might live in the technology sector. I've never been there, but I'm sure it has thousands of homes. What do you want me to do? Knock on every door until I find him?"

"I want you to follow God's lead."

"I don't see him leading me anywhere."

His blue eyes twinkled. "He led you to me. He'll lead you to Henry."

She exhaled. "Okay, when do I start looking?"

"After I pass from this world."

"And do you know when that will be?"

"When God decides it's time, but I feel it will be soon. Tell Ruth I love her." His eyes misted over.

"Ruth, your daughter? How? All I know is her first name."

"You will know." He reached for Rory's hand and clutched it until he slid back into the coma.

Time with Mr. Abrams seemed to fly, as did time at home. Ruby flourished. Her family believed the Aztavix magically relieved Ruby's symptoms. Rory didn't enlighten them. Terror held her tongue. After she questioned the theory of evolution, the Order held her dad for two days to scare him into teaching his daughter proper loyalty. After his release, he didn't speak to her for a week. He would explode if she told him of her faith. Ruby would believe and maybe her mom, but what if telling them put them in danger?

All in all, life ran smoothly until Friday, January 28, when Rory overheard Amethyst in the locker room. "Can you believe the chief hospital pharmacist would steal drugs?"

"Who'd have thought you could be executed for stealing meds?" Costas shut his locker.

Rory broke out in a cold sweat. "What are you talking about?"

Silence filled the room. The students stared, shocked that she'd spoken to them.

"Ancil Drummond was executed yesterday." Costas broke the hush. "He was arrested about a week ago. Don't you watch the Order Reports?"

"No." Her family barely had enough electrical power to run appliances. They rarely turned on the home monitors.

"Maybe you should," Amethyst said as she admired her reflection in the mirror.

"I didn't think they would execute you for stealing one pill. I thought they would jail you or something ... less fatal." Rory's heartbeats increased, making her lightheaded.

"I doubt he stole just one." Aryan's tone was patronizing.

"They're probably making an example out of him since pharmacists have access to meds. They probably think this will keep us all in line. You look really upset." Costas gazed at Rory with raised eyebrows. "Were you friends?"

"No. It's just upsetting to hear about someone being executed." Nausea bubbled in her stomach. She rushed from the room and left the group to question her bizarre behavior.

With her hand covering her mouth, Rory shot through the restroom door. The moment she reached the commode, she hurled, then shuddered with chills.

Officials of the Order thought Mr. Drummond stole the Aztavix and executed him. He died because of her. The right thing would be for her to confess and tell them they made a mistake. But would they execute her? How would her family survive without her credits? How would Mr. Drummond's family survive without his? She had been naïve to believe it was a victimless crime. It was too late now. He was already dead. Her confession wouldn't bring him back. What should she do?

She sipped water from the faucet to rinse the vile taste from her mouth. As she pulled paper towels from the dispenser, her pale reflection stared back from the mirror. Who was this hollow person? A murderer. She was a murderer. She'd murdered Mr. Drummond.

Mr. Abrams would tell her what to do.

Rory ran full steam to room 377. The bed had been made, and it was empty. Where did they move him? She sprinted to her station, retrieved her e-notebook, and pecked at the keyboard. Mr. Abrams expired at 3:12 a.m. No, this wasn't the time for God to take him. She couldn't do this without him. Her temperature spiked. Her stomach stirred. She couldn't breathe. The room began to spin. The floor rose and smacked her in the forehead. Darkness smothered her.

***

Rory's eyes fluttered open to the scent of ammonia. Dr. Bourland held her head off the tile floor while he waved a small bottle under her nose.

"What's wrong with her?" Amethyst asked as she bent down for a closer look.

"Maybe pregnant? She looked like she was going to puke earlier, and now she's fainted? One plus one equals two." Costas held up two fingers.

"I doubt it. Who'd have sex with her?" Amethyst wrinkled her nose.

"I might." Costas shrugged. "She has a brooding sexuality about her."

"You've got to be kidding." The disgust in Amethyst's voice was unmistakable.

"It doesn't take much to excite Costas." Willow rolled her eyes.

"That's enough. Back up, give her room to breathe. Haven't you learned anything in the med program?" Dr. Bourland barked.

Heat rose in Rory's cheeks. Did she have to listen to these halfwits? Her forehead throbbed. Had she hit a brick wall? No, it had been a tile floor. She made an effort to rise.

"Don't you people have patients to attend to? Move along. Nothing to see here." Dr. Bourland shooed them. "I don't know how they were assigned to this program."

"We heard that," Amethyst said.

"I meant for you to." He helped Rory up. "What happened?"

"I ... I ... don't know. I felt sick to my stomach. I couldn't catch my breath. Then everything went black." It all came flooding back. He would be appalled if he learned the truth behind her episode. She stared at the floor.

"Could you be pregnant?" He assisted her to a chair.

"No!" It escaped a little too harshly.

"If you are, there's no reason to be ashamed."

She was ashamed because she'd killed a man, but she couldn't say that. "If I were pregnant, I wouldn't be ashamed. I'd be depressed."

"Why?"

Because she would not bring a child into a world controlled by the United World Order. Because a man was executed. Because she was a thief. Because she couldn't lead a rebellion while pregnant. But she offered a less controversial answer. "I barely have enough energy for studying. I couldn't throw a child into the mix. It doesn't matter. I can't be pregnant. I've never had sex."

"Really? I mean, it's surprising at twenty, especially since you're engaged."

She shrugged. "So, I shouldn't be embarrassed if I'm pregnant, but I should if I'm a virgin at my age?"

"I didn't mean to imply anything. Why do you think you fainted?"

"Stress, sleep deprivation, skipping breakfast. Take your pick."

"Any one of those is a possibility. Your blood sugar is probably low. Rory, you're a physician student. You know the importance of a healthy diet. You're not a healthy weight."

There it was. He finally said it. He pitied her. Anger or disappoint would have been fine. Anything but pity.

"Sit here while I get you something to eat."

With no energy to protest, Rory leaned her head against the wall. Mr. Abrams was the only person who could have advised her on what to do about Mr. Drummond, but he was gone. What were her options? She was too cowardly to confess. Drummond's death had brought out her true nature, and it was ugly.

Everything was messed up. *She* was messed up. There was no way God still wanted her for anything.

Dr. Bourland returned with a bowl of oatmeal and a banana. "Your forehead is bruised. You must have hit it on the floor. It's a good thing you have a hard head."

Rory mustered a sad smile. "Thank you. I'll buy lunch to pay you back."

"Don't worry about it. Give yourself a few minutes for it to digest, then go home. Get some sleep."

"I can't."

"You're checked in." Dr. Bourland glanced around to make sure no one overheard. "I'll check you out at the end of the day. No one will be the wiser if you don't tell them."

"No, I don't want to get you in trouble." She had caused enough trouble.

"There'll be no trouble. When you're a doctor, what will you tell a patient presenting with similar symptoms?"

"That's not fair."

"Doctors make the worst patients. Go home, eat, get some rest. That's an order. You'll feel like a new person tomorrow." He grabbed his e-notebook and headed down the hall.

He was wrong. She wouldn't feel like a new person tomorrow. She would still be a murderer. The second hand slowly circled the face of the wall clock while she sat. Should she stay, or should she go?

Twenty minutes later, Dr. Bourland returned with her coat and ushered her toward the exit. "Leave through the side entrance. Go home. I'll expect you first thing in the morning."

After she slipped her coat over her green scrubs, she slinked toward the stairs. She looked back. Dr. Bourland stood watching her.

"Go." He pointed toward the exit.

Inside the stairwell, she leaned against the wall and gasped for breath. Should she turn herself in? Why did God take Mr. Abrams now when she desperately needed him? It must be because he realized she wasn't the leader he needed.

Chapter 12

With nothing to lose and in no rush to go home, Rory boarded the trans to the tech sector. After choosing a seat next to a window, she glanced around. Eerily, she was the only passenger in the trans car.

After a forty-minute ride, the trans slowed down. Her eyes widened as she took in the sights and wonders of the tech sector. It was a different world. The massive homes constructed of bricks and stone were not cookie-cutter copies of each other. Surely, multiple families resided in each structure. One family wouldn't need all that space. These homes dwarfed the medical sector homes, and she had considered them mansions. Doctors and nurses saved lives, but technology experts were obviously held in higher esteem.

A picturesque, open area of flowers, shrubs, trees, a pond, and benches sat nestled between housing groups. A sign designated the area as Reflection Park. Rory followed a stone path to a bench and sat. Squirrels scampered and climbed trees. Absorbed in the beauty of the area, she allowed her problems to drift away. A deep breath filled her nostrils with the sweet scent of flowers and trees. Why didn't labor sector residents deserve parks?

Suddenly, the air buzzed with energy. The hair on her arms stood on end.

"Tidings." The deep-toned greeting came from behind her.

Rory jumped up and whirled in the direction of the voice. A tall, attractive man stood confidently, watching her. His well-groomed long dark hair and beard, coupled with smooth and flawless skin, made it impossible to gauge his age. He could be thirty, forty, or fifty. His loose-fitting clothing was so white it glowed. What kind of laundry detergent did he use? Actually, his skin glowed. Was the glow symptomatic of an illness?

"Good morning?" Her greeting came out as more of a question.

"Whom do you seek?"

Her heart raced. Was she in trouble? Was the park only for tech people? She lifted her gaze. The man's eyes pierced her as if he could see into her soul.

When she didn't reply, he answered his own question. "You seek Henry Leeman."

How did he know? Her heart raced. She'd stopped checking the hospital recordings after the second day. Maybe the camera recorded the conversation when Mr. Abrams told her to find Mr. Leeman.

"I am Gabriel."

"Gabriel who?"

"Just Gabriel. Do not fear. I am not here to arrest you."

His denial failed to slow her racing heart, but she might as well broach the question. "Do you know where I can find Henry Leeman?"

"Yes." But he volunteered no details.

"Are you going to tell me?"

"I am ... not."

Just her luck, a wise guy. "You know I'm looking for him, you know where he is, but you're not going to tell me?"

"Correct."

Operating on auto-pilot, she fired a lethal glare, but it was deflected by his mesmerizing gaze. She shook her head to break the trance. "Why are you here if you aren't going to tell me?"

"I bear tidings."

Tidings? Who used that word? "Who sends these tidings you bear?"

"The Lord God—"

"You can't say that." She jumped back. Her eyes darted, searching for anyone who might overhear.

"Do not fear. No one is around. As I was saying, the Lord God Almighty sends this message: 'Fear not. Trust me and obey. Lead my people back to me. I will do more than your wildest imagination.'"

Her pulse roared in her ears. She scanned the area once more. "I don't know. My imagination is pretty wild."

"Trust me. God can surpass anything you imagine."

His glowing skin was really odd and so was his speech. Could he be? "Who exactly are you? I mean, what is your occupation?"

"I am a messenger from God, an angel." His smile sparkled.

Her knees buckled, and she sat on the ground. An angel, sent by God, was speaking to her, Rory Rydell. She rubbed her eyes. This had to be a dream.

"Just breathe. You are not dreaming."

"This is so unreal. God healed Ruby to prove he called me. I'm grateful, I really am, but I can't deliver anyone. There has to be someone more qualified."

"True—"

"Yes, thank you! Finally, someone's listening. So, you'll tell God I can't do this?" Her breath whooshed out as her hand went to her heart.

"Your capabilities do not matter. The Lord uses you as a vessel. David was a great warrior, yet he did not win battles. His strength came from the Lord. The Order will suffer defeat by God's might and your obedience."

"David was strong and looked like a leader, even if God did the work. Someone who looks like David is the kind of person people will rally around, not someone like me." Her shoulders drooped.

"God desires those who trust and obey. Just as through faith, Abraham took Isaac to the altar, Moses led Israel out of Egypt, and David faced Goliath, you must step out in faith to face the Order."

"All those guys are better than me. I'm not special. I'm not even good." She looked at the ground.

"Stop listening to the devil."

"What?" She looked up.

"The devil tells you that you are unworthy. He is a liar." Gabriel's eyes sparkled as he gazed into hers. "When the devil speaks, rebuke him in the name of Jesus."

"I can do that? I can make the devil stop talking? But the things he says are true. I've made terrible mistakes."

"God does not use you because you are righteous. He does not deliver the people because they are righteous. He delivers them because of his love for them and the wickedness of the Order. You only need to step out in faith. All those that you consider better made mistakes. All were ordinary people asked to do extraordinary things. Empowered by the Holy Spirit, they accomplished great things, as you will." Gabriel pointed to his eyes and then to her. "God sees you not as you are but as you can be."

She stood and wiped the dirt from the seat of her coat. "Mr. Abrams told me that, but I'm scared. I wish I could see this person that you say I can be."

Gabriel smiled. "I see someone who is beautiful inside and out."

Her cheeks burned. "Thank you." She leaned closer. "Your skin is so … Why does it glow?"

Gabriel chuckled softly. "You observe a reflection of the Lord's splendor."

The fact that God sent a radiant angel to speak to her raised a question. "How can God want me after what happened to Mr. Drummond?" Tears stung her eyes.

"Dry your tears. God loves you unconditionally. It is not earned. You do not deserve it. He chooses to love you, regardless of your faults."

She scratched the ground with her foot. "But you don't know what I've done."

"You did not kill Ancil Drummond. He is not dead."

Her heart leaped. "The Order lied about executing him?"

"He lives in heaven."

His words crushed her momentary redemption.

"They executed him because they thought he stole the Aztavix, but I'm the thief. I should be the one they executed." She averted her eyes again.

"Do not assume."

Her heart fluttered. "What do you mean? He didn't die because of me?"

"All things happen for a reason."

"Mr. Drummond didn't die because I stole the capsule? Or he died because I stole it, but it's okay because, for some reason, it fits into God's plan?"

"The reason does not matter."

Her gaze fell to the bottom of his shining garment. Raising her head, her glance was met by his clear, grace-filled eyes. "It matters to me. I need to know if I'm responsible."

"What good comes from this knowledge? What is done is done. Do not grieve for Ancil. He dwells in paradise."

"If Mr. Drummond died because it was God's time, it's fine, but not if I made it happen before his time."

"Believers discover true life when they pass from this world. Remember the peace you felt when Jesus spoke to you?"

It was hard to remember. So much had happened since then. "Mr. Drummond is happy he was executed?"

"He does not wish to return to this world." Gabriel gestured toward her with open arms. "Rory, your transgressions were covered when you surrendered your life to God."

"But all I did was say some words. Mr. Drummond died for something I stole. What I did was unforgiveable."

"Jesus accepted the punishment for you. Forgiveness is yours. You just have to accept it."

Was it that simple? "Okay, why did God take Mr. Abrams before he told me what I should do? I need him."

"You are far from alone."

"How can you say that? I am alone. Mr. Abrams was the only one who knew God called me, and now he's gone. I can't tell my family or anyone else because they'll think I'm crazy. I might be crazy. If anyone reports me, I'll be dead!"

"God is with you, and others will join. You are not alone."

"I don't see or hear God. And who are these others? Who will tell me exactly what I'm supposed to do?"

"Talk with God constantly. He will help you find your way. If you knew the Father's plan in its entirety, it would overwhelm you. You must trust and walk in faith."

"Not knowing overwhelms me." She sank onto the bench and hid her face in her hands.

"Faith means following God's direction when you do not understand where he leads. It means following his plan even if you are considered a fool. It means not fearing death because your reward is life everlasting."

Mr. Abrams said she needed to be prepared to suffer like Christ. Reality hit like a ton of bricks. God chose her because she was expendable. God didn't call her because she was special. She wasn't special. As a martyr, she would raise awareness for his cause. Her life didn't matter. "You said not to fear death. That's God's plan for me, isn't it, to die?" Her stomach swirled.

"You are special, and your life matters. Every human dies. Whether you follow God's plan or not, you shall pass from this world. Following his will is dangerous, but the rewards are out of this world." He flashed his pearly whites. "Humor."

Her head hurt. His mind-reading capabilities gave him an unfair advantage. "Why doesn't God protect the people who follow his plan? If he can do anything, why doesn't he eliminate all the bad people and leave only the good?"

He rested his palms together. "Good and bad are ambiguous terms. No one is all good or all bad. All people are varying degrees of each. A good person does not exist. If

God destroyed all the bad people, humanity would cease to exist."

His words sailed beyond her grasp. She squeezed her eyes tight. If she could just disappear, then this would all be over. She opened her eyes, but she was still there. "What happens if I refuse to answer the call? Will Ruby's virus return?"

"God chose you because he knows your heart. He knows you will choose to follow him. You are braver than you know. Many wait to aid you."

"Is Henry Leeman one of those?"

"He is involved."

"Okay, so he's involved, and you know where he is, but you won't tell me?"

A grin stretched his face. "Hunger makes you irritable. Purchase something to eat."

"I don't waste my credits on food. I save them for Ruby's medication."

"Ruby is healed. She no longer needs medication."

True. She had celebrated Ruby's healing, but the improvement to her family's finances had escaped her. Even so, old habits were difficult to break. "I still don't waste credits."

"Nourishment is not a waste of credits." He looked up as if his attention was caught by something else. "I must go."

The messenger disappeared. Where did he go? She had another question. "Mr. Gabriel. Sir Gabriel." She spun in a circle as she searched for him.

A tap on her shoulder alerted her to his reappearance.

"I'm not sure how to refer to you."

"Just Gabriel." He smiled his brilliant smile.

"Okay, just Gabriel—"

He winked. "Ah, humor."

"There are many ways to be executed." She shuddered as several methods flashed through her mind. "Some more painful than others. May I request to be executed quickly and as painlessly as possible?"

"You may."

"God agrees?"

"I cannot promise."

She stomped a foot. "This isn't funny. I'm serious. I'm afraid if the pain is too severe, I'll deny Christ. Then they'll kill me, and I won't fulfill God's purpose."

"You are stronger than you realize."

"You say that, but I'm not. I'm not strong at all. You don't know me. If they give me a paper cut, I'll tell them everything I know." Rory searched his face for understanding.

"God knew you when he formed you. He knows who you are, and who you will be in the ages to come. He chose you. God does not make mistakes. Rory, God loves you with an everlasting love. He has forgiven you. Do not dwell on past mistakes." He cupped her chin in his hand and gazed deeply into her eyes.

At his touch, strength flowed through her body, and a scene appeared before her eyes. Hundreds or thousands of people knelt during a raging storm. The multitude of people surrendered their lives to God. The scene was clear—the Order would suffer a resounding defeat.

Breathing heavily, she blinked. The scene and Gabriel vanished. The air buzzed with a strange energy. Every fiber of her being declared the magnificence of God. Now she just needed to find Henry Leeman.

After an hour, Rory's confidence wavered when she didn't run into Mr. Leeman. What was she doing? She couldn't knock on every door. Gabriel hadn't confirmed that he even lived in the sector.

Her stomach growled as she approached a small grocery shop. Inside the store, she browsed the aisles of neat shelves. She selected a package of cheese and crackers and proceeded to the counter.

"You are beautiful," said the young man behind the register. The tag on his black shirt indicated his name was Wyatt.

Rory glanced behind her. No one was there. In fact, she and Wyatt were the only souls inside the store. This was strange. Beautiful was not an adjective normally used to describe her. Her cheeks warmed. "Thank you."

Wyatt pushed his long brown hair behind his ears. "You have a beautiful glow."

Was that his standard line to customers? He was nice enough. She smiled.

Wyatt returned her smile, revealing a dimple in his left cheek. He scanned the package. "Are you looking for someone?"

Her jaw dropped. "Yes, Henry Leeman. You don't know him, do you?"

"I do. He's a regular."

"Can you tell me where I can find him?"

"I can." The clerk entered information into the register. He wrote on a notepad, tore off the sheet and handed it to her. "Here's his address, 312 Prosper Lane."

"Thank you. You've been more helpful than you know." She handed him her account card.

"My pleasure." He returned her card and purchase, then walked her to the door and gave her directions to the address.

"Thanks again." This had to be the reason Gabriel told her to buy something to eat. It couldn't be coincidence.

The directions led her straight to the address. The door to the brick and stone two-story home was beautifully crafted from wood, iron, and glass. She stood on the sidewalk and stared at the magnificent home. What was she doing? The homeowner wouldn't invite a complete stranger inside. She turned to leave and almost bumped into a man.

"What are you looking for?" growled a sixtyish, paunchy man with gray-streaked scraggly brown hair and beard. He wore rumpled khaki pants and a white button-down shirt. A brown paper bag was in his hand.

"I found it, thank you." Was the man Mr. Leeman?

"I haven't seen you before. I would remember." He eyed her suspiciously. "There's something odd about your face."

"Excuse me?" She touched her cheek.

"Your face, it's shiny."

What was with all the talk about a glowing face? "Excuse me, I need to go."

"What are you doing here?" Desperation laced his voice. He watched as she approached the door.

Her courage evaporated as she raised her hand to knock. What would she say? Would Mr. Leeman believe her? Half the time, she didn't believe. She turned to skulk away. The man stood blocking her path. Should she stay or go? She stood paralyzed.

The front door opened. A slight woman with perfectly coiffed silver hair rescued Rory.

"May I help you?" The woman's brown eyes widened as she got a good look at Rory. "Your face … you … are you …?"

Rory's mouth dropped open.

The woman noticed the man on the sidewalk. "Come in." She gently pulled Rory inside and closed the door behind her. "You're positively glowing. What's your name, dear?"

"Rory."

The woman called over her shoulder, "Henry, come quickly. It's her. She's the one!"

Chapter 13

A lean gentleman entered the room and eyeballed Rory. He towered over her and the woman. The creases in his forehead ran deep, and his jaw was rounded with age. After a few moments, he shook his head of thick white hair. "Have you lost your mind? Look at her. She probably doesn't weigh forty kilograms soaking wet. She can't be the one."

The woman's eyes were kind. She patted Rory's arm. "Don't mind him. You're exactly the kind of person God chooses."

"Athelene," the man admonished.

The woman frowned at him and helped Rory remove her coat. She hung it in a closet off the entrance. "If God chose a big hulking man, people would credit man for our release. God often chooses the least likely person."

Rory glanced around the room. The wood and tile floors were polished to a high gloss finish. Rich beige fabric treatments adorned the windows. The cream brocade sofa looked as if no one had ever sat on it. At least they had colorful paintings, strategically placed sculptures, and decorative pieces to pop a little color into the otherwise colorless room. Everything in the labor sector was varying shades of gray. No artwork or decorations were assigned to brighten her home's décor. The term décor didn't even apply to labor sector apartments.

"Come, please sit." The woman directed Rory to the sofa.

"It's too nice. I can't." No one should sit on it, except maybe Gabriel in his bleached white clothing.

"Don't be silly. That's what it's for. Are you all right? Your forehead's bruised."

Rory touched her forehead. It was tender. "I'm okay, just clumsy."

"Are you a nurse?"

"I'm in the physician training program." She smoothed the wrinkles from her scrub top.

"Yes, green scrubs are for doctors. Where is my head? You look familiar. Have we met?"

"No. Are you Mr. and Mrs. Leeman?"

"Yes," she replied. "I'm Athelene, and the grumpy one over there is Henry."

Grumpy scowled, solidifying his designation.

"Mr. Abrams instructed me to find him." Rory nodded her head in Henry's direction.

The color drained from the couple's faces.

"David Abrams," she clarified.

The man cleared his throat. "That's impossible. He's been dead longer than you've been alive."

"He died this morning." She pushed the words out through a lump in her throat.

"David Abrams was executed over twenty years ago," Henry said.

"They tried, but they couldn't kill him." She recounted the narrative Mr. Abrams shared about the failed execution attempts. Their faces expressed shock and disbelief.

With his hands clasped behind his head, Henry looked like he'd just lost his best friend.

Athelene pressed her hands together and touched her fingertips to her lips, almost as if praying. "All these years, we thought our friend was dead, but God miraculously saved him from execution."

"You believe me?"

"Of course. Henry, why do you look sad? God's finally on the move."

"How can you be sure she's telling the truth?" He spoke softly, but Rory heard.

"David sent her. He told us he would meet *the one* and send him, rather her, to us. I've had a feeling something good was about to happen. This is it."

"So she says."

"Look at her. What else could explain it?"

What did that mean? Explain what?

"With all the excitement, I've forgotten my manners. Would you like something to eat?"

Rory was starving. But it was probably frowned upon to accept food when she'd showed up uninvited. She smiled politely. "No, thank you. I had some cheese and crackers."

Athelene waved her hand. "Cheese and crackers are a snack. No wonder you're thin. It's just leftover pot roast. We have plenty. We'll just end up throwing some of it out. The kitchen's this way."

It must be nice to have more food than they could eat.

In the kitchen, Athelene pulled a wooden chair from a table with a glass top and directed Rory to sit. She retrieved a container from the huge refrigerator and spooned a generous portion of roast and vegetables onto a plate.

"That's too much." Rory held up her hands. "I'll never be able to eat it all."

Athelene put the plate of food in the warming oven. "Leave what you can't eat." She leaned closer and set the timer.

The aroma of savory pot roast wafted from the oven. Rory's mouth watered, and her stomach rumbled. After Athelene set the food before her, it took all her self-control to resist stabbing a slice of roast and gnawing it from the fork. On her best behavior, she politely cut a bite. She moaned as the flavors exploded on her palate while she chewed. Her gaze shot to Mrs. Leeman. "I'm sorry, but this is the best food I've ever tasted."

The woman blushed. "I'm glad you like it."

"Athelene, can I speak to you privately?" Henry summoned his wife from the kitchen entrance.

Rory's ears perked, but she couldn't hear their conversation. With his cynical attitude, Mr. Leeman paled in comparison to Mr. Abrams. Her shoulders fell.

Savoring each bite, she chewed slowly. After she swallowed the last morsel, she picked up the plate to lick it clean. Her eyes darted to the doorway. What if they walked in and caught her in the act? God probably didn't choose plate lickers to lead revolutions. Then again, Mr. Abrams had told her about Gideon. God instructed him to separate the men who lapped water like dogs from the ones who knelt to drink. God chose the dog lappers to serve his purpose and sent the other men home. God probably would choose plate lickers. She smiled at the memory of Mr. Abrams chuckling as he told the story. He got a kick out of God selecting the less than desirable. That must be why God chose her.

The couple returned. Mrs. Leeman exuded excitement, while Mr. Leeman looked like he'd just sucked a lemon.

"Would you like more?" Athelene looked at the empty plate.

"No, thank you. I can't eat another bite. It was delicious. You're an excellent cook." She carefully folded the fabric napkin and laid it beside the plate.

"You're sweet." Mrs. Leeman set the plate in the sink. "How did you find us?"

Rory briefed them about meeting Gabriel, and then her exchange with Wyatt.

"I knew it. Your glow is from being touched by an angel." Athelene's face lit up.

"Everyone keeps mentioning a glow. Do you have a mirror? I'd like to see what the fuss is about."

"Of course." Mrs. Leeman led her to a large mirror on the wall in the formal living room.

Rory jerked at the reflection of her glowing face. No wonder people kept talking about it. Her hands and feet were nice and dull. Only the skin on her face shined as Gabriel's had. Her face wasn't warm. The glow didn't rub off. She examined her face from various angles, and she glistened from them all. "Will my face light up like a beacon forever?" Her peace from meeting Gabriel melted as her stomach cramped. "This will draw a lot of attention."

"I imagine it will fade," Athelene replied calmly.

"When? Both the clerk at the store and the man on the sidewalk saw me after I met Gabriel. What if they report me?" She gestured to her face. "How will I explain this?"

"Wyatt was the young man at the store. He's one of us. He won't report you."

"What about the man on the sidewalk?"

Athelene glanced at Henry. "Bane was on the sidewalk when Rory arrived. If he reported it, what would he say? He saw a young woman whose face was glowing? Who would believe him?"

Henry rubbed his brow. "Everyone knows he drinks. That will discredit him."

Athelene held a finger beside her temple. "When God gave Moses the Ten Commandments, Moses's face glowed. He covered it with a veil so he wouldn't frighten the people. I don't recall scripture saying how long it lasted. Cover your face for a day or two."

"I can't work at the hospital with my face covered." Rory massaged her temples.

"Have faith. God sent an angel to speak with you. He'll protect you. Take a deep breath." Athelene put a consoling arm around her shoulders.

The food started rising in Rory's stomach. "I'm going to be sick."

Mrs. Leeman ushered her to a restroom and closed the door for privacy.

Rory hung her head over the bowl. The turmoil in her digestive tract slowly calmed. It would be déjà vu, except this bathroom was much nicer than the hospital facility. The countertops were granite, the floors marble, and the sink and light fixtures looked like gold. Her stomach settled, until she stood. Her glowing reflection in the mirror illuminated like a neon sign that read: Arrest Me. The food boiled up from her stomach to her esophagus.

Despite her best efforts, she couldn't throw up quietly. She wasn't making a good impression on her hostess. After her stomach was empty and her shivering subsided, she approached the sink, carefully averting her eyes from the mirror.

"Are you all right, dear?" Mrs. Leeman looked concerned as Rory emerged.

"Yes. I'm sorry."

"You have no reason to apologize. I'm sorry the pot roast made you sick."

"No, no, it's my nerves about my face glowing and leading a revolution." Rory smoothed her hair.

They walked back to the living room where Mr. Leeman was staring out the window.

"You've taken in a lot today. Jesus says not to worry about what will happen tomorrow."

She took a deep breath. "Yes, he does. So what now? How is this revolution going to work?"

Athelene shrugged. "I have no idea."

"Why was I supposed to find Mr. Leeman?"

"Before David was arrested for the bombing, he told us he would be convicted and sentenced to prison. He also said he would meet the person God would use to free us from the Order. He planned to send the leader to Henry. He didn't know why but said God would direct us. We were devastated when the Order announced David's execution before he sent *the one*. But now, here you are. God works in mysterious ways. You are truly blessed."

Rory rolled her eyes. These people were not helpful.

"God has the plan. He does the hard work. You just have to listen for his direction. We'll continue teaching you the Word until God reveals more. This is so exciting. God's moving, and we're alive to see it." She looked at her husband expectantly, but he stared at Rory with a solemn expression.

"From what Gabriel told me, I'll be a martyr, so forgive me if I don't share your enthusiasm." Her bottom lip quivered.

Mrs. Leeman stroked her hair. "No wonder you were sick. Could you have misunderstood?"

"He told you that you'll be martyred?" Henry narrowed his eyes at Rory.

"He said things like I shouldn't fear death, we all die, and death's not the end. Oh, and any pain I suffer is nothing compared to the reward in heaven. Things like that."

"He was probably just trying to ease your fear," Mrs. Leeman suggested.

"His words didn't calm me, but when he touched me, I felt like I could do anything. That all fizzled after I saw my reflection in the mirror."

"Just thinking about your encounter sends chills up my spine." Athelene shivered. "Come have a seat. Let's get your mind on something else." She patted the sofa.

Rory sat and glanced around the massive house. "Who else lives here?"

"Just the two of us." Her cheeks reddened. "It's a waste. We don't need all this room."

"Why did they give you such a big house?"

Henry answered, "Because they chose me to oversee the design and implementation of the Order's information system. They consider me essential."

"They don't know we teach Bible study in small groups. Those small groups teach others. We keep the meetings moving to different locations to keep suspicions down. We have no idea how many active believers there are at any time because of the precautions. There must be more than we suspected." Her brown eyes flashed.

"What's your occupation?"

"I used to teach. I'm not employed now."

"But the Order dictates that all able-bodied people must be productive."

Athelene shifted on the sofa. "They never required employment of the technology spouses. I hadn't taught in years when they took over. It's a good thing they didn't make me return to teaching. I don't think I could teach their lies. Not working allows me time to mentor Christians."

It was common knowledge the Order didn't enforce rules equally, but encountering this was like being slapped in the face. No sense stewing over it. "The man in front of your house, is he a tech guy?"

"Yes. He lives a few houses over. He lost his wife and young son not long after the formation of the Order. It was very sad. They were executed."

"Rumor was Tabor turned them in," Henry said. "He's haunted with guilt over betraying his family. He's a little crazy. Stay away from him."

Rory jerked. What kind of man ratted on his family?

Athelene shook her head. "I don't think he turned them in. I think he's haunted because he misses them."

"My wife thinks most people are better than they are."

She slapped his shoulder. "What does that say about you? I married you."

"We both know you could have done better. In any case, our guest here should keep her distance from Tabor." He looked out the window. "At least he's gone now."

After Mr. Leeman excused himself, Athelene discussed scripture with Rory. She was almost as good a teacher as Mr. Abrams.

As Mrs. Leeman started winding down, Rory brought up the one question she hadn't gotten around to asking. "Do you know where Mr. Abrams's daughter lives? He asked me to give her a message."

Her expression fell. "No, I lost track of her after the Order assigned everyone to housing."

"Do you know her name?"

"Ruth Rydell."

Rory's jaw dropped. "Rydell is *my* name."

"What are your parents' names?"

"Randa and Rydge."

A light flashed in her eyes. "That's why you look familiar. You look like your mother. She has those same beautiful blue eyes and blond hair."

The woman knew her mother?

"The Order outlawed prominent religious names. Your mother would have been required to choose a name other than Ruth. I lost contact with her after everything. I didn't know Randa was the name she chose." The woman looked down, then returned her gaze to Rory. "David was your grandfather."

Her hands trembled. "No, my grandfather died before I was born. His name was Judas Iscariot."

Athelene brushed Rory's hair from her face. "The Order changed the names of many prominent religious figures to names which would humiliate them. Judas betrayed Christ. Being called Judas Iscariot was a terrible insult to David."

She stood and shook her head. "Why wouldn't my parents tell me his real name?"

The woman stood and rubbed Rory's arms. "They were probably afraid you might repeat his name around someone you shouldn't. Then you and your family would come under scrutiny. They probably thought they were protecting you."

Mrs. Leeman was talking like a crazy woman. But Mr. Abrams had called her granddaughter the first time he'd spoken. He hadn't been delirious. He'd been telling her he was her grandfather, but she hadn't understood. All that time with him. He could have told her that her mother was his daughter. Why keep it secret?

"Your mother, Ruth, and your father were married a short time before the Order took over." Athelene looked away. "I let her down. After David's conviction, I promised that I would be there for her. Things were chaotic. The Order moved people around, and some people changed their names. I lost track of them. I should have tried harder. I'm sorry."

Rory's world flipped. Her parents had lied about everything. Whom could she trust?

"Your grandmother, Grace, was my best friend. Your mother was the closest thing I had to a daughter. She met your father, because he was a junior pastor at the Kingdom Church."

"I don't understand. My parents never told us about God or that Dad ever had another job, much less as a minister." The information started sinking in. "It makes sense. He's too intelligent to be a sanitation worker."

"I can see this is a shock, but it's true."

The avalanche of information buried her. "I can't believe they knew about God and heaven and never told us. I was worried about telling them I believe, but they knew and never said anything. My sister could have died without knowing God. I could have. We could have spent eternity separated from him." Bile rose again in her throat. "I should go."

"Let's pray first." Athelene called up the staircase, "Henry, where are you? Henry, please come pray with us."

"Why are you yelling that at the top of your lungs?" He shot her a harsh look while he descended the staircase.

His wife grabbed his arm. "Henry, her last name's Rydell. She is Ruth and Rydge's daughter. That makes her David's—"

"Granddaughter." He finished her sentence and stared at Rory.

After a few seconds, Henry took his wife's hand and held out his other hand to Rory. She tentatively grasped it and Mrs. Leeman's when she offered hers. The couple closed their eyes and bowed their heads. Rory followed their lead but opened an eye to watch over Henry.

Athelene led the prayer. "Heavenly Father, thank you for allowing Rory to receive instruction from her grandfather. You truly are an awesome God, protecting us during these dark times. Thank you for sending Gabriel to encourage Rory."

Encourage wasn't exactly the word that came to mind.

"I am thrilled when I think about all you've done and are preparing to do. You are faithful even though we were not. We don't deserve your loving mercies. We have waited a long time to be rescued from the Order. We long to live where we can worship you without fear. Reveal to us all we should do. Grant us strength and wisdom. Fill Rory with your Holy Spirit to guide and comfort her. Forgive me for breaking my promise and not staying in touch with Ruth and Rydge. Help them to forgive me. Give freely of your Spirit to all your people. Nothing is too difficult for you. To you be glory and honor forever, amen."

"Amen," Henry said.

"Amen," Rory repeated.

Rory's shifts consisted of three days at the hospital from 6 a.m. to 6 p.m. and then two days off. Unfortunately, she had one more work day before her days off started. If she was still luminous tomorrow, she would be forced to use a sick day. Athelene suggested that she return on Monday for more study and prayer. That would give a few days for the glow to fade.

From the coat closet, Athelene pulled a lovely turquoise scarf and matching coat. "Wrap this scarf around your face, and I think the coat will fit you too."

Rory had never seen such colorful clothing before. "I can't take your coat."

"I don't need three. It's snug on me but should fit you nicely." Holding it at arm's length, Athelene admired it. "This one's a holdover from before the Order. They don't make clothes like this anymore. Clothes used to have personality. They came in a variety of colors and styles. Once the Manufacturing Council took control, they declared that too many color and style choices produced waste, so they eliminated all but a handful of basic colors and utilitarian styles. It's a shame." She clucked her tongue as she handed the coat to Rory.

The color and style of clothing was the least of her worries. But the woman was kind, so she replied politely. "You're very gracious, but it's too nice for me. You should keep it."

"Don't be silly. It just hangs in the closet." Athelene waved her hand in dismissal. "Here, try it on."

She slipped into the coat and flexed her shoulders. "It fits."

"You look beautiful." Athelene clapped her hands.

"I'll never be able to repay you. Thank you for everything—the coat, lunch, and information."

"My pleasure. Henry, drive her home so no one sees her glow."

His jaw stiffened. "I don't know how to get to the labor sector."

"Rory will direct you." Athelene put Rory's old coat in a bag and handed it to her.

A sharp pain stabbed behind her eyes. Sit captive in a car with him? No way. Better that someone notice her glow. Even if someone on the trans noticed it, they wouldn't know her identity. "I rode the trans here. I don't know how to get home by the streets. I'll wrap the scarf around my face. I'll be fine."

"Okay, but Henry can drive you to the station." Athelene held Rory's face between her hands. "I'm thrilled to meet you. You're beautiful. Tell your mother I'm sorry."

This was Rory's first automobile ride. She opened the front passenger's side door and stepped in. It was a nice car. The dials and lights intrigued her. She rubbed her hand across the seat, the fabric was expensive leather.

Before he backed out of the garage, Henry smiled and waved to his wife.

"She's very nice."

After the garage door lowered, he swiveled to face Rory. The friendly smile had vanished. His face adopted a frightening expression. "She is very nice, and if you put her in danger, I'll make sure you regret the day you were born."

"You're a little late. Most days, I regret being born." What was wrong with him?

"A smart aleck too. You could be a spy for them. You could be trying to flush out believer groups."

She clenched her jaw. "Why would you think that?"

"You show up out of the blue claiming David sent you when he was executed years ago. Your story's outrageous."

"Honestly, I have trouble believing, and I'm stuck in the middle of it. But how would I know the things I told you if he didn't tell me?"

"David could have broken and told the Order before they executed him."

"Okay, why wait twenty years? And don't you think they'd send a big, strong dude? And how could I fake this?" She tore off the scarf.

"I don't know. I suppose they could have developed some kind of glowing dye."

"Mrs. Leeman believes me." Carefully, she rewrapped the scarf.

He shifted the car into drive and stared straight ahead as he accelerated. "I've waited over twenty years for *the one*. You certainly don't look like you can lead anything. You don't have a plan. You're asking me for advice. This is not what I expected."

"Not what you expected? I certainly never expected any of this. God led me to you. All I knew was that you had been a computer programmer. I expected you to have answers. You're a disappointment."

He flinched as if she had struck him. "This is a very dangerous assignment. You likely will die. People around you will die. Why do you want to do this?"

"You think I want to do this? Unbelievable. I tried to reject it, but then an angel touched me and made me shine like a torch. How can I say no?" She looked out the window. "I am aware I will die ... most likely. I don't plan on endangering anyone, but I have no idea how this is going down. I thought I was sent to you because you knew something."

Silence dragged out the remainder of the car ride. Henry pulled up at the station and stared out the windshield. "I apologize. I'm still trying to process you and your ... story. After all these years, it's hard to believe the Order will fall. I thought the revolution died along with David. Athelene would be devastated, if she knew, so I go through the motions. I have access to information, and the Order says believer activity is rising. They plan to increase arrests, so I'm nervous. Athelene and I will discuss where to go from here. Wait until your face stops glowing before you return."

"Sure, never mind that I have to walk around like this." She exited the car without looking back.

As the trans sped toward the labor sector, her anger simmered. The trans was crowded for her return trip. She collapsed onto a seat in an unoccupied area. A few people stared in her direction. When her face had been dull, she had the car to herself. Now at least thirty passengers accompanied her. She faked a disgusting cough and pulled the scarf tighter. Most of the passengers relocated farther from her. It was possible that her turquoise coat and scarf were drawing the unwanted attention. Wearing the colorful clothing with a glowing countenance was a big mistake.

What should she do about Mr. Drummond? Gabriel indicated she shouldn't feel guilty about his execution, but how could she not? She'd stolen the capsule before she knew about Jesus. If her parents had told her about him, maybe she wouldn't have stolen it. How dare they keep Jesus from Ruby and her. How would their lives have been different if her parents had told them the truth?

Chapter 14

Her anger had reached a full boil by the time Rory burst through the apartment door. "Why didn't you tell us the truth about God?"

Utensils clanged to the floor. Terror streaked across her father's face. Her mom raced to slam the door. Barricading the door with her back, she trembled.

"What's wrong with you?" Dad jumped up, knocking over his chair.

"Me? What's wrong with you?" Rory stuck her finger in his face. "How could you hide the truth about God from Ruby and me? The night I died, I heard Mom say you should have told me."

"What are you talking about?" Her father's face paled.

"That freezing night. I *died*. I woke to a bright light. I heard Mom say you should have told me, and you said there wasn't anything to tell. She was talking about Jesus. You should have told me Jesus died for my sins. I was out of my body. I looked down and saw all of you trying to revive me. Then, Jesus spoke and said I had to return and wait for his call. I was sucked back into my body, and you know the rest."

The events she had carefully guarded spewed out: meeting her grandfather, Ruby's healing, meeting Gabriel, and finding Henry Leeman. When she finished, she collapsed in a heap on the floor.

Her family stared silently at one another.

Tentatively, her mom touched her shoulder. "Your grandfather died over twenty years ago. The Order executed him. I have his ashes."

Rory exhaled heavily. Her hand waved as she spoke. "They lied. They tried to kill him, but God protected him. Grandfather was held in solitary until the night I died. That same night the Order transferred him to University Hospital."

"I used to believe in God, but that was before I understood the Order is correct. He doesn't exist. A god would have stopped them long ago." Dad turned his back to her.

"He wanted to, but people weren't willing to take a stand. You abandoned him." Her voice quavered, and her body trembled.

When he spun around, Dad's eyes danced wildly. "I didn't abandon God. He doesn't exist. It's not bad enough that I was jailed, and you were beaten? Is it going to take getting us killed to get it through your thick skull?"

"So what if they kill us? Death is better than living like this."

He leaned toward her with fury contorting his face. His hand cracked across her cheek.

Tears welled as stars circled before her eyes. Her hand flew to her cheek. She ground her teeth and clenched her jaw.

Mouth open, he stared from his hand to her. He mumbled under his breath and stormed out the front door.

"Rydge!" Her mother pursued him.

This wasn't the first time that he had mentioned that he blamed her for his detainment by authorities. His reminder stung more than the blow.

The door opened, and her mom returned. She stroked Rory's hair. "He didn't mean to hit you."

Rory blinked back tears. "Yes, he did. He's hated me since his arrest. I didn't know asking a question would cause so much trouble."

"He knows, and he loves you. Life has been difficult for him since the Order."

"Life is difficult for everyone." Rory huffed.

"Your face is glowing because an angel touched you?" Her mom studied her face. "What happened to your forehead?"

Rory filled in a few more details of the day but censored some, like how Mr. Drummond died because she'd stolen the Aztavix. She also omitted the martyr thing because it would be too upsetting for them.

A light rap on the door caused the group to freeze.

Another rap was followed by their neighbor's voice. "Randa, are you okay?"

Her mom touched Rory's arm, then pointed toward the bedroom. Rory nodded and disappeared from the room.

"Mrs. Turnbull, we're fine," Mom called as she walked to the door.

The door opened with a creak.

"I heard shouting and … well, I just wanted to make sure you're all right."

"I'm sorry we disturbed you. Rydge had a bad day. He was blowing off steam. It really isn't like him."

"He's usually so quiet. It didn't even sound like him. At first, I thought it was the Gillespis. They're always yelling about something. Then I opened my door, and I could tell it was coming from your apartment. I was afraid maybe someone was breaking in."

"You're brave to come over when you thought someone might be in the apartment. You're a good neighbor."

Rory rolled her eyes. Such a good neighbor that she waited until they could all be dead before she checked on them.

"I just wanted to make sure you're okay. Where's Rory?"

"She'll be home soon. I'm glad she wasn't here to witness her father's little scene. It was bad enough all the neighbors heard. Thank you for checking on us."

"Ruby, you're looking good. How're you feeling?"

"Very good, thank you."

"You're lucky they have medicine for it."

The woman was an idiot. They were lucky for medicine they couldn't afford, and which would eventually stop working?

"Yes, we are," her mom replied quickly.

"Would you like me to wait with you? Maybe Rydge will be nicer if company's here when he gets back."

"Thank you, but I'm really tired. I'm going to bed."

"Well, come over if you need anything."

"I will. Again, thank you."

After the door closed, Rory released her captive breath.

Relief covered her mom's and Ruby's faces as they entered the room and sat on the bed.

Her mom sighed. "Luckily, she didn't see you. I don't know how we'd have explained your glow."

Rory joined them on the bed. "Do you think she heard me screaming about God?" Her heart palpitated quickly.

"I don't think she can hear that well in her apartment. Even if she did, she wouldn't report us. She's my friend."

"She probably asked where I was because she thought the screamer sounded like me." Rory flopped onto her back and closed her eyes.

"I told her you weren't home, so if she reports anyone, she'll report me. They can arrest me so you can fulfil God's plan."

Rory shot upright. "No! I couldn't let them arrest you!"

"I was supposed to teach people about God in secret. I haven't held up my end, so if the military shows up, I'll take your place."

"No. That's not going to happen."

"Let's not worry about things that might happen." Drained, her mom looked at her. "Ruby is really healed? I want to believe, but it's so incredible. You met my father? I wish I could have seen him. Told him I love him." A tear rolled down her cheek.

"I wish I could have met him," Ruby added.

A pang of guilt struck Rory. "I'm sorry, I didn't know who he was until Mrs. Leeman told me."

Glued to her every word, they listened as Rory recounted her meetings with her grandfather. Her mom broke down when she shared the love he expressed for his daughter, Ruth.

"I offered to find her and sneak her into his room. He refused. He said it was too dangerous for both of us. That's probably why he didn't tell me his true identity. I would have taken you to see him if I'd known. I'm so sorry."

Mom dabbed her eyes. "How could you have known? I never told you about him."

"He sent me to Mr. Leeman who is supposed to help me start a revolt. Except Mr. Leeman doesn't know what we need to do. God is ready to do something." She shook her head. "When I say it out loud, it really sounds stupid."

Ruby hugged her. "No, it doesn't. It sounds exciting. I knew God is real. Remember? I told you. What can I do? I want to help."

"No!"

Ruby blinked at the harsh tone, then her eyes watered.

Rory tried to assuage Ruby's feelings. "This is dangerous. God protects those he calls. He hasn't called you." She winced. Even though God had called her, protection probably wouldn't be guaranteed.

Obstinately, Ruby crossed her arms. "Maybe God has called me. I had dreams."

"Look, I don't have any idea what I'm supposed to do. Maybe you can help when I figure it out." *No way.*

Ruby took Mom's hand. "Tell us about Grandfather. Why was he in prison?"

With her eyes closed, Mom traveled back to the worst day of her life. "My dad was falsely accused of bombing a mosque and killing hundreds of people. His trial was a joke. He stayed so strong through the ordeal. At his sentencing hearing, he warned the judge and prosecutor to repent before it was too late. He warned everyone that God would turn his back on them if they didn't stand up for him. I hated the prosecutor. He was arrogant and lied about Dad. I prayed for God to strike him down. It broke my heart when the judge sentenced Dad to the death penalty. Right after the verdict, a tornado struck the building and flying debris killed the judge, the prosecutor, and some of the jury and court employees."

Rory's and Ruby's eyes opened wide.

"That's like God pronouncing vengeance on them for wrongly convicting Grandfather," Rory said.

Mom nodded. "Dad, his attorney, the Leemans, your father, and I were the only ones left with the bodies. Everyone else fled the courtroom. I tried to convince Dad to run because God had rescued him. He refused. He said God needed to use him in prison, and your dad and I were to teach God's word in secret during the reign of the Order. I was so angry with him for staying. In my selfishness, I accused him of abandoning us."

"After witnessing the storm, people didn't believe?" Rory asked.

"At first, they accused Dad of bombing the courthouse. They never charged him though. I think after his sentencing hearing, they were afraid to put him on trial, because they feared God might be real."

"I'm sorry you went through all that." Ruby snuggled against their mom.

Mom put her arm around Ruby and kissed her forehead. "Afterward, people avoided us like the plague. We were in no position to teach anyone. The Order kept former religious leaders under surveillance."

Something clicked. Rory put a hand on Mom's arm. "Is that why I never had friends? People were afraid to be seen with us?"

"Yes, we were pariahs."

Rory lowered her eyes. "This must have been awful for you. I never knew how much you went through."

"I thought I was protecting you." Her mom hung her head. "We stopped speaking of God in the apartment because of rumors that the Order installed listening devices."

Terror seized Rory. "Bugs? The apartment is bugged? Crites! Is someone listening to everything we're saying? Dad was right. I'm signing your death warrants. What have

I done? I am stupid, stupid, stupid." She banged her fists against her head.

Her mom grabbed both of her hands. "It's believed they stopped listening shortly after they started. No one can effectively listen to recordings in all homes."

"What if you're wrong? What if they're still listening?"

She stroked Rory's hair. "Even if we're bugged, remember how you said the hospital cameras didn't pick up your conversations with my dad?"

"True." But just because God protected her once didn't mean he would continue.

Her mom didn't look worried. "The Order allowed me to teach but assigned your dad to sanitation. He tried to make the best of it, but he suffered with depression. We didn't want children while the Order ruled, but God had a different idea. I got pregnant despite using birth control. At first, we were devastated. Then we decided it was a sign that God was freeing us soon. We chose your name to honor God and hoped the birth registrar wouldn't reject it."

"How does it honor God?" Rory looked at her mom.

Mom pulled her feet underneath her and leaned against the wall. "Jesus came from the line of Judah, and lions were their symbol. Lions roar, so we named you Rory. We were terrified the registrar would recognize the significance and not only deny it but arrest us. Approval took longer than normal. Every time the phone rang or someone knocked at the door, we thought it was the military coming to arrest us. Then the approval arrived in the mail."

A loud knock made them jump. An authoritative, masculine voice announced, "Military Police, open the door."

"I told you Mrs. Turnbull heard me and reported us," Rory whispered. She grabbed her mom's hand. "Promise me you won't tell them it was you."

"Let me find out what he wants. You stay out of sight." Mom pointed at Rory and closed the bedroom door behind her.

Ruby opened the door to their tiny closet, and Rory squeezed into the farthest corner behind the clothing. The front door creaked open. Her head swam. Was this the day she would be arrested? It was too soon.

The man's voice filtered through the thin apartment walls. "Hello, ma'am, I'm Officer Jeffries. We received a report of a disturbance. I'm here to check it out."

The voice sounded concerned. Was it a ruse to build false trust?

"Yes, officer, we're fine. Everything's fine. Thank you for checking. I'm sorry we disturbed the neighbors and that you came out for nothing."

Rory's heart beat so loudly the officer could probably hear it.

"Tell me what happened, ma'am."

"My husband was upset. He stormed out. One of the neighbors checked on us. She thought maybe there was a burglar. He just needs a little time to cool down. It will be fine."

"Why was he angry?"

"He ... he ... thought I spent too much on groceries. Our credits have been tight since I left my job to care for our ill daughter. She's better, and I can return to work soon, so I splurged."

"Is this your daughter? She doesn't look sick."

If only he had seen her a few days ago. Sweat broke out on Rory's hands and face.

"She's much better."

"A woman's voice was also reported. Was that you?"

"Yes, officer, I guess it was." Her mom gave a nervous laugh.

If Rory could just have a do-over. They were all going to be arrested because of her. She was so stupid.

"Do you mind if I look around?" Officer Jeffries asked.

"Of course, go ahead. What are you looking for?"

"I don't know. Just making sure everything's okay."

The silence grated on Rory's nerves. A door opened, probably the closet in her parents' room. Was he looking in every closet? The military boots scraped on the concrete.

She couldn't breathe. They stopped outside her closet door. If he opened it, her feet would be exposed.

"My closet's a mess," Ruby said.

The door swung open.

With a stifled gasp, Rory closed her eyes and pushed against the opposing walls with all her strength. She leveraged her feet above the clothing line. A few seconds later, her muscles quivered, and her grip weakened. Unable to support her weight, she slid down the walls in slow motion and plunked on top of a few pairs of worn shoes. She clenched her eyes shut. Maybe the officer had closed the door and missed her descent.

No such luck.

Chapter 15

"Well, what have we here?" Officer Jeffries sounded amused.

Rory opened her eyes. The officer had squatted and now studied her curiously. A pang of fear burned in the pit of her stomach.

The officer took her hands and extracted her from the closet.

Trembling, she could barely stand.

He easily lifted her and sat her on the bed.

"Is this the sick daughter? Her face is flushed. Why was she hiding in the closet?" The officer looked at her mom.

Her mom wrung her hands. "We panicked when we heard you at the door."

"Why?" He touched Rory's forehead and then her cheek. "Strange, she doesn't feel warm. She's not flushed. She's glowing." He stepped back. "What's going on?"

Ruby and her mom stood wide-eyed.

Rory's heart pounded against her chest. When a massive cardiac event didn't rescue her, she stood and held out her wrists. "They don't have anything to do with this. It's me you want."

"Why?"

"An angel touched me, hence the glow." Rory waved her hand across her face.

Her mom stepped between them. "Don't pay attention to her. She's delirious."

The officer let out a low whistle. "Angels aren't real."

"Then how do you explain this?" Rory made a "duh" expression.

Officer Jeffries flipped on his flashlight and shined it in her face. Rory squinted against the beam.

He pinched her cheek. "I can't explain it. So, how did you meet this angel?"

"Rory, don't say anything," her mom cautioned.

"I wasn't feeling well, so my supervisor sent me home. I was sitting on a bench, and an angel appeared." She looked at the ceiling as she volunteered the bare facts.

"Rory." Her mom's gaze telegraphed for her to shut up.

Ruby looked faint.

"What did this angel say?"

She glanced frantically from her mom to Ruby. She couldn't mention the rebellion. "He said God loves me."

"An angel appears, and all he says is 'God loves you'?"

Not trusting her voice, Rory nodded.

"You paused. If that was all he said, why didn't you spit it out?" The officer's expressionless face masked his thoughts.

"He said some other stuff, but it didn't make sense." She waved her hand to dismiss the question.

"What didn't make sense?"

"Something about people suffering and life being short."

"What did you say?"

"Nothing. I was in shock."

He studied her glowing countenance from different views. "Could you have been dreaming?"

A little too quickly, she said, "Yes. Yes, I think, I dreamed the whole thing. I wasn't feeling well. I'm still not. I probably dozed on the bench. When I woke up, it felt real. Has that ever happened to you? You wake up from a dream, and it feels real?" She chewed her bottom lip.

"Sure. But how do you explain the glow?" He tapped her cheek.

The officer was toying with her. The slug. "I can't. That's why I hid. I can't explain this."

"Who else saw your glow?"

"No one."

He folded his arms across his chest. "How did you get home without anyone seeing?"

"I wrapped my scarf around my face."

"How did you know your face was glowing if no one saw it and told you?"

"I saw my reflection in the window at the station and thought I looked feverish, so I covered my face. I didn't want people thinking I was contagious. Mom asked about it after I got home." Her chest tightened. He was too smart to buy any of this.

"That's right. She didn't know she was glowing until I told her." Mom was going to get arrested for lying for her.

"Is this what the domestic argument was about? Her face shining?" He addressed the question to Mom.

"Yes." She paused. Anyone could see she was formulating her story. "We asked about the glow, and she told us her dream. When she mentioned an angel, my husband blew up and stormed out."

He looked at Rory. "You should have led with the dream. It's less convincing when you toss it in at the end, while you're chewing on your lip."

Rory's stomach leaped into her throat. What a jerk to raise her hopes just to crush them.

Officer Jeffries held Rory's shoulders. "Listen carefully. This call is officially a domestic situation over a grocery bill. You don't want to raise any suspicions, so stay out of sight until the glow disappears. Do not discuss the dream with anyone. You did not tell me this story, and your face never glowed. Got it?"

The three nodded in unison.

"Got it," Rory said, even though she didn't. Her knees gave out, and she sat hard on the bed.

"I'll see myself out." As he left, he took the radio from his shoulder. Static crackled then he spoke. "Officer Jeffries, badge 7340. This is a domestic dispute. The outburst reported was the husband—" The remainder of the transmission was cut off when the door closed behind him.

What just happened? Rory slid from the bed to the floor and buried her face in her hands. The weight of the events threatened to crush her.

Her mom embraced and rocked her. "Shh, it's okay."

She pulled out of the embrace. "No, it's not. It's my fault that officer showed up. Mrs. Turnbull reported my tantrum. We could all have been arrested."

"We don't know who reported it."

"Well, regardless, I almost got us arrested."

"Rory, get hold of yourself." Ruby stood with her hands on her hips. "God sent an angel to speak to you. An officer could have arrested you but didn't. Don't you see? God sent Officer Jeffries because he believes. You should thank God instead of making up reasons to worry."

"You're right," Rory admitted. "I should be thankful. God should have chosen you." Maybe that was the plan. She would be the martyr, and then Ruby would lead.

Grabbing both of them in a tight hug, Mom gazed heavenward. "Jesus, thank you for protecting us tonight. I'm so sorry I failed you. Please, watch over Rydge. Heal his heart. Please, forgive me. Amen." She sobbed quietly.

After a few moments, Mom wiped her eyes. "When I was pregnant with you, your dad and I agreed we would wait until you were old enough to understand the consequences before we told you about God. But you were inquisitive. Your questions got you in trouble. Fearing for you, your dad refused to tell you.

"Then, after Ruby contracted LI, excessive absences put both of our jobs in jeopardy. Since teachers accrue more credits than sanitation workers, we decided he would quit. But the Occupation Committee forced my resignation."

"Why?" Rory reached for her mom's hand.

"Officially, they said sanitation workers were in short supply and teachers weren't. But they wanted to break him. His heart hardened, and he doubted God. Either God didn't exist, or he didn't care." Tears trickled down her face. "The Order made it difficult for us to provide for you. Maybe when you're a parent, you'll understand why this is so hard on him. He's the provider and protector of the family. He feels like he failed."

"He didn't fail," Ruby said. "We're fine."

"We've gone to bed hungry, and he hated that we couldn't afford the Aztavix you need ... needed." She stroked Ruby's cheek with her thumb. "I wish you could have known him before. He was kind and loving. That's why I fell in love with him. If the Order had never happened, we would have had a wonderful life." Mom sucked in a deep breath and ran her hand through her hair. "There's no sense crying over things we can't change."

"Tell us about God. What's he like?" Ruby asked.

The three of them snuggled on the bed as Mom reached into the recesses of her mind to pull up the lessons she learned long ago.

"God is the creator of everything that was, is, or is to come."

Ruby's eyes widened in wonder while she listened. Some of the stories Rory had heard from her grandfather. Some were new, but all were wonderful. Ruby drifted off around midnight.

"Where do you think Dad is? Do you think he's reporting me?" Rory tucked the blanket around Ruby.

"No, of course not. I am worried, though. I don't know where he could be." She looked away.

"I hope he's okay." What if something happened to him? It would be her fault. Everything was her fault. She had been too hard on him. Now he was who knows where doing who knows what. Why couldn't she have chosen a less confrontational approach?

Chapter 16

Fortunately, Rory's skin appeared dull and boring in the mirror the next morning. With dark circles under her eyes, she looked like crap, but at least she didn't glow. After a benign day of hospital routine, the next day crept as the acid gurgling in her stomach continually interrupted her studies. What if Athelene and Henry couldn't help her figure out God's plan?

At 11 a.m. on Monday, she ducked behind a column at the trans station and watched for anyone who might have followed her. She would die before she led the authorities to them. Maybe die was a bit extreme. Suffice to say that she would make a great effort to protect them. Unfortunately, wearing the turquoise coat made her very conspicuous. But if she arrived wearing her old coat, Athelene would be offended. With precise timing, she leaped onto the train as the doors were closing. If anyone had tailed her, she had lost them. Not bad for a novice. After she finished patting herself on the back, she dropped onto a seat in a vacant area. A few passengers cast quizzical looks her way. Probably because of the darn coat.

After Rory exited the train, she stepped to the side to let everyone pass. When she was convinced no one was following her, she hesitated. Which way to the Leemans'? On her previous visit, she had roamed the area until the store clerk directed her. Possessing no sense of direction, she searched for anything familiar. With no other option, she enlisted help from God and headed to her right.

She had been walking for about fifteen minutes when the grocer where Wyatt worked came into view. From there she retraced her steps to Prosper Lane.

That same man stood outside the Leemans' home when she arrived. After a deep breath, she walked quickly and looked away from him.

"Hey. What are you doing back here?" Tabor asked.

"I'm returning a scarf." She kept her head down.

"You're not shiny anymore. That's why she loaned you her scarf isn't it, to hide your shine?"

Rory stopped and gave him the evil eye. "What are you talking about?"

The man's hair and beard still looked wild. So did his eyes. "Last time, your face was shining."

She winced but didn't respond.

"It wasn't a natural shine. It was supernatural."

Stopping, she feigned concern. "Are you all right? Do you need to see a doctor?"

"I'm not sick. Something strange is going on. There's something strange about you." He pointed at her.

"Excuse me, you're frightening me."

Mrs. Leeman opened the front door as Rory hurried up the walkway.

"You don't need to be afraid." The desperation in his voice chilled her to her bones.

After she closed the door, Mrs. Leeman peeked out the window. "Bane seems to watch for you. I think it best if you don't visit for a while. I'm sorry."

Great, her grandfather sent her to them, and now they didn't want anything to do with her. She was on her own.

"I wanted to wait for you to eat, but if Henry doesn't eat by eleven, he gets cranky. He's upstairs working. I'll warm something for you."

Maybe that explained his attitude during her last visit. He was hungry. "Please, don't go to any trouble."

"It's no trouble."

Rory trailed her to the kitchen.

"Sit down, dear." Athelene dished out a hearty portion of baked chicken, mashed potatoes, and green beans.

As the food warmed, Rory filled her in about her dad storming out and the good conversation she had with her mom. She explained her parents' rationale for choosing her name.

"How clever." The woman nodded.

"Oh, and Mom said she would love to see you, but she thinks it's too risky right now."

Athelene looked like Rory had knocked the wind from her. She broke down in tears.

Rory awkwardly hugged the woman. "Don't cry. Mom's not upset." Why had she said anything?

Mrs. Leeman dabbed at her eyes with a kitchen towel. "I don't deserve her forgiveness. She's so gracious not to hold a grudge." She removed the plate from the warmer and placed it before Rory.

"She didn't think you abandoned them. The Order watched them and probably you too. It would have been dangerous to be seen together. She's glad you and Mr. Leeman are well." Rory took a bite of chicken.

"The guilt I carried all these years was so heavy. You just lifted my burden, thank you." Athelene clutched her chest.

"Uh, I didn't do anything. Mom's the one not holding a grudge."

"You delivered the good news. Hopefully, God will take care of the Order soon, and we'll be able to get together." She sat across from Rory and composed herself. "Where were we? Oh yes, I've arranged for you to meet with a believer who is very knowledgeable in the scriptures. Are you scheduled at the hospital on Wednesday?"

Rory nodded.

"Good. He'll pick you up on University Street outside the hospital at 6:15 in the evening. Is that a good time for you?"

"Yes." She scooped a bite of mashed potatoes.

"Look for a black pickup truck. He's tall with short brown hair, handsome ... and single. He would be a good catch." Athelene winked.

"I'm engaged." She held up her left hand to show the thin band on her ring finger. Although she wouldn't be engaged much longer. She set her fork on the plate. The topic extinguished her appetite.

"Is he a believer?"

"No." She picked up the fork and stared at the plate while she picked at the food.

Athelene sat across from her. "Do you think it's a good idea to be engaged to a nonbeliever?"

Rory glanced at her. "He might believe if I tell him everything that's happened." Probably not, but there was a chance.

The woman's face softened. "Why haven't you told him?"

"He was sent away for eight weeks of training for his job about the time I started believing. He's not allowed to talk to anyone while he's there, so I can't tell him until he returns." She glanced at the ceiling. "And I guess I'm scared to tell him. Scared he won't believe me. Scared he might report me."

Athelene placed her hand over Rory's. "God is in control, even when it feels like he's not. What's his name?"

"Darius."

"God desires all souls to accept him, but he allows people to choose. Worrying changes nothing. Pray. God will lead you." Athelene opened a drawer, pulled up a false bottom, and retrieved a small notebook. After she opened it to the middle, she scribbled a line. Then she turned it for Rory to see. "It's my prayer notebook. I pray for all the names in it."

Darius's name was written beneath a dozen others, including her own. Athelene flipped the pages, showing the previous pages filled with names.

"Does Mr. Leeman know about this? How will you explain it if the Order discovers it?" The woman was recklessly creating evidence.

123

Mrs. Leeman glanced toward the stairs. "No, he wouldn't like it. If they find it, then it's my time to go. I've walked this earth long enough." After she returned the notebook to the drawer, she rearranged the items above the panel and closed the drawer.

"I want Darius to know the truth and to know God, so I have to tell him about Jesus." Rory closed her eyes. "But if he doesn't believe, I'll have to call off the engagement. He's loyal to the Order. I shouldn't marry anyone anyway, since I'm going to be, you know, martyred."

Trouble clouded the woman's eyes.

"Don't be sad. I have to believe my death will be for the greater good." Rory smiled weakly.

"For the record, I don't feel God telling me you're going to be a martyr."

A tiny blossom of hope bloomed, but Rory stomped it out. It was just wishful thinking on Athelene's part. She pushed her plate away.

"You don't like it." Athelene's face revealed her disappointment.

"Oh, I do. It's delicious. It's just that I overate last time, and I don't want to repeat my performance."

"I'll pack up the leftovers for you to take home." Mrs. Leeman scraped the uneaten food into a plastic container. "How did things go with your father after he returned home?"

"He's not speaking to me. He won't even look at me. So, I don't talk to him either. I guess I should apologize." She shrugged.

Athelene gave her a hug. "Give him time. I believe God will bring him around."

"There is something else." Rory took a deep breath and told her about the incident with the officer.

A strange look crossed the woman's face.

Rory's pulse raced. "You think the officer didn't believe me, don't you? Do you think he followed me? I tried to make sure no one did, but I don't know how to do this. I'm so sorry." She rose to look out the front window for anyone skulking around.

Athelene grabbed her arm. "Sit. I was thinking how great our God is to protect you."

"You don't think anyone followed me?"

"I'm not worried in the least." Athelene folded a dish towel. "I'm sad that we won't be visiting anymore, but I don't want to do anything to endanger you. Hopefully, this will all end soon."

"That would be great." Except she probably wouldn't be around to enjoy it.

Henry never came down, which was fine with her. After a short biblical study, Athelene prayed, gave Rory the leftovers, a big hug, and walked her to the door. "Will you be okay walking to the station?"

"Yes." Rory grimaced as she pulled on the turquoise coat. She might as well be walking around with a target on her back. Once she arrived back at home, she would retire it for good. "Wait, what's the name of the person I'm meeting on Wednesday?"

With an odd grin, Athelene said, "He wants to surprise you. You'll recognize him. Just watch for a black pickup truck."

"It's someone I know?"

"You've met." The woman rushed her out the door.

Rory walked to the trans station while mulling over Athelene's words. Who could this mystery man be?

Chapter 17

At precisely 6:15 p.m. on Wednesday, Rory waited on the curb of University Street. She tapped her foot while she scanned the street for a black pickup. A couple of vehicles meeting the description whizzed past. When a black truck slowed on its approach, her breath caught in her throat. It eased to a stop beside her. The passenger window lowered.

"Surprise." The driver grinned from ear to ear.

Rory went numb as she recognized him. "Off-Officer Jeffries? I'm waiting for someone." She turned abruptly and continued walking down the sidewalk.

The truck cruised slowly beside her. "Me. You're waiting for me. Climb in."

She stared straight ahead and quickened her pace.

"It's 6:15, this is a black pickup. What do you need, a formal introduction?" At the corner, he turned, blocking her path with the truck. "After I left your apartment, I contacted Athelene about your dream. She already knew because your grandfather sent you to them. She suggested l meet with you so you wouldn't have to commute to visit them."

Yeah, right. Henry couldn't care less about making things easier on her. He didn't want her seen entering his house.

A car honked. Rory flinched.

"Crites! Stop being so stubborn. Get in already. You're holding up traffic." Jeffries leaned across the seat and opened the passenger door.

Another car approached. Rory stepped in as the car honked again.

He looked in the rearview mirror and then accelerated the truck. "Put the seat belt on. Call me Jaxon."

She snapped the belt in place then turned to face him. "Why didn't Mrs. Leeman tell me I was meeting you?"

"I asked her not to. I thought this would be more fun." He flashed an annoying grin. "I wouldn't want to miss that look on your face when I pulled up."

Rory popped his shoulder with her fist. It didn't faze him, so she hit him again.

He leaned away from her. "What's that for?"

"Because you scared the crap out of me when you stopped beside me, and you didn't tell us that you're a believer at my apartment." She hit him again for good measure.

"You didn't tell me you believe."

"I held my hands out for you to handcuff me. Then you asked, 'Are you sure it wasn't a dream?' I was scared to death. Why didn't you tell us you believe? I've been worried sick you were going to show back up and arrest me."

"You could have been a spy trying to trap me. A guy can't be too careful." He glanced sideways at her.

"But I was glowing. How could I fake that?" After a moment, her eyes opened wide, and she whispered, "Is it safe to talk?"

"Why wouldn't it be?" he whispered back.

"The truck could be bugged. The Order provides it."

"No," he answered in a normal voice.

"How can you be sure?" she continued whispering.

"I know someone, and he sweeps it regularly. In fact, he went over it right before I picked you up. I'm not taking any chances." His brown eyes flashed.

That guy had better be good. In a normal tone, she said, "My mom says they used to bug the homes of people they suspected of believing."

"They did. Now they only listen in on citizens they receive intel on."

"Are they listening to our apartment because you were called out?" Her pulse ratcheted up.

"No. The ticket was closed after my report. You're welcome."

She relaxed a bit. "Thank you."

"This is it." He pulled to a stop in front of a concrete building with four metal overhead doors and high windows. It was only a few blocks from the hospital.

"It looks abandoned. What is this place?"

"A warehouse the Order had no use for. A few of us turned it into a gym." He looked over at her when she didn't immediately exit the vehicle. "Hey, are you okay?"

"Why does God even need us? Why doesn't he just say 'Poof' and the bad guys die? That would be so much easier."

"That's the point."

She furrowed her brow. "What's the point?"

"People need skin in the game. History shows that we don't appreciate anything we get too easily." The guy blinked at her like this was obvious.

"I still prefer the *poof* idea. So, how is this going to go down? More specifically, what am I supposed to do?"

"Not sure. I'm just helping you get ready."

"I don't understand how I can ever be ready."

"We'll figure it out together." He raised his eyebrows.

After he climbed out of the pickup, he pushed the back of the driver's seat forward and grabbed a plastic cooler. She followed him as he ambled to the metal door, unlocked it, and held it open for her.

Inside, she blinked to allow her eyes to adjust to the dim light produced by the battery-operated spotlight. Scattered across the floor of the large warehouse were metal bars of various heights, rings, and weights. Small and large burlap-covered punching bags occupied a corner of the room. Metal shelving units lined a wall, and several cardboard boxes were stacked in random areas.

Jaxon walked to one of the shelving units, removed his shoulder holster and gun, and set them on a shelf.

The cool temperature made her shiver. But it wasn't the only reason for the icy sensation snaking down her spine. They were isolated and alone, supposedly training for her date with death. With weights? The only thing this place could train her for was how to withstand a lot of pain.

"Sorry, since we don't have permission to use the warehouse, the power's off. You'll warm up when we start working out." He rubbed his hands together. "Did you bring sweats?"

"No. Why would I? I thought we were studying scripture."

"No problem. I'll loan you my sweatshirt." Their eyes met and held for several seconds. "You have the bluest eyes I've ever seen."

Her cheeks burned, but she threw her shoulders back. "My, what brown eyes you have?"

"You're a little sarcastic."

"You started it with the blue eyes comment. What did you want me to say?"

"A simple thank you would do." Laugh lines crinkled around his brown eyes.

His laughing eyes conjured up pain from years of peer ridicule, but his face held no trace of malice. Maybe he was different.

"Brown eyes are common, but baby blues are unusual, and I don't think I've ever seen eyes as blue as yours. Do you wear lenses?" He leaned closer and peered into her eyes.

She looked away. "No. My mom and sister both have them. They aren't that unusual."

"As blue as yours?"

"You saw them the other night. You didn't notice?"

"I was a little preoccupied with your glow. I didn't notice your eyes, much less theirs. Your eyes are beautiful, but I'm sure you hear that all the time."

She shrugged one shoulder. "Not really. Uh, thank you."

129

"Do you work with blind people?" When she didn't respond, he pointed to the plastic cooler. "You're probably hungry. I brought roast beef sandwiches. We'll eat while we discuss scripture, and then we'll get our blood pumping. Let's give thanks first." He bowed his head, and she followed suit. After a brief prayer, he handed her a sandwich and a paper napkin.

"Thank you."

Jaxon's legs stretched the length of the mat where they sat. He shared stories from the start of Jesus's ministry. His biblical knowledge was impressive.

She studied his face as he spoke. His jawline was strong and his chin sharp. He wasn't particularly handsome until he smiled. His infuriating grin transformed him into a captivating slug. Perhaps he wasn't a slug. The jury was still out.

After the lesson's conclusion, he stood and slipped his jacket off. "Do you work out?"

"Of course ... not. Does this look like a body that works out?" She waved a hand from head to toe.

"Hard to tell under all those clothes. Anyway, looks can be deceiving. You're studying medicine. You know how good working out is for you."

He thinks he knows everything. "Knowing what's good for you and having time to do it are two different things."

"Excuse me," he retorted.

Undeterred, he removed his sweatshirt and tossed it to her. *Fine.* She shed her nondescript, old coat and pulled his sweatshirt over her scrub top. It swallowed her. His tight T-shirt revealed his taut muscles. Looking at Jaxon certainly didn't hurt her eyes. Suddenly overcome with warmth, his sweatshirt might not be needed after all.

He led her through a battery of strength training exercises. Rory struggled and strained and failed miserably.

"Come on, you're not trying."

"I can't do this."

"Then you have no muscle at all."

"Then I have no muscle at all," she mocked. "It's easy for you with your huge biceps and triceps. You probably did chin-ups in the womb."

He squeezed her upper arm. "You really don't have any muscle. Didn't you climb trees or playground equipment as a kid?"

She crossed her arms and glared.

"What, you stayed inside and read books?"

"The other kids bullied me, so I kept to myself. This is a waste of time." The pain from old wounds throbbed more than any physical pain she would suffer from his stupid drills. She stomped toward the door.

Jaxon cut her off with his long strides. "Why did they bully you?"

"I don't know. Maybe because their parents told them to avoid me because my dad had been a minister. Or maybe they just didn't like me. Who cares?"

"I'm sorry—"

"You have no reason to be sorry. Kids are cruel. Adults are cruel. So, I have no muscle, big deal. You're supposed to teach me scripture, not this push-up crap."

"This explains a lot."

"Explains what?" She lobbed a piercing glare in his direction.

"You reject before you're rejected. It doesn't hurt as much that way."

She pointed a finger at him. "You know nothing about me."

"I'm trying. I know God chose you, so you're special."

His confident smile rubbed at her raw nerves. "Well, I'm not. God made a mistake. His first, I suppose."

"God didn't make a mistake. You're hanging out with the wrong people."

What an idiot. "Like I have a choice. The Order tells us where to live and work. By default, they determine the people we're around."

"Not entirely. You're hanging out with me. They have nothing to do with this. In fact, they wouldn't like it. You put too much pressure on yourself. Relax, let God take control."

"I didn't choose to be around you. I didn't know I was meeting you, remember?"

"True, but look at what a great time we're having."

Rory locked her jaw and shot her dagger eyes at him.

He threw his hands up in surrender. "Rory, I'm not the enemy. We're on the same team. I want to help, but you have to let me."

The exasperation in his voice threw her over the edge. "You think I'm not allowing you to help because I can't do a push-up? What does exercise have to do with anything? It's not like I'm going to fight. That would be ridiculous."

"When you tried to hide in the closet, you didn't have the strength to hold yourself up. If I wasn't a believer, you'd be sitting in Gibbons. I'm trying to help you develop that strength. Someday, you might need to pull yourself over a fence to get away. As it is, you don't stand a chance. You'd easily get caught."

"That's the plan, genius. I'm not supposed to stand a chance. I'm supposed to get caught and die for the cause. Everyone will rally around the memory of poor Rory who died because she didn't deny God." She collapsed onto the hard, concrete floor and closed her eyes.

Jaxon lowered himself beside her. "Athelene told me you think you're going to be a martyr. I think God has plans for you to lead and teach. I don't think you're going to die, in the near future anyway."

"Oh, so you can see the future?" She sat up. "Look at me. You said it yourself that I have no muscle. I have very little knowledge of God. What am I good for, except to be a martyr? I figured it out when Gabriel spoke to me. I was chosen because I'm disposable. After I'm executed, the public will be outraged. Believers will unite, and God will use them to defeat the Order. It's the only thing that makes sense."

He tilted his head and narrowed his eyes. "God can make anything happen, so his plan doesn't have to make sense to us."

She waved a hand. "Whatever."

After a few moments, Jaxon stood. "Enough for tonight. When you're at home, work on push-ups, jumping jacks, running in place, or anything that gets your heart pumping."

She rolled her eyes. This guy just didn't get it.

He grabbed her hands and pulled her up. "How do your shifts work?"

"I work tomorrow, and then Friday starts my two days off."

"Your shifts are the same as mine. That can't be a coincidence. This is a divine match." He grinned that devastating grin again.

She groaned.

Jaxon proposed that they meet three times a week. Rory agreed to two. They worked out a preliminary meeting schedule while Jaxon gathered his belongings.

"God should have selected someone more like you. You're physically fit, and you know scripture. You should take my place."

"God didn't send an angel to speak to me. He sent Gabriel to you. Anyway, what else do you have to do? We can continue with the biblical studies, and why not work out? You never know when it might come in handy. You might even start to enjoy it. Bring sweats next time."

She lunged for her out. "I don't have sweats, and I don't have extra credits to buy any. We might as well forget the working out part."

"You don't get off that easy. I bet I can find a pair in lost and found."

"Ew."

"Sheesh, I'll launder them. I can pick you up at your apartment and give you a ride when we meet on our days off."

"It's not a good idea for people to see you picking me up. Everyone in my neighborhood is curious about anyone with

133

a vehicle, so you would be noticed." The less time they spent together the better.

"What's the harm of being seen together?"

"When I'm caught, you'll come under suspicion."

He nodded. "Or vice versa. Okay, we'll just meet here. Come on, I'll drive you home."

"That's not necessary. I'm perfectly capable of getting home on my own. I do it every day."

"Crites! Can you be any more bull-headed? Fine, take the trans, but I'm driving you to the station if I have to carry you to the truck. It's dark, and this is not a great area."

Rory opened her mouth to protest.

"This is non-negotiable. I'm driving you to the station."

She tore off the sweatshirt, grabbed her coat, and stomped toward the door. A quick glance over her shoulder captured him shaking his head before he tugged the sweatshirt over it.

He extinguished the spotlight and locked up.

The moonlight provided a clear path to the pickup.

Rory stood by the passenger door and tapped her foot while she waited for him to unlock it.

The thump of the tires hitting the pavement was the only sound as Jaxon drove to the trans station.

The jury had reached the verdict. He was a slug. He'd called her bull-headed, but had he looked in a mirror lately?

When he pulled to a stop in front of the station, she opened the door and stepped out without so much as a glance back.

"You're welcome," he called after her.

She set her jaw and walked straight ahead.

While she waited for the trans, her anger cooled. Loneliness threatened to suffocate her. Her grandfather was gone. The Leemans didn't want her coming around. She couldn't confide in her family. Like it or not, Jaxon was all she had. If she drove him away, she'd have no one.

Besides, she wasn't really angry at him. She was angry at God. Why did she have to be the martyr? Sure, she wanted the Order to fall, but why did she have to be involved? *God, I need your help. Don't let me push away the only person willing to help me.*

Chapter 18

The sun colored the sky with brilliant pinks and reds as it sank to the horizon. The temperature was cool but nice as Rory strolled the few blocks from the hospital to the gym. The pleasant mid-February evening matched her mood. She swung the bag that held the workout sweats Jaxon had given her at their second meeting. After her attitude improved, she and Jaxon eased into a friendly banter. Over the last three weeks spent sharing scripture with him, she'd blossomed in biblical knowledge. Her physical fitness even improved, a little.

Her lips curled upward in anticipation of their meeting. It was always just the two of them. The survival of the entire community of believers, not just Jaxon and her, depended on anonymity. For Rory's protection, Jaxon and Mr. and Mrs. Leeman decided that no other believers should know she existed until they understood more about her calling.

The majority of believers knew of only a few others. The precautions were designed to limit the number of believers who could be compromised in the unfortunate event one of them was arrested and tortured. Key believers like Henry and Athelene were more informed. If they were arrested, the information they could give up would devastate the cause.

Unoccupied brick warehouses, pocked with broken windows, lined the street—victims of the Order's business closures. The area was deserted. What had it been like during its heyday, when businesses had breathed life into the buildings? Vehicles would have filled the parking lots, and people would have milled around. Now, the lots were empty, and half of the streetlights were dark.

Suddenly, a large man with scraggly long hair and a beard appeared from nowhere and stepped in front of her, cutting her off.

He shoved her into an alley and slammed her head against the brick wall. Pain erupted in fiery splinters along the back of her skull. With her head throbbing, she only half-heard him as he demanded her account card and access code. His breath reeked of alcohol, and his overwhelming body odor gagged her. He shook her and again ordered her to hand over her card.

She reached into her coat pocket and fumbled for it. "I don't have many credits."

"Liar. You work at the hospital. You have lots—" He stared at her a moment and then shook her again. "It's you! You got me fired!" He leaned into her and pinned her against the bricks.

She struggled in vain. "I've never seen you."

His face reddened. "I worked security at the hospital. You reported me."

Oh no. He was the security guard who wanted to see her breasts the night she stole the Aztavix. "I didn't report you. Anyway, you were out of line. It was your fault."

At her words, his dark eyes flashed with rage. "They won't give me another job because of you. You ruined my life. Now, I'm going to ruin yours." He pushed her harder against the wall.

A spike of adrenaline shot through her body. He intended to kill her. With her heart in overdrive, she struggled, but she couldn't budge the man. "Help! Someone!"

The man's greasy hair slapped across her face as he whispered in her ear, "Scream all you want. No one is around to hear you."

"Please. Don't do this." If she had paid attention to her surroundings as Jaxon had taught her, she wouldn't be in this situation.

He laughed sinisterly. "Now you're begging me. Let's see what I can do about that."

The man pressed his lips against hers. The touch of his slimy lips made her gag. Bile rose in her throat. She jerked her head to the side and spat the liquid on the ground.

He slapped her. But the slap lost its sting on her numbed senses.

"You think I'm gross? You think you're better than me?" His spit showered her as he spoke.

"You don't want to do this."

"You're wrong. I do want to do this." A crazed look crawled around in his eyes.

"You'll go to prison. You don't want that." She tried to appeal to his reason.

"Not if they don't find your body. It's hard to get a conviction when there's no body."

Her muscles seized up. This wasn't the way she was supposed to die. Her death was supposed to matter. She was supposed to die for Jesus, not for the twisted desires of a psychopath.

"And if they do find your body, at least in prison, I'll have a bed and food. That's better than I have now, which is nothing, thanks to you." He pressed his fingers against her throat.

She trembled. She would never see Jaxon again. She would never get the chance to tell him how much she appreciated him. No, this couldn't be how she would die. "Jesus, please help me!"

The man grinned and slowly encircled his hands around her throat. His fingers applied pressure, cutting off her oxygen.

"Help me, Jesus," Rory mumbled and pushed once more in desperation.

His fingers dug deeper. She couldn't make a sound. Could Jesus hear the plea inside her head? Of course, he could, but he didn't seem to be doing anything to help.

Bright spots appeared in the periphery of her vision. She would black out soon. *Jesus, please let me wake in heaven.*

A vicious snarl and a high-pitched shriek pierced the air. The former security guard stumbled backward.

She coughed out a breath and then seized the opportunity and bolted. *Thank you, Jesus.*

As her feet flew, she risked a glance back. A large pale dog had his teeth clenched on her assailant's groin. Her mind was a blur until she came to the gym. Jaxon's truck was parked outside. *Praise God.*

She burst through the door and doubled over with her hands on her knees. "A man tried to kill me." She wheezed for breath.

A storm brewed in Jaxon's dark eyes. He grabbed her shoulders and surveyed her up and down. "Are you okay?" His gaze zeroed in on her bruised neck and cheek.

"Yes, no, I don't know." She coughed.

"Were you followed?"

"I don't know. A dog attacked him, and I ran."

He strode to the shelf and grabbed his holster. Drawing the pistol, he checked it, then snatched a flashlight and switched it on. "Stay here. Lock the deadbolt behind me. Get down behind those boxes. Don't unlock the door unless you hear me call out all clear."

Rory grabbed his arm. "Don't go. He's long gone by now."

"I hope not. I swear, if I find him, he'll never hurt you again."

His icy voice sent a chill through her. The avenger who stood before her was a stranger.

"Describe the perp."

After she described the man, her stomach somersaulted as Jaxon threw the door open and exited with pistol and flashlight raised. She turned the dead bolt, scrambled behind the boxes, and got down on her knees.

The air in the warehouse was stuffy. She gasped for breath, still coughing through a raspy throat.

Time crawled. Where was Jaxon? What if he never returned? *Jesus, please protect him.*

After an eternity, a knock at the door almost made her throw up. She cried when Jaxon called, "All clear."

Quick as lightning, Rory jumped up, ran to the door, and threw back the bolt. She wrapped her arms around Jaxon's neck and shook uncontrollably.

He dropped a bag on the floor, then lifted her into his arms. "I found the alley where he attacked you. You dropped your sweats."

The sweats were the last thing on her mind. Her muscles relaxed in his strong embrace.

"I scoured the area, but I didn't find anyone around there or here."

"I was so afraid … something would happen to you." Her words were barely understandable between sobs. "I don't know what I'd do if—"

"It's okay. You're okay." He carried her to the mat. "You don't weigh anything."

She ignored the comment.

Jaxon lowered himself to the mat, pulled her onto his lap, and stroked her hair.

She leaned the side of her head against his hard chest. The rhythmic beating of his heart soothed her overstimulated nerves. His familiar scent mingled with sweat filled her nostrils. Who knew sweat smelled so good? If the world froze at this moment, she would never ask for anything more.

"I was stupid to let you walk here alone. I know this is a shady neighborhood."

"It's not your fault. You offered to pick me up. I didn't want us seen together."

"I should have insisted. If they arrest you, they might as well arrest me. We're in this together. Are you up to telling me what happened?" Tenderly, he brushed her unruly hair from her face. The gentleness of his touch and his calloused hands were a contradiction.

She told him everything.

The color drained from his cheeks. "Did he hear you ask Jesus for help?"

"I don't know. That was about time the dog attacked. I'm sure that distracted him."

"He knows who you are. But even if he heard, he can't report you. What would he say? He heard you call out to God while he was attacking you? They would assume he concocted the story to get out of assault charges. Still, you need to file a report."

She shook her head. "I don't think that's a good idea, and besides, I don't remember his name."

"The hospital can provide it."

"If I file charges and they arrest him, he might report me. Then, they might listen in on our apartment. You said they do that to people who come to their attention. It would be very bad if they listened to my apartment."

"I can't let him get away with this." A lethal glint hardened his eyes.

Scratching noises at the door silenced them. Her eyes widened while Jaxon's narrowed. He grabbed his pistol.

At the sound of a whimper, Rory sprinted to the door.

"Wait," Jaxon warned. With his gun ready, he turned the bolt and slowly opened the door. A cream-colored dog nudged his way in.

"That's him. He saved me."

Cautiously, Jaxon stepped outside. He returned shortly and secured the bolt. "I didn't see anyone." Then he rubbed the dog's head. The dog rolled over and offered his stomach for a rub. Jaxon obliged. "Thanks for rescuing my friend. He's a Lab. He looks well cared for, not a stray. I don't see any tags, though." The dog licked Jaxon's face. "What should we call him?"

"Hmm. Guardian, Hero, I don't know. Suggestion?"

He studied the dog. "What do you think about Brave?"

"I love it. Brave's a great name."

Brave wagged his tail in affirmation.

"Are you hungry?"

Rory shook her head. "There's no way I can eat … after everything."

Jaxon broke off a piece of sandwich and commanded Brave to sit. Brave sat immediately and received a chunk of sandwich as a reward. By the time Brave passed several commands, he'd managed to eat the whole sandwich.

"Someone trained him well."

"I bet someone misses him." Rory hugged the dog's neck. He licked her face. "Is there a way to find his owner?"

"I can check the missing pet log. I'll take him until we find his owners."

"No, I want him. He saved my life. I can love him until we find them."

"We don't have to try to find his owner. You could see if they find you."

She mulled it over. "That would be selfish. I think we should try, but I hope we don't find them." She buried her face in his neck.

"I still think you should file charges."

"I know you do. I'll think about it, and thank you for looking for the attacker."

Jaxon pulled her close. His gaze fell to her lips. She held her breath. What was happening?

He lowered his lips to hers. Her heart thumped against her chest as her lips eagerly met his. Butterflies took flight throughout her insides, and she collapsed against him. His lips were soft and sensuous for someone so muscular. The kiss sent chills through her, but it was wrong. He leaned his head back and gazed questioningly into her eyes. She looked away.

"What's wrong?" He ran a gentle finger down her cheek.

His touch evoked feelings she'd never experienced with Darius. She pulled away and stared at the floor. "I'm sorry. I shouldn't have kissed you. I'm engaged."

"You never mentioned a fiancé."

"It didn't come up." After realizing the unlikelihood of Darius accepting the truth, she had removed her ring weeks ago. The truth was, ring or not, Darius hadn't crossed her mind since she'd started training with Jaxon.

"Do you love him?" With his hand under her chin, he tilted her head up.

Rory couldn't look in his eyes. "I'm engaged, of course, I do ... I mean ... I did when he proposed. So much has happened, I don't know anymore."

"Does he believe?"

"No."

"Does he know about you?"

"Of course not."

"The Bible says we shouldn't marry someone who doesn't share our belief in God."

She let out a heavy sigh. "I didn't know God when I accepted his proposal. Besides, I don't expect to live much longer, so I'm not going to marry anyone. But I need to tell him that God is real. If I don't, how will he know? That's the Great Commission, to spread the good news."

"Why haven't you told him?"

"I wasn't sure I believed. At first, I thought I hallucinated everything. Then, he was sent to training for eight weeks about the time I decided God was real."

"What's his occupation?"

"Courier."

"They're training him to look out for people practicing religion. As a courier, he's in and out of businesses all day. They're training him to recognize suspicious behavior. They're brainwashing him, telling him religious people are dangerous."

She slapped her forehead. "Of course, I should have realized. Why would a courier need eight weeks of training to deliver packages?"

Jaxon encircled her in the safety of his embrace. "You don't have experience with the military. You wouldn't know. You've got to end all contact with him right away. Whatever you do, don't tell him you believe."

"But if I don't tell him, he'll never know. I don't know if I love him, but I care for him. I don't want him to live or possibly die without knowing God."

"If you tell him, he'll report you. It doesn't matter if you are his fiancée, wife, or mother. He's taking an oath to turn in anyone he suspects of treason. Your calling is bigger than him. You can't risk it."

"Maybe that's the way it's supposed to happen." Rory snuggled into his chest as she tried to hide from reality.

"What do you mean?"

"Maybe I tell him, and he reports me. I'm arrested and martyred, and then all the believers rise to overthrow the Order."

Jaxon shook his head. "No, that doesn't feel right. Don't start things in motion on assumptions. Promise me you won't say anything until we have an answer about this. Promise me." He held her shoulders firmly.

"This is too hard. Why didn't Gabriel just tell me if I'm supposed to tell Darius the truth or not?"

"Promise me."

"Okay, I promise. But can you trust my promises? I promised Darius that I would marry him. I'm breaking that one."

"Your world has changed since you promised. You can't be held accountable."

Was he right? In any case, her nerves were too raw to sort it out at the moment. "I don't know, but we've wasted enough time. Let's work out." She pulled the sweats from the bag that she had dropped in the alley.

"I thought we'd take the night off."

"Are you kidding? After everything that's happened, I need to train harder." She stepped behind the boxes to change. "Can you teach me some self-defense moves?"

"The first lesson in self-defense is pay attention to your surroundings. If you do that, you can avoid needing to defend yourself. Walk confidently and look people in the eyes. Random attackers look for victims who aren't paying attention. They don't want to be identified."

She emerged from behind the boxes. "I realized too late that I wasn't paying attention."

"Why were you preoccupied? You were thinking about me, weren't you?"

"You're so full of yourself." Rory shoved him playfully.

"So, you were thinking about me." He raised his eyebrows but then turned serious. "You shouldn't walk on deserted streets alone. But if you find yourself in that situation, don't daydream, even about me. Pay attention." Jaxon tapped her head. "Scan the area while you walk. When approaching an alley, look down it for movement."

At the hanging punching bag, he demonstrated the proper way to punch and kick and the areas to target. After a half hour of hard training, he asked, "Is this enough for the night?"

"Enough self-defense, but I want to do some fitness."

Jaxon petted Brave as Rory pushed herself up and squatted until she could squat no more.

"I'm driving you home tonight. No arguments." He placed his finger over her lips.

Rory shivered at his touch. "I would appreciate a ride home."

"I like the new you."

After they locked up, she imitated Jaxon as they walked to the truck. While she was scanning the area for perpetrators hiding in the shadows, she bumped into his backside.

"What was that?" he asked, turning around.

"Sorry, turns out I can't pay attention to my surroundings and where I'm going at the same time." The absurdity hit her. Rather than cry, she broke down in a fit of laughter.

"What's so funny?"

"Nothing, I don't know why I'm laughing. It's not funny at all. I can't even walk behind you without running into you. I'm hopeless."

The laughter was contagious. Jaxon joined her. Once he gained control, he said, "You're not hopeless. You just have a lot to work on."

She wiped the tears of laughter from her eyes. "Life is weird. A few hours ago, I was a sniveling mess, and now I'm laughing uncontrollably."

"Laughter is the best medicine, right, Doc?"

Jaxon opened the truck door, and Brave jumped in. Rory followed.

"Hang around the hospital after your shift tomorrow, and I'll drive you home."

"Not necessary."

"Your attacker knows where you work. He can follow you until he gets you alone."

"He wasn't waiting for me tonight. It was random."

"It was random until he recognized you. You got lucky tonight. It might make him more determined. Obviously, he's not stable. If he wants to find you, it won't be hard."

Rory opened her mouth to protest, but he interrupted. "This isn't open for discussion. Wait for me tomorrow."

Her scared streak overruled her rebellious streak. "Thank you."

"That was easier than I expected."

"Oh, shut up."

"That's my girl." His grin infected his whole face.

His girl. The reference gave her goosebumps. If only they had met in a different place under different circumstances, then she would be his girl. Except she didn't deserve someone as wonderful as Jaxon. Under the cover of darkness, she blinked back a sad tear. "Do you remember where I live?"

"What kind of officer do you think I am? Of course, I do."

When they'd first met, Rory didn't consider Jaxon attractive. Now, she studied his profile in the dark. He was drop-dead gorgeous. And when they kissed, the world and all its problems disappeared. He transported her to another dimension. The real question was what did he see in her? She wasn't attractive, and honestly, her personality left a lot to be desired.

He parked in the space closest to her family's apartment. As they stepped out of the truck, he reiterated that she would wait for him the next day.

"Aye, aye." She saluted, then reached into her coat pocket for her key.

He leaned against his pickup while she led Brave toward the apartment.

At the door, she turned abruptly, ran back, and pecked his cheek with a kiss. "Thank you for everything."

"Anytime." He flashed a heart-stopping grin.

Fighting the magnetic pull toward him, Rory dragged herself away and unlocked the apartment door. He was a wonderful guy, but her future wouldn't accommodate love.

"A dog." Ruby squealed and ran over to pet Brave. "Is he ours?"

Brave's tail wagged a million kilometers per minute.

"Crites! What do you think you're doing bringing that animal here?" Surprisingly, her dad spoke to her.

"It's the least I can do." Rory patted Brave while he licked her face. "A man jumped me, but Brave attacked him and chased him away."

Her mom's hand flew to her mouth. "Are you all right?" She took Rory by the shoulders and looked her over. "Your cheek is bruised and your neck. Did he choke you?"

"Yeah, then Brave came out of nowhere and chased him away. I ran to the gym and met Jaxon."

"I told you that you have no business dabbling in heretics," her dad said. "If you weren't going to meet that man, you wouldn't have been attacked in the first place. Learn your lesson before those meetings get you killed."

Brave bared his teeth and growled at her dad.

Veins popped on her dad's neck as his face turned deep red, almost purple. "You bring a vicious dog into my home. We barely have enough credits to provide food for us, and you want us to feed that?"

"He's nice to nice people. I don't want you to use any of your food for him. He can eat mine. He saved me, not that you care."

Her mom jumped between them. "You both need to calm down. We don't want to disturb the neighbors. Brave rescued Rory. We owe him a warm place to sleep. We can discuss this further tomorrow. Since Ruby doesn't need medication anymore, we have enough to eat. I'll return to work soon. Rydge, you've had a long day. Why don't you go to bed?"

"Don't tell me to go to bed!" He stared stonily at her.

Brave growled low.

Rory and her dad locked eyes in a standoff.

Dad broke the silence. "I'm going to bed because I want to, not because you told me to." He stomped into the bedroom and slammed the door.

As soon as he retired, Rory relaxed. Brave licked Ruby, and she giggled.

"Did you report the attack?" her mom asked.

"Jaxon will file it tomorrow. He looked for the guy, but he was long gone. Then, Brave showed up outside the gym."

"I don't like the idea of you walking alone to meet Jaxon."

"He doesn't either. From now on, he'll pick me up to take me to the gym. He's driving me home tomorrow after my shift."

"I like this Jaxon." Her mom smiled and hugged Rory.

Rory liked this Jaxon too.

Chapter 19

Rory's muscles screamed in protest when she rose early the next morning. In her zeal, she'd overdone the exercises. Her reflection in the mirror made her flinch. The angry blue and purple bruises adorning her neck and cheek were going to darken. The neck discoloration was the worst. She tore through the contents of the bathroom drawer as she searched for something to conceal the bruises but found nothing. The scarf draped around her neck looked ridiculous with her scrubs but better than the skin beneath it. She left the apartment early enough to avoid the other students in the locker room.

But she couldn't hide from Dr. Bourland's penetrating gaze. "What's with the scarf?"

"I just thought I'd accessorize." Rory continued staring at her screen.

The doctor set his coffee on the counter and walked around to face her. He stood silently. A full minute passed. He wasn't going to go away until she gave in. Finally, she looked up. With a finger under her chin, he turned her face to the side with the bruise. She pulled away. He reached over and removed her scarf. "Crites, Rory! Who did this to you?"

She launched into the story she had rehearsed about being mugged on her way to the grocer.

"You should have stayed home today."

"Why?"

He pinched the bridge of his nose under his glasses. "To recover from the traumatic experience."

"Staying busy helps keep my mind off it. If I stayed home, I would've been depressed."

"Don't you need to report the attack?"

"I did last night."

"Okay, then, let's start rounds and keep your mind occupied. Put the scarf back on. You don't want to scare the patients with those bruises." He tossed the scarf back to her.

Dr. Bourland was the first educator to validate her intelligence. She was fortunate that he had chosen to train her. Life would have been miserable if she had been paired with the condescending Dr. Ahmid. She should tell Dr. Bourland about Christ. But would he report her? Maybe he would believe. Per the Bible, believers were to share the gospel with everyone. But Jaxon said she shouldn't set things in motion before God's time. Was that even possible? Jesus or Gabriel or someone needed to tell her to whom she should and should not share the gospel.

The hospital indeed provided the needed distraction. The day flew by in a flurry of activity. By the time she had the chance to sit down and look at the clock, her shift was over.

A few people milled around the main lobby waiting room as she entered. Jaxon was waiting. He hadn't seen her yet. She seized the opportunity to admire his chiseled features. When he caught her staring, she smiled. "You're early."

"I was in the area. The scarf's a nice touch." He turned her chin to view her cheek. "Your bruises are much more noticeable today. I'm sure they were the talk of the hospital."

"I managed to avoid most people. Of course, Dr. Bourland noticed. He thought I should have stayed home to recover from the trauma."

"He's a good guy. Let's get out of here." With his hand on the small of her back, he guided her through the exit. The touch of his hand kindled a warm sensation that spread through her core.

The streetlights illuminated the parking lot on the mild evening. Jaxon scanned the area as they walked to his truck.

Once they were safely inside, he produced a picture from a folder. "Is this your attacker?"

The man's likeness sparked a chilling memory of the assault. "Yes." She shuddered and pushed the file back. Looking away, she tried to erase his image from her mind.

Jaxon put the truck in gear and pulled onto the road. "His name is Theodus Maneson. I went to his last known address, but he lost his housing after he was terminated. The station's database doesn't show another address. He's probably living in one of the abandoned buildings by the gym. According to the hospital's personnel director, he was warned and counseled twice before Dr. Chase Bourland reported him for harassing you."

"You filed a report? I told you I don't want my name circulating around the Order." Rory fired a piercing glare.

"I didn't." He kept his eyes on the road.

"Then how did you get this information?"

"I walked into the hospital personnel office in uniform and asked about a security guard who'd been terminated about a month ago. She was eager to help. After that, I drove by the address on file. When he wasn't there, I went to the station and searched for another address."

"Why are you trying to find him? You can't arrest him without charges."

"He doesn't know you didn't file charges. He probably thinks you did. If I confront him, and he thinks he's being arrested, he might give me a reason to defend myself."

"You can't just kill him."

A dark expression flashed in Jaxon's eyes. "Hopefully, he would give me a good reason. We can't take a chance and let some loser ruin the plans."

Rory scowled.

"Don't give me that look."

"A loser can't ruin God's plans."

"He almost did."

"God protected me. He sent Brave to attack him. God will protect me," she swallowed hard, "until it's time not to. God says to leave revenge to him. He will take care of Maneson."

Jaxon's grip on the steering wheel tightened. "Sometimes God wants us in the battle. God could overthrow the Order right now, but he's using us. I believe he wants me to take care of Maneson."

Her jaw clenched. "Last night you warned me against setting things in motion that aren't God's plans. You should take your own advice."

"If God doesn't want me to take care of Maneson, he won't let me find him."

"Oh, so you just go ahead and do whatever you want and force God to stop you, instead of asking him what you should do? I'm praying you don't find the guy."

"Don't waste your prayers on him."

"It's really you I'm praying for." She glanced over and their eyes locked.

He merely shrugged as he pulled into the Cinders parking lot. "Would it be okay if I come in and say hi to Brave and your family?"

"Sure." She chewed on her lip. How would her dad react to Jaxon?

The aroma of stew and an overenthusiastic Brave met them when they entered the apartment. Jaxon knelt, and Brave licked his face.

"Mom, Ruby, you remember Officer Jeffries."

He stood. "Call me Jaxon. It's nice to see you again under better circumstances."

"Yes, you certainly scared us last time." Her mom dried her hands on a towel and took Jaxon's hand in both of hers. "You and Ruby do have those beautiful blue eyes like Rory."

Ruby and Mom acted like smitten schoolgirls. With goofy grins, they glanced back and forth between each other and Jaxon. Thankfully, Mom let go of his hand.

"That's how to respond to a compliment," he whispered so only Rory heard.

She elbowed his side.

"Jaxon, thank you for taking care of Rory last night and driving her home tonight." Her mom ran a hand over her hair.

"It was my pleasure."

"Rory tells us how much you know about God and the Bible," Ruby gushed. "I exercise with her at home."

Jaxon squeezed Ruby's arm. "I think your muscle is bigger than your sister's."

Ruby beamed.

The front door opened and Brave barked.

"When are you getting rid of that mangy mutt?" Dad grumbled.

"No!" Ruby wrapped a protective arm around Brave.

"Hello, Mr. Rydell. I can take him if he's a problem." Jaxon extended his hand. He stood a head taller than her father.

Dad ignored Jaxon's hand.

Keeping one eye trained on her dad, Rory quickly introduced the two men.

"So, you're the man she's been meeting who's filling her head with lies. It's not bad enough you're going to get yourself killed. You're going to take her and all of us with you. They're not going to believe we're not in on this. You're encouraging her to think she can lead a rebellion. You know good and well she can't."

"She won't be alone. God is by her side."

"There is no God." He moved dangerously close to Jaxon. "If there was, we wouldn't be living under the United World Order."

Jaxon replied calmly, "Before the Order, most people were simply going through the motions. God allowed the Order in an effort to humble people."

"Humble them? They weren't humbled. They were destroyed. God told Abraham he wouldn't destroy Sodom if there were at least ten righteous people. There were a lot more than ten righteous people in the United States when the Order took over."

"I'm certainly not smart enough to understand God's ways, but God didn't create the Order, people did. The children of Israel had to wander in the desert for forty years because they lacked the faith to take the land God gave them. He waited for all the naysayers to die before he let them enter the Promised Land. Time after time, they turned to idol worship. Not all of them did, but enough that God stopped protecting them. The children of Israel fell under Babylonian captivity for seventy years. Before the Order, people might not have worshipped idols of wood or metal, but they worshipped themselves. Christians sat back apathetically and allowed it. God didn't prevent the Order, but it was man who allowed the Order in."

Rory's mom stepped between the two men as a buffer. She placed her hands on Dad's shoulders. "Rydge, Ruby and I believe also. If something happens, and we're caught, so be it."

He pushed her hands off. "So be it means execution. You're all crazy. I'm not going to be a part of this." He turned toward the door.

"Don't leave, Mr. Rydell. I'll go. Come on, Brave."

"Rydge, don't be this way." Mom spoke quietly to Dad.

He stormed out before Jaxon could gather Brave.

"I'm sorry. I didn't mean to cause a problem."

"It's not your fault." Rory's mom took Jaxon's arm and led him to the sofa. "He just needs some time to cool down. Please, stay for dinner. It's just stew, but we would love for you to join us."

"Thank you, but I should go in case Mr. Rydell comes back."

"Please stay," Ruby begged.

Jaxon raised his eyebrows at Rory.

"Please stay," she said.

"Okay, since you said please. But if your dad returns, I'll grab Brave and go."

While they brought the food to the table, Jaxon looked around. "You have a nice home."

Rory burst out laughing. Then her mom and Ruby joined in.

Regaining her composure, Rory said, "That was the only thing you could think to say? Oh yes, concrete floors, saggy furniture, and bare cinder block walls are so nice."

His cheeks turned bright red for a change. "Nope, that's the best I could come up with."

"Don't mind her. She has a sarcastic streak. Gets it from her father." Her mom gave Rory a mind-your-manners look.

"Yeah, I seem to recall her knocking my hand off her shoulder the way Mr. Rydell did yours." He grinned at Rory.

It was her turn to blush ... again.

"It's the thought that counts, so thank you. Hopefully, they'll reassign me to a teaching position now that Ruby's healed. Then, we should be assigned back to the academic sector."

As they sat down to dinner, her mom asked Jaxon to give thanks. In addition to thanking God for the food, he asked Jesus to open her dad's eyes and heart.

Her mom squeezed her hand. Rory glanced over. Her red eyes glistened.

The beef stew and corn bread never tasted better. Maybe it was the company. They ate, talked, and laughed. This was how family should feel.

"Thank you for asking me to stay. You're quite the cook, Mrs. Rydell. I hope you're teaching Rory your secrets."

Mom waved her dishtowel at him. "And you are quite the charmer."

"Tell your daughter that." He winked at Rory. "I should head out. Come on, Brave."

"I'll walk you out." Rory grabbed her coat. Jaxon held it for her. "Such a gentleman," she teased.

Bowing, he extended his arm.

"Bye, Jaxon. Please, come again and bring Brave," Ruby said as she gave Brave a final hug.

"I will, maybe when your dad isn't around."

Outside, Jaxon sidled next to Rory. "So, you wanted to get me alone."

"What? You thought I wanted to walk *you* to your truck?" She knelt and hugged the dog. "I wanted to say goodbye to Brave. But seriously, thank you for taking him. It removes a stressor. And I'm sorry about Dad. It's so embarrassing the way he acted. I should have known better. I should have brought Brave out to see you."

"Then I would've missed out on dinner." Jaxon opened the door to his truck, and Brave jumped in.

Rory gave Brave's ears a good scratch and stepped back. Jaxon closed the door and gently pushed her against it. A flock of birds flapped their wings in her stomach. Her mouth went dry. What was wrong with her?

"You aren't responsible for your dad. I had a great time. We'll pray harder for him to come around."

He leaned in with his lips almost touching hers. His warm breath made her temperature rise. She should resist, but the closeness of his lips taunted her. They had already kissed once. Just one more wouldn't be that much worse, right? She closed her eyes and leaned toward him as he backed away, leaving her awkwardly puckering her lips.

"You want me, even though you pretend you don't. I'll behave until you have a chance to break it off with your fiancé."

She shifted and started to rebut his accusation.

"Don't bother denying it. He'd better return soon. I don't know how long I can keep myself in check. You should go before I lose my willpower. Bring your sweats tomorrow, and we'll run after I pick you up. Same time, same place. Good night, Rory." He grinned like a Cheshire cat.

"You're impossible." She turned in a huff and left him standing by his truck.

"Impossibly attractive."

True, so true. His charisma had captured her heart despite her best efforts to resist. Love definitely complicated everything.

Ruby was waiting for her at the door when she returned. "Jaxon likes you."

"He likes us all. He said he really enjoyed tonight."

"No, he *likes* you, like *loves* you." Ruby's eyes sparkled.

"I'm engaged, remember?"

"Well, I like Darius, but he doesn't believe in God. You should marry Jaxon."

"Darius is pro–Order, and he won't be open to your new beliefs." Her mom put an arm around Rory's shoulders. "You have to break off the engagement."

"I know. I'm going to call it off. Since I'm going to be mar—" Rory almost let the martyr thing slip. She couldn't burden them with that. Instead, she discussed her struggle about whether to share her belief in God with Darius.

"Sweetheart, these are tough questions." Her mom brushed the hair from Rory's face. "What I do know is that marriage is tough when you share the same beliefs, and when you don't, it's impossible." Her countenance fell.

"You're talking about you and Dad, aren't you?" Rory asked.

Her mom choked back her tears. "He used to be different. He wasn't angry all the time."

Ruby handed her mom a tissue and hugged her. "It'll be okay. God will fix him."

"We need to concentrate on Rory's predicament. I understand you want Darius to know about God, but this doesn't seem like the right time. Let's pray for the Lord to give you the words to cancel the engagement." She gazed sadly into Rory's eyes.

"When will it be the right time?"

Her mom shook her head. "I don't know."

In heaven, would she remember Darius and realize he wasn't there? Heaven was supposed to be paradise, so maybe she wouldn't, but she had to give him a chance.

"You're not responsible for Darius. Let's turn him over to God." Her mom took her hand and clasped it.

Mom led a prayer for Darius and Dad. Rory had a difficult time concentrating. Darius needed someone to tell him about God, and who would do it, if not her?

"After God delivers us, you and Jaxon should get married." Ruby hung on to the idea like a pit bull.

The problem with Ruby's idea was that Rory wouldn't be alive after God delivered them. Neither guy would get the girl. Still, she should let Darius down easy. She owed him that. But every time she tried to focus on Darius, Jaxon's face appeared—his lips a breath from hers, teasing her with the kiss she hadn't received.

Chapter 20

The next few weeks flew by. Rory silently prayed for her patients. Jesus enabled her to diagnose difficult conditions and prescribe successful treatment plans. All of her patients recovered. Her superstar reputation quickly spread throughout the hospital. She wasn't the brilliant student they assumed, but she couldn't admit Jesus was behind the recoveries. Or maybe she should?

The other physician students began to discuss patients with her. Finally, she enjoyed respect from her peers, even though it would be short lived.

Depending on their schedules, Rory and Jaxon met most afternoons or evenings. They worked out twice a week at the gym during their allotted times. On off nights, Jaxon drove to a remote location where they jogged a few kilometers. He deviated locations to avoid a pattern.

On one particular afternoon, Jaxon drove to a dirt and gravel road surrounded by fields of tall grass and shrubs. He stretched while Rory pretended to do the same.

"Let's go, I'll give you a head start." Jaxon hung back with Brave.

Rory engaged her core and ran lightly on her toes. It wasn't long until Jaxon and Brave caught up and sailed past, leaving her in their dust. Her core disengaged, and her feet struck the ground harder. She rested her hands on her hips and dipped her head.

To overcome the pain, she surveyed her surroundings. Patches of dry grass indicated the area needed rain. To her right, the trail of an overgrown gravel driveway led up to a dilapidated two-story house. Most of the first floor was hidden by huge bushes and tall grass. The Order must have decided no one needed to live on the property.

Who had lived there before? A rancher? The house and property would have possessed a quaint charm during better times. How had the family felt when they had been forced to leave? Had they resisted? Her parents had been forced from their home. A pain stabbed her chest. Perhaps the pain was sympathy for her parents, or it could have been sparked from running.

Jaxon and Brave stood at the finish line, cheering her on. His victory dance was so lame. He handed her a water bottle as she crossed.

They cooled down while they walked back to the truck. When the trio passed the abandoned house, she asked, "After the fall, how will businesses and property be returned to people? Like this property. Who gets it?"

He shrugged. "I'm sure God has a plan."

"But if people have to implement the plan, we need to know it."

"God will reveal the plan when the time's right."

"Don't you like to plan?" How could he be so cavalier?

He grinned. "Nope. I do my best work in the heat of the moment with my adrenaline surging."

"Do you think they'll try to return businesses and property to the previous owners?" The pain of those who had lost property resonated with her.

"Maybe. Or maybe God will give it to the most qualified and deserving."

"That's another option." What was fair? Allocating it to the most deserving sounded too much like Order propaganda. How would the new government know whom God considered most deserving? Oh well, it wouldn't be her problem. She would be long gone by then.

"Luckily, we don't have to figure it out." He patted her head.

"You're patting me like I'm a dog." She leveled a sharp look at him.

He bent down and patted their canine friend. "Brave, she acts like it's an insult to be treated like a dog."

Rory shoved Jaxon. Brave wagged his tail.

They relaxed on the tailgate of the truck under the shade of a large oak tree. The light breeze cooled Rory's flushed skin. She sipped water and admired Jaxon's rock-solid physique. Desire rose as she glanced at his lips. Her pulse soared. Quickly looking away. Heat blossomed up her neck and into her cheeks. *Come on, get a grip.*

Oblivious, Jaxon sipped water and shared the parable of the talents. "As a master prepared to embark on a long trip, he entrusted three servants with one, two, and five talents, or coins. The servants who were given the two and five talents invested them and doubled their value. The third servant hid his one coin. When the master returned, the first two servants presented the coins left in their care, including the earnings. The master told them that since they proved themselves worthy with the little charged to them, he would trust them with more. He celebrated their success. The third servant explained that he hadn't wanted to lose the talent because he knew the master was harsh, so he hid it. He proudly returned it. The master called the servant lazy and said he should have invested the talent to return it with interest. The master took the coin from the lazy servant and gave it to the first servant. He threw the lazy servant into outer darkness."

Rory released a deep breath. "It seems harsh to call the servant lazy. The master never instructed them to invest it and return more than he gave them." She might have hidden the coin, not because she was lazy, but because she wasn't knowledgeable about investing.

"The master represents God. He knows our thoughts and intentions. So, if the master says the servant was lazy, we know he was."

"You brought up this parable to support your theory that God will restore property to those who are most deserving."

"Your question brought the parable to mind. The Bible is our reference book. When we grapple with questions, scripture is the best glimpse into God's will. Doesn't it make sense that businesses should be awarded to those who are competent and will make them successful?"

"Well, when you put it like that."

Jaxon leaned toward her. The electric surge from his close proximity took her breath away. Her gaze fell on his lips. Would he tease her again? *No, you don't.* She grabbed his shirt and reeled him in until their lips touched, and a tingling sensation shot to her core.

He slid his arms around her. His lips responded eagerly. Intoxicated by his familiar scent, her mind clouded while butterflies flitted in her stomach. A warning blared in the recesses of her mind. This wasn't the kind of person she was. Pain pierced her heart as she tore her lips away.

"What's wrong?" Jaxon whispered. His warm breath against her ear caused a shiver to run down her spine.

Gasping, she looked away. "I'm sorry. I started this, but I shouldn't have. I haven't broken up with Darius. This is wrong."

He took her hands. "You have broken up with him. He just doesn't know yet. If he wasn't incommunicado at training, you would have told him. You're not cheating. It's already over." He kissed her hand and then her wrist.

A tingling sensation soared up her arm. "True, but—"

"But what?" He nuzzled her neck.

Her resistance shattered as her mind shut down. His afternoon beard prickled her fingertips as she clasped his face, guiding his mouth. When his lips hungrily covered hers, sparks flew.

Guilt tried to rise, but she quickly pushed it down. Sacrificing herself for the cause should entitle her to savor a kiss or two with the man she loved, right?

Chapter 21

Head over heels in love, the passing weeks were marked by time at the hospital and time with Jaxon—until March 14—the day Darius returned from training. Rory jumped at the dreaded knock. She fought her instinct to hide and pretend no one was home. To delay the meeting only prolonged the angst. She was ready to shed her guilt.

She opened the door and pain stabbed her stomach when Darius greeted her with a huge smile and a beautiful bouquet. From his tanned face, he'd enjoyed some sun on his trip. The white polo shirt looked nice against his bronzed arms. He grabbed her and kissed her passionately.

Her lips failed to respond. The kiss was wrong, like kissing a brother. Should she lead him on or blurt out the breakup the instant he arrived? Both choices were cruel.

"What's wrong?" Worry creased his brow. "Is it Ruby? Did she get worse?"

His concern for her sister hit her hard. He didn't deserve a broken heart.

"No, she's fine." Rory smiled weakly and took the flowers. "These are beautiful. You shouldn't have." He really shouldn't have.

"Of course, I should've. Beautiful flowers for my beautiful girl." He slid his arms around her waist and nuzzled her neck. "I missed you so much."

The touch that normally would have aroused her made her feel ill. She broke free. "Tell me about everything. What was it like flying in an airplane?"

"It was great. The seats reclined. The force of gravity during takeoff and landing made me nervous, but it didn't last too long. I sat by the window. It was really cool seeing everything from so high up and being surrounded by clouds."

"Wow, exciting. How was your meeting? What kind of things did you learn?" Her hands shook as she arranged the flowers in a glass of water. They didn't own a vase.

"The rooms were super nice, kind of like a small apartment. A maid cleaned the bathroom and made the bed every day. We ate in a cafeteria. The food was really good. The meetings were boring." He drew out the word boring.

"What kind of things did they discuss?" *How to recognize if your fiancée is a traitor?*

"You don't want to hear about it. Let's talk about us." He knelt on one knee and pulled a black velvet box from his pocket.

Her eyes widened as he opened it. "No. I asked you not to buy another ring."

"I know, but I want you to have a nice one, and I can afford it now." He removed a platinum band with a solitaire diamond and held it out. Was it a carat or two? At any rate, it was huge. He reached for her left hand.

Rory jerked her hand away.

He winced as if she'd kicked him in the stomach.

She held him at arm's length. "We need to talk.*"* He had forced her hand, and he wasn't going to take it well.

He stood and shifted his feet. "This doesn't sound good. What's up?"

"I'm sorry. There's no easy way to say this. We shouldn't marry." She couldn't look into his eyes. "We're … we're not compatible."

"What do you mean, not compatible?" His eyes clouded.

"You would be happier with someone else. Someone … more like you." What did she even mean?

"And you'd be happier with who? With a doctor? That's what this is about, isn't it? You've fallen for that doctor training you. Instead of telling me the truth, you say we're not compatible." His face reddened, and the veins in his neck bulged.

"No, I'm not seeing him. This is about you and me. We aren't compatible. What do we have to talk about? You don't understand what I do—"

Darius closed the distance between them but stopped short of touching her. "So, I'm not smart enough for you? Is that what you're saying? You think I'm too stupid to marry." He banged his hand on the table.

"No. It's not about either of us being smarter. It's about being different. We don't have common interests."

"I thought we had love in common. You've always been smarter than me. But we always talked. I don't see why it matters." His eyes bored through her. "Unless there's someone else."

She blinked back tears. Should she take back everything? What good would that do? She no longer loved him like she once had. There was no way to break off the engagement without destroying him.

"Did you know you were breaking up with me before I left? Is that why you told me not to buy a ring? Were you already seeing someone else?"

She'd never seen him this angry. "I wasn't seeing anyone before you left, but I was feeling that we aren't right for each other. I thought long and hard while you were gone."

Darius took her hand. "Is this about me not wanting to buy the medicine for Ruby? That's what it's about, isn't it? I changed my mind. I was going to buy it, but Ruby was better. I never should have said no. I'm sorry."

"No." Maybe she should tell him there was someone else.

"Then what does it have to do with? For eight weeks, the only thing I thought about was coming home and marrying you while you were thinking about breaking up with me." He threw the ring on the table and turned away.

"You don't want to marry me."

He whirled to face her. "Don't tell me what I want!"

165

She stepped backward. "You would call it off if you knew—" Her stomach clenched. Why did she keep talking? *Oh God, should she stop?*

"There's nothing you could do to make me want to call it off. Well, unless you believe in a god, but you don't."

Her eyes betrayed her secret.

His jaw clenched. "No. This isn't funny. Don't joke about this!"

Her silence confirmed his accusation.

"You can't. You can't believe in a god. You're smarter than that."

Her mouth opened and replied independently of her will, "God is real." She'd crossed the point of no return.

Darius grabbed her shoulders. "Who told you this? That doctor you're seeing?"

"God told me."

He shook her as if he could shake her belief away. "God couldn't have because there is no god. You know that. Why are you saying this?"

"I died and—"

"What do you mean you died?" His fingers dug into her flesh.

She abbreviated her out-of-body experience.

"You never told me any of this before I left."

"I didn't think you'd believe me."

"Because it's not true. This didn't really happen. Your mind does funny things when you almost die. You imagined it or something." His eyes bounced wildly. "Rory, I have to report you. I've got no choice. They trained me to watch for these kinds of things. I signed papers swearing I'll report anyone I'm suspicious about." He dropped his hands and balled them into fists.

She touched his cheek. "I understand. I couldn't bear you not knowing the truth. Jesus is real, and he gave his life so you can be saved. Just ask him to speak to your heart. He loves you and wants you to know him." Her eyes pleaded with him.

"This is the craziest story I ever heard. Why are you saying this? You're giving me no choice. You see that, don't you?" He leaned his head back and took a deep breath with his eyes closed.

"If you report me, it's okay. I'm going to heaven after I die. I'll forgive you. I love you, but this is why we aren't compatible. If you don't report me, and I'm arrested, I promise I'll never admit I told you." She touched his shoulder.

Darius recoiled. "Your parents and Ruby, do they believe?"

She felt like Peter as he sank while he walked on the raging sea. Drowning was inevitable as the water rose around her, but her family wasn't supposed to drown too. "No. I haven't told them." Her stomach churned at the lie.

"But you tell me?" He raised his eyebrows.

"I wouldn't have told you now if you weren't pressuring me to marry you."

He scratched his head. "Why are you so special that a god would speak to you?"

"I ask that question all the time. I can't be the only person God's speaking to because I'm not special. Maybe other people just aren't listening."

"Crites, Rory. You're putting me in a bad place. I love you, but it's my duty to report you." He struck the table again.

Rory flinched. "I'm sorry."

He rubbed his face. "The night this started, I think the cold did something to your brain, and you imagined the whole thing." He tapped her head. "You need to see a brain doctor. You need help."

She placed her hand on his arm. "There's nothing wrong with me. There's nothing a neurologist can treat. I need you to know the truth because I love you."

"No. Shut up. Stop talking about this. I have to report you. Crites!" Darius grabbed the ring and the box from the table.

Rory removed her original engagement ring and placed it in his hand. He looked at the ring, then back at her. Finally, he threw the ring on the table and stormed out.

She stared at the ring as it wobbled on the gray Formica. What had she done? Telling Darius was a monumental mistake. The problem was that once words were spoken, they could never be erased. They floated around in the universe forever. *God, please protect my family and don't let Darius turn them in.*

To avoid speaking with her family, Rory retired and pretended to be asleep when they returned from the grocer.

The devil whispered that she should tell Darius she had been wrong about God to protect her family. She was too drained to rebuke him. Like an inmate on death row, she wallowed in the fear of what lay ahead and waited for the inevitable.

Chapter 22

The next afternoon, Jaxon comforted Rory. "It had to be done. Are you okay?"

She refrained from discussing the details of the crushing blow she had delivered to Darius and certainly didn't mention her deadly confession. What was done was done, and worrying Jaxon wouldn't change anything. "I'm just glad it's over."

"Henry wants to meet with you on your day off on Thursday."

She swallowed hard. She would probably be in custody by then. Her fate rested in Darius's hands. If Mr. Leeman had an inkling about her confession, he'd never allow her near his home. "Why does he want to meet?"

"He didn't say. I have a special meeting until noon. I told him I'd drive you over afterward, but he wants you at his house at eleven. If you take the trans there, I'll pick you up after."

"Yeah, sure."

Rory worked out harder than normal. Post-workout, she and Jaxon relaxed on the mat. She leaned against his chest, savoring his presence. All was right with her world.

Jaxon lightly kissed her neck. "Since you broke off your engagement, there's no reason to pretend you don't want me so much it hurts."

Her love for him was intense, but she had ruined everything with her big mouth. A soft sigh escaped from her lips. "Don't you think it would be a distraction to our calling?"

"No." He kissed her ear. "I don't find this distracting at all."

Her tears broke through the dam where she had locked them deep inside.

"What's wrong?" he asked.

"I don't know. I guess the uncertainty of everything."

He wiped her tears away. "Well, God says not to worry about tomorrow. It will worry about itself." He kissed the top of her hand. "Rory, marry me."

A shiver of desire raced through her. "This isn't fair. I can't think clearly."

"There's nothing to think about. Just say yes." His lips pressed against hers.

"I don't want you to be arrested because you're my husband." Arrest was a real possibility, especially after last night.

"If you're arrested, I'll turn myself in. Whatever happens, I'll be by your side. I'll go down to the bowels of hell with you, if necessary."

She couldn't allow that. "You're too valuable. The cause needs you."

"If I'm so valuable, God will protect me. I don't know what tomorrow holds. But I do know that I want to spend whatever time I have left with you. Then we'll spend eternity in heaven."

Rory looked down. "You could do so much better. You could have someone with a beautiful face and a hot body."

He held her shoulders and gazed into her eyes. "Listen to me, you are beautiful inside and out. I don't know why you can't see it. Your face is beautiful, like an angel. And your body ... well, we'd better not talk too long about that." He raised his eyebrows. "Besides, heart is more important, and you have a huge heart. You accepted God's call, even though it's dangerous and scary as hell. That's beautiful."

Obviously, he didn't know her as well as he thought. "I accepted in theory. I tell myself I'll do whatever God asks, but I can't be sure I won't choke when the going gets tough. Your idea of who I am is generous."

"I know exactly who you are, Rory Rydell. You are my future bride. You might as well say yes. But if you don't, I'll wait. Mark my words you will say yes."

"You sound pretty sure of yourself." His words launched her heart into orbit, even though they wouldn't likely come to fruition.

"I've never been more sure of anything." He winked.

She settled back down onto his chest with a lump in her throat. Her heart ached for the life that would never be.

The next few days, Rory constantly watched over her shoulder, afraid an officer would pop up to arrest her at any moment. When she was still free on Thursday, she boarded the trans to the tech sector. Selecting a window seat, she stared at the passing scenery. Had Darius reported her? She covered her mouth and coughed, trying to expel the burning sensation climbing up her chest to her throat.

Since Rory had allowed more time for travel than was necessary, she arrived early for the meeting. Cumulus clouds dotted the blue sky. The sun kissed her skin with warmth, and a gentle breeze rustled the leaves in the trees. The gorgeous day persuaded her to loiter in the park. If she encountered Gabriel, she would ask him if she'd made a mistake when she told Darius about Jesus. He probably wouldn't tell her, though.

"It's a beautiful day, isn't it?"

Rory whirled toward the voice and found herself face-to-face with Bane Tabor. He resembled a psych ward patient with his unkempt hair and beard and his frantic eyes.

"Please tell me you believe in God." Desperation laced his voice.

After Rory scanned the area and verified the coast was clear, she spoke in a hushed tone. "I can tell you no such thing. You'll be arrested for talking about this."

"I don't care. Let them kill me. What do I have to live for? My wife and son are gone. Initially, I believed God would redeem us, but it's been so long. I've given up."

The man's despair tugged at her. With no specifics on God's plan, there wasn't a lot she could share, even if she wanted to.

Tabor dropped down to the grass and hung his head in his hands. She joined him.

"Mary was my wife. She was beautiful, more beautiful than I deserved." He stared at the ground with his hands clasped between his knees. "We attended church regularly. I wasn't really a Christian, but I knew I didn't want the United World Order regime. Mary was distressed about living in a world where God was outlawed. We decided to take a stand as a family and choose execution. I agreed. Then one day, while I was at work, Mary used my email account. Pretending to be me, she reported that she and Caleb were believers. When I asked her why, she claimed God told her I needed to stay to develop the computer system for the Order, so I could code backdoors to enable me to access it. Then after God overthrew the Order, I would assist the believers with the system. She said the Order would trust me more if I turned them in." His shoulders heaved.

Was the revelation true? The anguish on his face appeared genuine.

After a moment, he composed himself. "I begged her to let me die with them, but she was adamant. I was so angry. How could she do this? The email had been sent. I couldn't undo it. I know she believed she was doing God's will. I figured it was my punishment for not being a Christian. They made me watch … the injection." Tears streamed down his furrowed cheeks, off his chin, and fell in dark circles on his pants. "They went to sleep and never woke up. I live with that image every day. I can't do it any longer. I did my part. I coded the backdoors. It took seven years to complete. At first, I thought it was my fault God hadn't overthrown them because I hadn't finished. I did my part, but I haven't seen hide nor hair of God. Then several weeks ago, I saw you and your shining face. I knew you were special, that you were a sign, but you denied it."

His story tugged at her heart. Should she tell him God was preparing something? What if he was lying? He was really good if he was. *God, what should I say?*

Rory tentatively touched his shoulder. He jerked.

"The day I first saw you, I had a bottle of antidepressants and whiskey. I planned to sit in this park and mix pills and booze." He forced a sad grin.

"You were going to commit suicide?"

"Loneliness torments me night and day. I was going to go to sleep and never wake up. Then you showed up with your shiny face. It was like nothing I'd ever seen before. I thought you were an angel. Are you?" Tabor looked hopeful.

She laughed. "You obviously don't know me. I'm no angel." She scanned the area as she bit her lip. "But I was touched by one in this very park."

"I knew it. That's why your face was shining. What did he say?"

"His name was Gabriel."

Tabor's face lit in recognition of the name.

"He said to have faith and that something will happen soon."

"What?"

She shrugged her shoulders. "He said I would be overwhelmed if I knew, so I just have to have faith."

"Is that when your face started shining? After you met him?"

She nodded. "He touched me, and I felt this overwhelming peace. I guess that's when the glow started." What was she doing? First Darius, and now she was blabbing to a stranger.

"Did Gabriel tell you to visit the Leemans? Are they believers?"

Henry's warning not to endanger them blared in her head. "When I visited them, they didn't say anything about believing." The lie brought a lump to her throat.

"What did they say about your face shining?"

Her cheeks felt warm. "Nothing. They didn't mention it. When you brought it up, I thought you were unstable. But when I used their restroom, I saw my face in the mirror. I was horrified. I wondered why they didn't say anything."

"Maybe only believers can see the glow."

"Maybe." Everyone who had mentioned the glow believed. Maybe she hadn't needed to cover her face. If he was right, this meant he was a believer.

"I would've bet my life that Athelene believed. It doesn't surprise me if Henry doesn't."

"I don't really know them, but they seem nice."

"Good church going folk," he said with a sarcastic edge. "The Order used me as the poster child of a model citizen for turning in my family. I was an outcast. I never had many friends, but after that, everyone went out of their way to avoid me. Henry had been an elder at the church we attended, and I tried to confide in him, but he refused to speak to me."

Tabor would recognize her parents since he'd attended her grandfather's church. She must proceed carefully.

"Why do you visit them?"

She paused to formulate her answer. "A patient in the hospital where I'm training was very ill and asked me to let them know." A patient *had* asked her to find them.

"Who was the patient?"

Thank goodness for privacy rules. "I can only give a patient's name to persons they have specified."

"I thought maybe the patient is connected to God's plan."

Her pulse quickened. Spinning lies, even for good reason, was making her nauseous. "I don't think so. He didn't make it."

"Why are you here today?"

"To tell them their friend died."

"How many times have you been here?"

"Three." She chewed her lip. Why was he asking so many questions?

"I run into you each time you visit. That must mean something, don't you think? It must mean you and I are connected."

The man desperately sought a bond with someone, anyone. Although, he might have a point. "Maybe. I don't really understand any of this."

Tabor took her hand. "Thank you so much for telling me. I have a reason to live now. Are there a lot of believers?"

"I don't know any others, but Gabriel indicated there are many. I don't think God would move if there weren't."

He brightened. "Where are my manners? I'm Bane Tabor."

"Rory." She gently pulled her hand away.

"Does Rory have a last name?"

"Of course."

"It is?"

Looking around, she said, "You know, I'm a little uncomfortable—"

"How can I contact you if I don't know your full name?"

"I don't think we should contact each other."

He looked stricken. "It's obvious that God brought us together."

"God brought us together three times. If we are meant to meet again, he'll make it happen. I'm sorry. I need to go." She jumped up and hurried away while he struggled to his feet.

"You don't need to be afraid of me."

"I'm not. I'm just late," she called over her shoulder.

Why had it upset Tabor when she wouldn't share her full name? Was he genuinely thrilled to meet another believer or to meet a believer to report? She was in over her head and taking on water fast.

175

Chapter 23

Mr. Leeman answered the door, looking dapper in neatly pressed khaki slacks and a button-down, long-sleeved blue shirt. Not one of his white hairs was out of place. "Come in, dear."

What was up with calling her dear? The last time they'd met, he had barely been civil. Perhaps Mrs. Leeman had threatened him to be on his best behavior.

"Did you have trouble getting here?" He glanced up and down the street before he closed the door. Was he looking for Tabor?

"Sorry, I'm late. I arrived early, but I walked through the park. It's such a beautiful day. I lost track of time."

"Did you run into Gabriel again?" He perked up as he led her to the sofa.

"No." The pleasant Henry Leeman was barely an improvement over the unpleasant one.

As she sat on the sofa, her mind wandered back to Tabor. Could a loving husband and father go through with such a ruse? God asked Abraham to sacrifice his son, but then stopped him. She chewed her bottom lip. Tabor had played her. She was such an idiot.

Henry cleared his throat. "Rory, are you listening to me?"

"Huh? What did you say?" She wiped her clammy hands on her pants.

"I said you should know that the Order is picking up rumors of a revolutionary leader gathering troops. They're on high alert. They are actively looking for you."

Nausea bubbled in her stomach. It was bad enough when they were looking for general citizens with religious beliefs, but now they were specifically looking for her. The rug flew out from under her, and her psyche fell hard.

"They are calling this long-awaited leader the Lion of Judah."

Her eyes widened. "They're not looking for me? Whew, God figured out that I'm not a leader? Who is this lion?" A vision of a fierce lion saturated her mind, followed by the pride with their teeth bared, pursuing the Order forces.

"You are the Lion of Judah."

"Me?" The image shifted to her alone and frightened in a jail cell. "Who is calling me this and why?"

He smiled and waved a hand. "Here's the beauty of it. They don't know Rory Rydell is the Lion. Against my wishes, my dear wife started a rumor that God has spoken to the Lion, and this Lion will help God deliver us from the Order. After you shared how your mother came up with your name, she coined the phrase." He stared out the huge window.

Rory allowed the revelation to marinate. "Isn't that a little misleading?"

"More than a little. They undoubtedly imagine a tall, strong, male, and she doesn't correct them. She feels they need hope. As much as I was against the ploy, I have to admit, it's best for you. Everyone, including the authorities, will be on the lookout for someone like Jaxon. You will walk in plain sight, and they won't even see you. My fear is that if believers learn your identity, they won't believe you can lead them."

"A valid concern. So, now what?" She stood and began to pace.

"Have you received any messages from God?"

"No. Have you?"

"Why would I?" He pointed at her. "You're the Lion, the one chosen by God. No one has appeared to you since we last met?" His voice was edgy.

She stopped pacing. "You know I'm no lion. Why did Grandfather and Gabriel instruct me to find you? You're clueless. You don't even believe God chose me. I doubt you even believe in God."

He flinched. "We expected rescue years ago. And you're not who I expected God would send. You showed up at our house with a glowing face for Pete's sake. I can find no explanation other than that God has chosen you for something." His eyes darted to her, then quickly away. "Do you still believe you'll be a martyr?"

"Yeah. That seems most likely."

Henry looked sad. Maybe he liked her after all. "Did Gabriel say anything about how the Order will learn your identity?"

"No." There was a good chance that Darius or Tabor would report her. One of them might be reporting her as they spoke.

"You don't look well."

"Discussing martyrdom tends to do that."

He held her shoulders. "What did Gabriel say that made you think you'll be a martyr? It might mean nothing to you but will to me. Perhaps this is how I help. Think."

His tone made her back away. Recalling Gabriel's exact words was difficult. She closed her eyes. "Something about how I'm stronger than I know, not to fear death because we all die, and afterward, we live in heaven. Why would he mention not to fear death unless this calling was going to kill me?"

"That's it? That's all he said?" His mouth held a hard line.

"He said a lot of stuff. Oh, he said I can ask not to die a painful death, but he couldn't guarantee it." She sighed.

"Did he say why you should find me?"

She shrugged. "Something about many people will help me. I asked if you were one of those people. He said you're involved. I'm pretty sure that's what he said."

From his expression, the cogs were turning in Henry's head. If he knew about her conversation with Tabor or Darius, those cogs would spin so fast they'd explode. At least she'd told Tabor she didn't think they believed in God. Then again, he probably hadn't believed her. She chewed on her lip.

The doorbell rang. Henry excused himself and then returned with Jaxon in tow. Another man who would be unhappy with her if he knew about her confession to Tabor. So, she wouldn't share. Jaxon looked handsome in his jeans, black polo shirt, and big smile. He leaned down and kissed her cheek. Heat crept up her neck.

Their host scowled and raised his eyebrows as he looked from her to Jaxon. "Is something going on between you two? Earlier, when you didn't hear a word that I said, you were daydreaming about Romeo here, weren't you?"

A huge grin popped onto Jaxon's face. "You were daydreaming about me?"

"No." A stupid response because she couldn't share the subject of her preoccupation.

"Well, she tries to pretend she hasn't fallen for me, but we both know that's a lie." He threaded his fingers through hers.

She pulled her hand away. Jaxon firmly retrieved it.

"This is a terrible idea," Henry said solemnly. "It makes you vulnerable."

"Really?" Jaxon asked.

"Really. You're a tough guy, and if you're arrested, you might be able to hold up under torture. But when they threaten to hurt her, what will you do? You'll tell them everything. The Order is ruthless. You know that. You're military. This isn't a game." His face grew red.

This revelation elicited a cloud of concern on Jaxon's face and confirmed what she already knew. This was not a time for a relationship. She had to end it. Her heart cracked right down the middle.

Jaxon wrapped a protective arm around her. "Are you ending it with Athelene?"

"For Pete's sake, we were married before the Order was even an idea. I can tell you that if we weren't married, I certainly wouldn't in this climate."

"So you say. You really don't know what you would do until you're in the situation. God brought us together, and he'll protect us."

"Athelene brought you together."

"You think it's coincidence that I responded to the disturbance at her apartment? It was God uniting us."

"The apostle Paul said it's better to remain unmarried."

"Paul was compelled to stay single and *suggested* unmarried believers remain unmarried. Jesus never commanded or suggested believers remain single. We already fell in love. Paul would be happy for us." He shot a lethal glare Henry's way.

Henry shot the look right back. "You think your love is indestructible. Well, it's not. If you recall, in Romeo and Juliet, the star-crossed lovers died tragically. God has allowed many good people to die since the formation of the United World Order. Your love will end as another tragic love story. Fall out of love."

"If we die, we'll live in heaven. As believers, we don't need to fear death. Have you forgotten that?" His gaze was as hard as steel.

Henry pointed at Jaxon. "You're a loaded gun. Do you care about the others you'll destroy with you?"

"If we go down, why does that affect others?"

"Because she can't hold up under interrogation, and if they threaten to hurt her, you'll break."

"You underestimate us. Is this why you called us here? To tell us to break it off?" Jaxon's voice had a knife-sharp edge to it.

He waved his hand. "No, I had no idea anything was going on between you."

"So, why are we here? Let's get on with it."

"I asked to meet with Juliet. You invited yourself."

"Okay, then why did you want to meet with Rory?"

"To give her a heads up. The Order is diligently following up on rumors about a new leader who is planning an attack. They are aware of and actively looking for her. The both of you need to exercise extreme caution."

"And they're calling me—well, not me really, but the leader who they don't know is me—the Lion of Judah. Which is good because who would think I could be a lion, right?" She raised her brows at Jaxon.

Jaxon stood and rubbed his hand over his face. "The purpose of our *special* meeting was to brief us about the Lion rumor. They have no real information, no name, no description. Currently, they are treating it as hearsay. But they are afraid someone will decide to assume the title and start a revolution. We're supposed to keep our eyes and ears open for anyone who might know more and bring them in for questioning. No one knows Rory is the Lion except us and her family, right?" He glared at Henry.

Henry clenched his jaw and stared at Jaxon. He probably interpreted Jaxon's words as an accusation. The room's temperature was rising. The man finally spoke. "Athelene sent out anonymous messages to people she knew would spread the rumor. The messages were encrypted and can't be traced back to us. But with things heating up, I'm going to tell Athelene we need to break the two of you up and have someone else study with Rory."

"All that does is give her identity to one more person. You can tell Athelene anything you want, but God wants me to work with and protect Rory." Jaxon tugged her arm and pulled her to her feet. "Come on, let's go."

Rory looked back and forth between Jaxon and Henry.

Henry's face was hard like granite. "Rory, I see it in your eyes. You know I'm right. End this. You two are concentrating more on your love than God's plan."

Jaxon pulled Rory down the hall, out the door, and along the sidewalk. She had to run to keep up with his long strides. When he opened the truck door, she quickly climbed in. He slammed the door shut after her.

His nostrils flared as he slid into the driver's seat. "That old fart. Who does he think he is, telling us we shouldn't fall in love? What did you discuss before I got here?" He started the ignition and then accelerated. The tires screeched against the pavement.

Rory filled him in on the discussion he missed.

After she finished, she gazed out the passenger window. "He's right. I've known all along, but you're so darned charming that I couldn't help myself."

He raised his eyebrows. "I am darned charming, aren't I?"

"This isn't funny. We're caught up in our feelings. Maybe it would be better if someone else worked with me." *And it would put distance between us when I'm arrested.*

"Who are we to break up what God brought together?"

"Jaxon, I'm very happy for all our time together, but maybe ... we should take a break." She chewed on her lip.

"This is not the time—"

Jaxon slammed on the brakes and threw his arm out in front of her. In the heat of the discussion, he'd missed a stop sign. Her hands flew to the dash to brace herself as the shoulder strap tightened across her chest. A car horn blared. The truck skidded to a halt seconds before it would have hit the car that whizzed by on the cross street.

"Are you okay?" His brows furrowed in concern.

She nodded.

"I'm sorry."

"I'm fine. Let's put this discussion on hold until we get home."

"Copy."

They rode in silence. The sun spread warmth through the windshield. It was a shame the day had been ruined. Why couldn't she be a normal person with a normal life who could enjoy a day in the sunshine?

Jaxon pulled into a parking space at the Cinders and shifted the truck into park. He swiveled in the driver's seat and reached out to pull her close.

She rested her hand against his chest, keeping some distance between them. "Please don't make this harder. Preoccupation with our feelings almost resulted in an accident."

"That was my fault. But God brought us together, and we fell in love." He gestured with his hands. "You, me, us, this can't be wrong. Let's pray about us."

"Ugh. How can I argue with that?"

"Exactly." He grinned and pulled her in for a kiss.

When they reluctantly parted, Jaxon clasped her hand, and they bowed their heads with their foreheads touching. "Heavenly Father, we love you with all our hearts. All things are possible with you. We know you brought us together to use us to deliver your people from the Order. Help Rory see that you intend for us to work together and for us to be romantically involved. Set her straight. Protect us as we serve you. In Jesus's name, we pray, amen."

Rory shoved him. Should she scowl or smile? Either one probably wouldn't make a difference. "What kind of prayer was that? Set me straight? What happened to 'Show us your will, Lord'?"

"I just cut to the chase."

She pursed her lips. "For now, let's be friends. Dad should be at work. Why doesn't my friend come in and visit?"

"After a friendly kiss."

"You drive a hard bargain."

The magic of the kiss evaporated as Henry's words replayed in her head. *You know I'm right, end this.*

Chapter 24

Two days after the meeting with Henry, Rory and Jaxon feasted on ham sandwiches and potato salad at the gym. The food and location were unimportant. The company made the meal perfect.

After they ate, he pulled her close. "God said no one should separate a couple that he has joined together. In the Song of Solomon, he says that rivers cannot wash away love. I can go on and on. We are meant to be together. Why do you fight it?" His gaze penetrated her soul.

She caressed his cheek, coarse with afternoon stubble. "If we met under ordinary circumstances, I would be Mrs. Jaxon Jeffries so fast your head would spin. Our calling complicates things."

"I've told you that I will stand by your side and go down with you, whether you're my wife or not." He knelt on one knee and took her hand. "Say you'll marry me. We can marry ourselves right here, right now, before God Almighty." His eyes pleaded with her.

"You're so romantic. What more could a girl ask than to marry a guy in an abandoned warehouse while wearing her favorite pair of sweats?" She jumped up and twirled in a circle.

"What do you want, a long white dress and lots of guests?"

"Who wouldn't?" She batted her eyelashes.

"We can have another ceremony with all the bells and whistles after the Order falls, but in the meantime, we can have our own private one now and enjoy the perks of husband and wife." He raised his eyebrows while he awaited her answer.

To hide the pain of her shattering heart, she wrapped her arms around his neck and whispered in his ear, "I'm sorry. We need to wait until the Order falls." She kissed his earlobe and added, "Say you'll remember me just like this as we are right now."

"What are you saying?" He pulled her from his neck to look into her eyes.

To shut him up, she covered his mouth with hers. A fire rose in the depths of her soul. The attraction was debilitating. She needed to put distance between them. She released him and headed toward the equipment. "I never thought I'd say this, but I need to work out."

Grinning wickedly, Jaxon teased, "A cold shower is more like it."

She walked backward and taunted him. "Sounds like you know."

"Believe me, I do." His gaze telegraphed his pent-up desires.

Heat rose in her cheeks. She blinked away tears born of intense longing.

Jaxon jogged up and slapped her backside. She shoved him, and then they got down to business. Her strength had improved greatly, considering where she'd started. After an hour of intense exertion, they collapsed, exhausted and sweaty, onto the mat. Her heart fluttered as she wiped the sweat from his brow.

"What's wrong?" he asked.

"If I'm arrested, will the Order listen in on my family's apartment?" She bit her lip.

"That would be protocol, and it's why we need to make sure you don't get arrested." He ran a thumb down her cheek.

She propped herself on her elbow. "What if we run away to a deserted sector and start a new life, just the two of us?" She wouldn't be arrested if she was hiding from her calling.

He rolled onto his back and chuckled. "You don't strike me as someone who can live off the land. Even if we could, it would take a lot of supplies. Supplies we can't get. Anyway, you wouldn't leave Ruby and your parents."

Tears rimmed her eyes. Why did everything have to be so complicated?

"We're called to help overthrow the Order. We can't do that if we run away."

"God will find someone else. Why does it have to be us?"

"You're asking the wrong question. Why does it *get* to be us? This is exciting. Not only do we get to see it happen, we get to participate. Remember what happened to Jonah when he ran from his calling. A big fish swallowed him. He sloshed around in its belly for three days and nights. Gross."

"There aren't any big fish on the way to the hill country."

"Maybe the ground would swallow us. We don't need to go to the hill country to start a life. We can do it right here." He threaded his fingers through hers.

"Aren't you scared?"

"To marry you? Yeah, a little. Your dagger eyes are terrifying."

She swatted him. "No, overthrowing the Order."

He shrugged. "I figure I win no matter what. If I help defeat the Order, I win. If I die trying, I go to paradise for eternity. I still win."

She snuggled against him. "I wish I was as brave as you."

"Maybe you're braver."

"Yeah, right."

"I'm not afraid, so maybe I'm not brave at all. You forge ahead in spite of your fear. That might make you braver." Jaxon wrapped his arms around her.

After a moment, Rory shook her head. "I wouldn't say I'm forging ahead. It's more like inching. Anyway, God likes you best."

"How do you figure?" He kissed the top of her head.

"God loved David best, and he wasn't afraid of Goliath or any of the enemy armies. He trusted God to deliver him, like you. I, on the other hand, want to run away like Jonah. God loved David more than Jonah."

"God rescued Jonah out of the fish's belly and counseled him when he was upset that the people of Nineveh repented."

"God loved Jonah, but he loved David more. He called David a man after his heart. He didn't say that about Jonah. But unlike Jonah, I'd be thrilled if the Order saw the error of their ways and chose to follow God. I really would."

As she cooled down post-workout, she shivered. Jaxon pulled a blanket from one of the boxes along the wall and tossed it over her. He slid underneath and gathered her in his arms. They discussed their hopes and dreams and what the world might look like when the Order fell. The steady beating of his heart comforted her. They fit together perfectly. This was where she belonged—with Jaxon on one side and Brave on the other.

***

Bright sunlight peeked through the windows and startled Rory awake.

She sprung upright and shook Jaxon. "Wake up. We fell asleep. Get up. You have to drive me home."

He stretched and pulled her on top of him. "We fell asleep, so what?"

"My family expected me home last night. They'll be worried. Come on." She yanked at him.

"They know you're with me."

"And they'll be freaked. They'll assume we've been arrested."

Brave barked as he sensed her distress.

"Okay, okay." Jaxon rose slowly and yawned.

On the way to her apartment, Jaxon suggested, "Maybe they're asleep and don't know that you didn't come home. Sneak in quietly, so you don't wake them."

"Maybe you're right." She chewed her lip.

"Relax until you know there's a problem."

"You obviously don't know me." She shot a dirty look in his direction.

He pointed at her. "I know that look very well."

Jaxon made small talk, but it was background noise to her. He parked in front of her entrance and pulled her in for a kiss. With her lips tight, she didn't reciprocate.

As she jumped from the truck, he leaned across the seat. "They'll see you're fine, and they'll get over it. Love you."

Without a word, she slammed the door and sprinted to her apartment.

The noise of her key in the lock made her cringe. The door creaked despite her efforts to open it quietly.

"Where have you been?" her mother demanded.

Mom stood a few feet from the door in her tattered robe. Her dark blond hair was pulled back in a ponytail. Her dad was drinking a cup of coffee at the table in his T-shirt and undershorts. Their bloodshot eyes betrayed their sleepless night.

"I'm sorry. We were talking after we worked out, and we fell asleep. We just woke. I came home right away." She probably looked like a wreck.

"Do you have any idea how worried we were? I woke around two and checked on you. When you weren't here, I woke your dad. We didn't know what to do, where to look. We didn't sleep a wink after that. We were afraid something had happened or ... you were ... were arrested." Mom gestured with her hands.

Her dad fired an evil eye at her.

Rory embraced her mom, who stood stiffly. "I'm so sorry. I didn't mean to worry you. I didn't do it on purpose. It just happened."

"At least one of us got a good night's rest. I'm off to work on no sleep." Dad looked like he could spit nails.

In attack mode, she opened her mouth to unload on him. But a glimpse of the fear burning behind his anger caught her off guard. He cared. She could relate. How many times had fear driven her over the edge in the last two months? He probably still loved God but was too stubborn to admit it. The discovery left her speechless as she watched him stomp to the bedroom.

"What do you think God thinks about this?" Her mom roused her from her stupor.

"About what?" She turned her head toward her mom.

"Sleeping together before marriage."

Indignation bubbled from her core. "God considers sex before marriage a sin, not sleeping together."

"I was being polite."

"I'm being literal. We slept. We did not have sex."

"I was young once. I know the desires of young—"

Rory cupped her hands over her ears. "Ew! We didn't act on our desires. Yes, I desire him, but we did not and have not had sex."

"What's going on?" Ruby entered the kitchen, rubbing her eyes.

"Nothing!" Rory and her mom yelled in unison.

Hurt, Ruby recoiled to the bedroom.

Rory took a breath. "You assumed wrong. Now, I need to shower and catch the trans."

She stormed into the bathroom. Her own mother thought she made them worry all night because she boinked her boyfriend. Boyfriend? He wasn't her boyfriend. But her mom thought he was her boyfriend. *He* thought he was her boyfriend. And he was the man she yearned to marry and live with happily ever after, but she couldn't because she had to sacrifice herself for the people. She jerked on the faucet and stepped over the side of the tub. Lifting her face into the stream of water, she shut her eyes. If only the water could wash away her calling.

Chapter 25

An interesting array of patients helped smooth the rough start to Rory's morning. When Dr. Ahmid sought her out to consult with her about a patient, she bit her tongue to restrain a sarcastic remark about how he didn't need advice from a physician student. It wasn't her knowledge he sought. It was God's. He just didn't realize it.

At lunch, she sat with the other medical students. They asked her opinion about their cases. The comradery filled a deep void within her. Amethyst sat the farthest from Rory and shot dirty looks in her direction. Rory attempted to draw her into the conversation without success.

The day proceeded nicely. Still, the expression on Jaxon's face when she'd slammed the truck door haunted her. She would apologize later. Her heart danced just thinking of him. *Thank you, Jesus. What have I done to deserve this?*

The physicians' open workstations occupied the area where the two hallways converged. The design allowed physicians to keep an eye on the corridors while seated at their desks.

After the trill of the elevator bell, the sound of heavy boots striking the tile floor made Rory's fingers freeze on her keyboard. Her eyes shot up from her patient chart notes. Mrs. Miller, the hospital's personnel director, led two intimidating military officers down the hall. Rory's extremities tingled. She had nothing to fear ... unless Darius or Tabor had reported her.

She forced a smile. The director's mouth held a tight line.

Rory bit her lip. A sense of foreboding smothered her, just as if a bag had been pulled over her head.

Jaxon had drilled her for the occasion. She would duck around the corner out of the entourage's sight, enter the stairwell, run down to the first floor, hug the wall to avoid the cameras, and exit through the loading dock. If she walked purposefully, she would be, in effect, invisible. As soon as she was safe, she would contact Jaxon. She snapped shut her e-notebook, grabbed it, and then stood to launch her escape.

"Dr. Rydell."

When the director called her name, a chill shot up her spine. Her feet turned to lead. Should she run? They would overtake her before she reached the stairs, and then she would look guilty. To hide her quivering hands, she clutched the e-notebook against her torso.

"These officers asked to speak with you." Mrs. Miller turned on her heels and returned in the direction from whence she came.

Fight or flight? It turned out that she defaulted to option three, paralyzed. Fear strangled her adrenaline.

"What can I do for you?" She spoke in a volume sufficient to be heard over her pounding heart.

"Are you Rory Rydell?" asked the taller one. He weighed in slightly heavier than Jaxon and stood a little taller. His dark hair was short like Jaxon's; however, the resemblance ended there. Jaxon's face was friendly. This officer's visage was hard like stone. More decorations adorned his uniform than Jaxon's, which indicated a higher rank.

"Yes." Mrs. Miller had just addressed her by that name. The officer was clearly a genius. She kept her opinion to herself because to deliberately antagonize him would be stupid. Of course, that had never stopped her before.

"We are to accompany you to Gibbons."

Her heart dove to her feet. She threw up a little in her mouth. A visit to Gibbons was usually a one-way trip.

"This isn't a good time. I have patients to see." She pointed down the hall. "How about I stop by after my shift?"

"This is not a request. You must accompany us, now." His expression grew ominous.

Dr. Bourland approached. "What's going on?"

"We're escorting Miss Rydell to Gibbons," the tall one answered. Either the shorter one couldn't or wasn't allowed to speak.

"Why? What's this regarding?" Dr. Bourland engaged his authoritative tone.

"She is summoned for questioning."

"What kind of questioning?"

The officer stood silent.

"She has the right to know why you're questioning her," the doctor persisted.

"She is accused of believing in a god."

Her knees turned to rubber. The fluorescent lights shined especially hot. Her face burned. Should she admit she believed in God? Deny it? Staff gathered to observe the spectacle. She was the freak show.

"That's preposterous. I've never heard her say anything to that effect." Dr. Bourland stood his ground before the tall officer. "Who accuses her?"

Would they arrest Dr. Bourland if he defended her?

"This is not your concern." The taller officer glared at the doctor.

Rory touched his arm. "It's okay. I'll be okay." If okay meant arrested and executed, she would be okay. "Thank you for everything."

The doctor looked at her. "What are you saying?"

"You have been the best mentor I could have had." What could she say to let him know Christ was real? "I hope the truth finds you." That was a stupid response. Moisture welled in her eyes at her missed opportunity to enlighten him and her friends.

Her destiny had always ended in incarceration. But why was today the day? If only she could have had a little more time.

The tall one grasped her shoulder. "Miss Rydell—"

She shrugged his hand off.

He grasped her firmly.

"I need to put this away." She held up the e-notebook, and he released his grasp but shadowed her.

Was this really happening, or was it a nightmare? Rory logged out and tucked the notebook in the cabinet like she would retrieve it the next day.

The taller officer zip-tied her wrists in front of her. He led, and the shorter one followed, creating a Rory sandwich. If she'd stood a chance to escape, she would have run, but instead she followed the officer into the elevator.

Dr. Bourland stood with his mouth open as the elevator door closed. Was he shocked? Appalled?

The elevator was so stuffy she could barely breathe. If the tall one hadn't had a firm hold on her arm, she probably would've collapsed.

Spectators lined the hall on the ground floor. Good news traveled fast. The crowd gawked as she and the officers filed by. Amethyst stood front and center with a huge smile covering her face. Rory should have shared Christ with her, but it probably wouldn't have made a difference.

The officer led Rory to a black military vehicle parked outside the hospital entrance. The tall officer opened the back door and pushed her head down as she crumpled inside. A cage barrier separated the front and back seats.

There were no inside handles to open the doors. She broke out in a cold sweat. Her pulse increased, and her mouth dried.

The two officers clambered into the front seat. They spoke quietly. So, the shorter officer *could* speak.

Resting her head against the seat back, Rory stared at the black fabric roof of the vehicle. She was spiraling downward and would hit bottom soon. If she was lucky, the fall would prove fatal.

She should have run. Who was she kidding? This was God's plan. It would have been futile to flee. They would have easily overtaken her, and she would still be sitting right here. They would probably have enjoyed chasing her. At least she hadn't added to their pleasure. Her lips curled up in celebration of the small victory, until the short-lived triumph was canceled by the tear that trickled down her cheek.

Chapter 26

Despair threatened to suffocate Rory as she pictured Jaxon's reaction to her arrest. Had anyone told him? He had insisted he would turn himself in. She prayed God would prevent him from keeping his promise. Why hadn't she professed her love this morning? What a terrible last image she'd given him. If she had accepted his proposal, they would have created precious last memories, but at what cost to him? Her nose ran as her eyes stung with tears.

God didn't need a crybaby. She awkwardly wiped her tears on her zip-tied hands. What should she say when they questioned her? How could she make her death matter? She needed Jesus to speak to her audibly.

She stared out at the landscape passing the window. Perhaps God would send a huge earthquake to overturn the vehicle and allow her to escape. It was stupid to hope for rescue. God didn't rescue Jesus from the cross, and he loved Jesus more than he loved her, as well he should. Jesus was perfect, and she, well, she was not. Henry said they would torture her to get the names of believers. She swallowed the lump in her throat.

The depressing prison came into view, and the vehicle halted at the entrance. A vise squeezed her stomach. The tall one opened the door. "Out!"

Something about his voice rang familiar. She looked closer but couldn't place him.

Her legs wobbled as she stepped from the vehicle. He steadied her. What a guy. The three of them fell in line just like before in the Rory sandwich.

Time slowed as her senses heightened. The sound of the boots against the hard floor reverberated in her ears. A musty odor permeated the air. Men and women in uniform stopped, stared, and whispered as they passed. All those years, she'd hated feeling invisible. If only she could be invisible now.

She jerked at the shriek of a buzzer. The tall one led them through a door, which banged with a thud behind them. He cut the zip tie from her wrists, grabbed an orange jumpsuit from a shelf, and dismissed the short one.

She rubbed her wrists to restore circulation.

The tall one opened a door to a small room and shoved the jumpsuit into her arms. He followed her inside and slammed the door.

"Change," he barked.

There it was again, the feeling that she knew his voice. She shook her head. "Do you mind waiting outside? It's not like I can escape." Whose voice was that? The pitch was several octaves too high for her.

"I have to make sure you're not concealing weapons." His smile made her skin crawl.

He didn't believe she had hidden weapons. He was playing a mind game to make her feel vulnerable and humiliated. It was effective. She lowered her scrub pants. What if he intended to violate her? Plastering on an exterior façade of strength to mask her crumbling interior, she glared into her captor's eyes. Something flashed in his dark eyes, disappearing as quickly as it appeared. She'd probably imagined it.

The jumpsuit swallowed her. Fortunately, she wasn't trying to make a fashion statement because prison orange washed out her fair skin.

She kicked the scrubs to the side. The officer grabbed her upper arm and pulled her through two doors with buzzers before they arrived at her final destination. She shuddered at the echoing clang of the cell door, a precursor of the end of her life.

The officer exited without so much as a goodbye.

She pressed her forehead against the cool metal bars. Where was Jaxon right now? And what about her parents? She ran through different scenarios of how they might find out about her arrest. None of them would be received well.

She closed her eyes, and her mind drifted into a numb shock.

How long had she stood with her forehead against the bars? Long enough for indentions to form where they had rested. She surveyed the area. The stark cell came fully furnished with a rudimentary cot, toilet, and sink. From the near-silent surroundings, no inmates occupied the other cells in the block. On the bright side, no prisoners to violate her. As the lone prisoner in the block, she must be special. She'd never been special before. Turned out that being special was overrated.

She ran a finger along the cool cinder block wall and broke down. The cinder blocks reminded her of her family's apartment. When she didn't come home, would they assume it was a repeat of last night? Would they think she was a slut and an inconsiderate daughter? When they learned of her arrest, her dad would say he'd told them this would happen. She'd treated her family awful before she left. If she could just have a do-over.

Who had reported her? If it had been Darius, she would have been arrested a week ago. Unless he struggled with the decision or if it took the Order time to act. The timing fit Tabor better. Did he report her visits to the Leemans' house? She chewed on the inside of her cheek. What was a plausible reason for her visits that wouldn't implicate them? With all the information they knew, their arrest would be devastating to the cause. She rested her head against the wall. They would verify any reason she offered. What would hold up to scrutiny?

In a catatonic state, she plodded to the cot and collapsed. The cot was as flat and hard as a board.

Her heart ached that she would never see her family or their crummy apartment again. As run down and bare as their apartment was, she would give anything to be there rather than here. Anywhere was better than here. Her grandfather's words came back to her. *You don't miss what you have until it's gone.*

They could lock her up, but she still had choices. If they asked her to betray other believers, she would lie. God would forgive her. He had to because she couldn't be the reason for anyone else's arrest.

How long until they executed her? Dreading execution was worse than dying, probably. Some citizens claimed the pain from lethal injection was inhumane. But it seemed more humane than most other options.

The silence was deafening. "Hello, anyone there?" She spoke just to hear sound.

She tucked her hands under her head and stared at the ceiling. Time was a strange concept. Time spent with Jaxon whooshed by. Here, a second drew on forever. Had she been in this cell for minutes or hours?

Footsteps in the corridor broke the silence. Her pulse raced. Were they coming to interrogate her? Something scraped along the floor. A tray of food.

Nausea suppressed her grumbling gut. She turned her back to the food and faced the wall. Refusing to eat or drink would hasten death. The quicker, the better. She would only survive three to four days without fluids. Eating and drinking were the only things in her control.

She closed her eyes, and suddenly, she was standing in the middle of a dim room, staring at Jaxon. As she reached for him, the floor gave way, and she slid into a deep, dark hole. She tried to plant her heels, but they slipped as despair grasped her ankles. Scripture indicated believers shouldn't fear. *God, please help me claw my way out of this pit of fear.*

Chapter 27

Rory awakened in a daze. Where was she? The bed was too hard. It wasn't her bed. Tears welled. Of course, she was at Gibbons.

She rolled off the cot, knelt, and whispered, "God, please rescue me."

When no answer came, she slid under the blanket and resumed her position facing the wall.

Why didn't God tell her what she was supposed to say when they interrogated her? Had he abandoned her? Had he left her to die alone?

Her grandfather described feeling abandoned when he was incarcerated. Everyone in prison probably experienced that. Was she in the same cell her grandfather had occupied? This could have been his cell before he was transferred to solitary. Execution had to be better than rotting in prison for over twenty years. She had never been a people person, but she missed people.

What if God sent horses and a chariot of fire to swoop her up to heaven as he did for Elijah? He could swoop her at the exact moment of her execution. How great would that be? No one who witnessed it could deny God existed. *God, are you listening? This is a great idea.*

Rory jumped at a touch to her shoulder. She rolled over.

She would recognize that glow anywhere. Bolting upright, she gasped, "Gabriel."

Of course, he must be here to open the prison doors as God did for Peter. Adrenaline surged. She jumped and ran to the cell door, waiting for it to fly open at her touch. It didn't budge. Desperate, she threw her shoulder into it. When it held firm, she banged her forehead against the bars and sank onto the cold, hard floor.

"You're not here to help me escape, are you?"

"No." His glow diminished slightly, or was it her imagination?

She put on a brave face. "It's okay. It's not like I have anywhere to go."

"Praise God for the opportunity to suffer for his glory."

Like a punctured balloon, she deflated. "Yeah, I know, Peter, Paul, Grandfather, all those guys did. I can say the words, but God knows I don't want to suffer. I will, though, if that's the plan."

"None desire persecution. Those you mentioned knew that Christ willingly suffered for all men, even for those who persecuted him. They rejoiced that their suffering led souls to Christ."

She stood and met Gabriel's gaze. It wasn't like she could conceal anything from him, so she might as well reveal her true self. "I'm scared to death, and I don't know how to change."

"Rory, when you face your enemies, do not be afraid. The Lord is with you. Praise him."

"Is that why you're here, to tell me not to fear and to praise God? No other reason?"

"I am not here to take you to heaven."

With that settled, the needle of the lethal injection vicariously pricked her arm.

"You torture yourself."

"What?"

"By dwelling on what you expect to happen, you experience the trial many times, instead of once when and if it occurs. You try to control the outcome. Relinquish control to God. His ways are better than yours."

"You say that, but while I sit here waiting for them to execute me, his ways don't seem so good. I imagine ways to be rescued, to keep my mind off ... the other option."

"I did not say your desire will not happen, but I am not here to open the prison doors at this time. Do not waste your energy trying to orchestrate events. Trust God and thank him for the good that will result from your arrest. Release your fears to him."

She leaned her back against the bars. "It's impossible for me to release my fears."

"Nothing is impossible for God."

"It's not impossible for God. It's me. I'm the problem. I don't deserve blessings. This morning, I acted awful to Jaxon and my family. I left without telling them I love them. Now, I'll never get the chance." She hung her head.

Gabriel lifted her chin. "They know you love them, and you know they love you. Ask the Father for forgiveness and remember it no longer. Concentrate on loving those here."

"Here? In Gibbons? You want me to love the people who are going to execute me? Are you crazy?" He was asking for more than she was capable of.

"Perfect love conquers fear."

"How do I get this perfect love?"

"By choosing God as your primary focus. Glorify and worship him, and that love will overflow to all, even those who persecute you. They need you to demonstrate Christ's love to open their eyes to the truth. When you lead a lost soul to Christ, you save him from death and cover many sins."

"Did you make that up? They're going to kill me because I believe in God, and you want me to try to convert them? I do need to cover a lot of sins, but this is suicidal."

"Love breaks down barriers. They need love to escape eternal darkness. Jesus loved you before you knew him. It is easy to love your family and friends; the true test is to love your enemies." He waved a finger in the air.

It wasn't always easy to love her family, but his point was taken. Jesus loved her enough to reveal himself to her. The least she could do was share his love with those at Gibbons. She sighed. "This will be hard."

"Love is a choice. If easy, all would love." His voice was calming like the murmur of a slow flowing stream.

"Can you tell me what to expect? What am I supposed to say when they question me?"

"Do not worry, the Holy Spirit will guide your words. You are chosen for this day." Gabriel took her by her hand, led her to the cot, and patted it.

She sat on the hard surface. Chills ran up her spine as he sat beside her. "How will I make a difference? How will I be executed?"

"The answers you seek have not been revealed. The Father, Son, and Holy Spirit know and are in control."

Even though he didn't answer her questions, his presence provided comfort.

"Can you understand fear?"

"I do not fear because I know God Almighty, the maker of heaven and earth and all that is on the earth and in the heavens. I have known him a very long time. I have witnessed amazing things beyond your imagination. There is nothing he cannot do."

She nodded as she tried to wrap her mind around his words.

"I may not understand fear, but I do understand your desire to know. If I knew, I would tell you, but I do not know the details of God's plan. Many will be inspired, and the Order will fall, but I do not know your fate. You wish to plan your future. but I promise, God's plan will be for the best."

"Should I have run when the officers arrested me?"

"The answer does not matter. Will knowing change anything?"

"No. I just wondered. Jaxon tried to train me to escape, but I froze. I didn't know what to do, so I did nothing. Is this where I'm supposed to be?"

"This is according to plan."

Rory gazed into his eyes. "I have a favor to ask. Please watch over Jaxon and my family and help them deal with the aftermath."

"As you wish." He grasped her hand.

Her muscles relaxed. "I really appreciate you coming."

"The pleasure is mine." He bowed his head toward her.

"Seriously? Visiting me is a pleasure?"

"I enjoy our conversations. You possess a ... unique wit and humor. I delight in observing you grow in knowledge and obedience."

An angel enjoyed speaking with her? Who would've thought?

"Lie down and rest." He stood.

She grabbed his tunic. "Please don't go. I can't bear to be alone right now."

"You are never alone."

"Yeah, yeah, but before you showed up, I felt alone. Right now, I need to see and feel you. Please."

He stroked her hair like she was a child. To him, she probably was.

"You are very wise."

"Many years make one wise."

"How old are you?"

"For me, time is immeasurable. I have existed since the beginning when God created me. It is difficult for you to understand."

"You can say that again. Most things are difficult for me to understand. But if it makes you feel better, you don't look a day over ... five hundred."

Gabriel chuckled.

"Really, if I met you on the street and you weren't illuminated, I'd guess you to be in your forties. You have held up very well. You're very attractive."

"Thank you, as are you." He placed his hands on both sides of her face. "You judge yourself too harshly. You are beautiful."

"I wish I could see me as you do. For the life of me, I can't figure out why Jesus chose to speak to me or to send you."

"God speaks in many different ways to all. Alas, many ignore him. You chose to hear."

"I don't know about that. He had to make a comatose man speak to get my attention."

"You always struggled with the Order's proclamation that gods do not exist. You believed, even if you did not realize it."

"Gabriel …"

"Yes?"

"I love you."

"I also love you."

Gabriel kissed her forehead. The cot became comfortable. Her troubles melted away. With Gabriel's hand over her eyes, Rory slipped into a deep, peaceful slumber.

Chapter 28

The scrape of a tray on the floor signaled the arrival of breakfast and awakened Rory. A sharp pain of anxiety pierced her chest. Gabriel was no longer here. She closed her eyes and attempted to conjure the peace from their time together.

An alibi for her visits with the Leemans drifted into her head. The Leemans wouldn't like it, but it was better than them being arrested.

The iron door opened. She rolled over. The tall and short officers had come to wish her a good morning, how nice.

"Don't you guys ever get time off?" Sarcasm proved therapeutic.

The officers exchanged startled looks and spoke quietly. "What?"

The tall one cleared his throat. "Commander Malvo wishes to speak with you."

"It's early. Could we meet later?" She rolled back over.

"It's not a request."

"Of course not." Taking her time, she sat up. Her socked feet hit the cold concrete floor. She fumbled under the cot for her shoes. Maybe their startled expression related to her bed hair. She ran her fingers through it.

It didn't matter what they did to her. She would go to heaven. If it hurt, it would be for a short time in the scheme of eternity. After a deep breath, she stood.

The tall one zip-tied her wrists in front of her. Like yesterday, they walked in a Rory sandwich.

The surroundings were unfamiliar because when she'd walked the halls the night before she'd operated in a daze. The general architecture, institutional, was similar to the hospital. But here, people were sentenced to die, or at least they wished they were dead.

Her feet moved mechanically toward her fate. Jesus hadn't said much after his arrest. Should silence be her game plan? It would be helpful if the Holy Spirit gave her a little heads-up.

Gibbons's employees glanced over as their procession passed. Many of the onlookers did a double take, and their jaws dropped. Some elbowed coworkers and pointed. She ignored them and smiled like she was privy to an amusing secret. In fact, she was. Her death would ignite a positive change. With renewed strength, she held her head high.

The tall one opened the door to a room with a bank of large windows. The windows were reflective as if they were made of one-way glass. Was someone watching from the other side?

The sparsely furnished room hosted a metal table with three metal folding chairs. The tall one pulled a chair from the table for her. She sat and rested her zip-tied wrists on the table. The cool room temperature made the hair on her arms stand at attention. The two officers stood at the wall facing her.

The tall one's dark expression complimented his sharp facial features. If he smiled, his face would probably break. He was somewhere in his thirties, young to be so bitter. His dark brown irises blended into his pupils, making his eyes appear black. The Occupation Committee had nailed his occupation. Or had the military changed him? Had he once been a nice, fun-loving guy?

In a fight, she would put her money on Jaxon, even if the tall one was bigger and meaner. If only Jaxon would crash through the door, overpower the officers, and whisk her to safety. Unfortunately, being whisked to safety wasn't in the plan.

The short one was muscular. He looked like God had squashed the tall one down a few centimeters and rounded him out. His softer face wouldn't break if he smiled. He probably smiled sometimes. The brown of his irises contrasted with his pupils, and his gaze was tentative, not angry. He looked uncomfortable with his occupation. His intimidating physique probably played a bigger role in the assignment of his profession than his test answers.

How was she supposed to make them aware that she loved them? The silence grew increasingly uncomfortable. Her eyes darted around the room. Finally, she blurted, "I love you."

The two officers looked at each other, then the tall one growled, "Shut up!"

Yep, shutting up was a better idea. Her cheeks burned. Awkwardness pulsed in the room. Would she receive a point for effort, even if it was a stupid attempt?

After an eternity, a short lean man with close-cropped graying hair burst into the room. He clutched a manila folder. Based on the creases that lined his forehead and the starburst of lines that peeked from under his glasses, he was in his late forties. Several stripes and pins adorned his pressed uniform, which indicated the high position of commander.

Both officers snapped to attention.

Rory sat taller.

"At ease," the commander said.

The two officers relaxed. Rory remained in her attention posture.

The commander perused the contents of the folder and spoke without so much as a glance in her direction. "Miss Rydell, I'm Commander Malvo. I trust we're treating you well?"

Seriously? "If by treating me well, you mean arresting me, forcing me to change clothes with that one leering," she nodded to the tall one, whose expression remained impassive, "and incarcerating me without formal charges, then yes, you're treating me well."

"You are in no position—" Malvo glanced at her and froze. He dropped the folder onto the table. "What happened to her face?" He removed his black-rimmed glasses and rubbed the lenses with a cloth. After he replaced his glasses, he moved in for a closer look.

"Sir, she looked like this when we arrived at her cell at 0700," the tall one replied.

"Did she look like this when you brought her in yesterday?" His voice rose noticeably higher.

"No, sir."

The commander turned to Rory. "What happened to your face?"

Of course, her face was glowing, which explained the earlier stares. Time for a little fun. "What are you talking about?"

"How are you making your face glow?" he demanded.

"My face is glowing? It must have happened when Gabriel touched me last night."

"Who is Gabriel?" Malvo rubbed her face with his thumb.

She jerked away from his touch. "An angel."

The pound of his fist on the table made her jump. "There are no angels. You don't want to mess with me."

In an amazingly calm voice, she replied, "You asked why my face is glowing. My best guess is God made my face glow so that you and everyone," she nodded to the two guards, "who sees the glow will know he is real."

"Rory Rydell, it has been reported that you believe in a god. You just corroborated the accusation."

Her heart raced, and her mouth was so dry she had no saliva to swallow. She looked toward heaven and pressed forward. "God loved you so much that he sacrificed his only Son. If you believe in him, you can enjoy eternal life. His Son, Jesus, paid the ultimate price for your sins. He gave his life. All you need to do is accept his gift and offer yourself to him." *Sweet Jesus, don't let me faint.*

Malvo stuck his finger in her face. "Unbelievable. You … trying to convert me. Do you think you're the first person to try to convince me that God loves me? I didn't fall for that lie before the Order, and I'm not falling for it now. I was ecstatic when the Order outlawed gods. They put all those self-righteous hypocrites in their place."

"I'm sorry, you must have had a terrible experience."

"Don't you understand I hold your life in my hands? I determine whether you live or die. Me!" He shoved his thumb toward his chest.

"God determines whether I live or die," she stated softly.

Malvo held his hand to his ear. "What did you say? Speak up. I thought I heard you say God determines if you live or die. That can't be right. You wouldn't be foolish enough to make such a statement."

The commander was wrong. She was foolish enough, and she repeated it, slightly louder. "God determines my fate. It's not foolish if it's true."

"Oh really? We'll see about that." He paced the length of the room. With a sigh, he turned to face her. "Your scores indicate you are intelligent. How can you believe in a god?"

"I don't believe in *a* god. I believe in *the* God."

Malvo's face turned bright red. If steam had escaped from his ears, it wouldn't have surprised her.

"When did this belief start?" he asked through clenched teeth.

"A few months ago."

"Liar." Malvo slammed his hand on the table. "You were reported when you were in high school."

"I didn't believe in God or creationism in high school. I merely questioned how single organisms could arrange themselves to produce advanced life. I was beaten and forbidden to ever question Order curriculum again."

"Apparently the punishment was insufficient. We should have arrested you then. For crying out loud, you work in science. Science and any kind of god cannot coexist."

"Science has never proved that simple cells randomly evolved into any life-form."

209

Malvo's face was so close that his coffee breath turned her stomach. "Where did this god come from? What created him?"

"God was not created. He was from the beginning."

He shook a finger in the air. "Aha. You believe in a god that has always existed, but you can't believe a scientific dynamic created life? Don't you hear how absurd that is?"

"Not any more than the leading scientific theories that say the original cells just existed. All theories require faith that their origins existed from the beginning. The idea of God designing life makes more sense than random cells colliding until they create life." She raised her bound wrists and pointed toward her face with her finger. "Plus, I have a glowing face to prove I was touched by an angel."

He clenched his jaw so hard he could have cracked a tooth. "If there is an all-powerful god, why didn't he prevent the United World Order?"

"God didn't let the Order take over. People did. The Order's originators created panic and terror. Then, they portrayed themselves as the great protector. People turned their backs on God and begged the Order to take control. The Order neglected to disclose that their endgame would be to disarm citizens, steal businesses, and strip away personal freedoms. They succeeded because they deceived the people."

Malvo clapped his hands slowly. "An astute observation. Deception was necessary. People aren't smart enough to understand they make poor decisions. Still, why did this god allow people to turn away from him?"

"For freedom. God allows people to choose what they believe. Now let me ask you a question. If God is a myth, why outlaw him? Why outlaw something that doesn't exist?"

"You know this. We don't outlaw gods. We outlaw the belief in gods. It's the people who believe in nonexistent gods who are dangerous. They kill in the name of these imagined gods."

"So, it's okay for the Order to kill citizens who simply express belief in a deity because they might kill? You took away all weapons. How would they kill anyone?"

"Surely, you're not naïve enough to believe that no citizens possess weapons. Everything is available to the highest bidder, even banned weapons. Also, there are military personnel who believe in a god. Isn't that right, Thacker?"

The short one's eyes darted nervously. "Are you asking if I do?"

Malvo waved his hand in the air. "No, no, Sergeant, I know you're a loyal Order soldier. I'm asking you to confirm that there are military personnel who hide religious beliefs."

"I would think they would be pretty crazy to do that, sir." His face flushed.

Did Thacker believe, or was he afraid that Malvo suspected he did?

She cleared her throat. "Believers don't need weapons. When they trust in God, he is faithful and will deliver them by his might. This is why the Order forbids citizens to believe in God."

"I was wrong. You are an idiot or insane. There are no gods. There will be no revolution. Nothing is going to happen other than a group of idiots might murder a few Order loyalists before they're defeated. Enough of this nonsense. Let's get down to business." Malvo pulled out a chair on the opposite side of the table and sat. "I'm going to ask you more questions. I know the answers, so there's no point in lying."

He was the one lying. If he knew the answers, he wouldn't ask. He was trying to trick her into giving him the answers he wanted. He was a good liar. Could she lie as convincingly?

"If you tell us the truth, things will go easier on you."

"Easier? You mean you'll execute me less dead?" The remark slipped out. It was not Holy Spirit inspired. It resonated of Rory Rydell. Perhaps the silent approach would have been best.

Thacker smirked.

The chair tipped over when Malvo stood abruptly. He strode over and yelled in the officer's face, "You think this is funny, Sergeant Thacker?"

"No, sir," he replied as his face sobered.

Malvo faced Rory and released a long breath. "If we believe you can be rehabilitated, we could choose to incarcerate you. You might even be released after a few years." He clasped his hands behind his back. "Are you the one referred to as the Lion of Judah?"

Rory blinked. She almost laughed.

"I know. You don't even look like the Pussycat of Judah, but our source named you."

Thank you, Athelene. Though it didn't really matter. Gabriel confirmed this was her destiny. But he didn't say she had to roll over and make it easy on them. She would make them work for it. "Why would anyone call me that?"

"Because you are going to lead believers in a revolt against the Order."

Locking eyes with him, she said, "I thought you arrested me because I believe in God. You seriously think I can lead a revolt? Did it ever occur to you that your source is sacrificing me to protect the real Lion?"

"The source has a long history with us."

She threw her hands up in surrender. "Okay, you caught me. I'm a lion."

"Who decided you're the Lion?"

"I don't know. Who's your source?"

He stuck a finger in her face. "I ask the questions. You answer them. Why would an angel visit you if you're not planning some kind of coup?"

"You said angels don't exist. So, no angel visited."

The veins in Malvo's neck bulged. "You *said* an angel visited you."

"Yes, but you said they don't exist. If they don't exist, I must have been mistaken."

His face turned beet red. He turned away from her for a few moments and then turned back to face her. "Tell me about Henry and Athelene Leeman."

The blood drained from her face. This was Henry's worst fear materialized.

"Are they the ones who told you I'm the Lion? If you're getting your information from them, you're in trouble."

"They aren't my informants. But tell me what you know about them."

"What do you want me to say?" He probably had a recording of her entering their house, so no point in denying she knew them.

"Do they believe in a god?"

"How would I know?" She stared into his eyes.

"Why did you visit them three times over the last few months?"

"I prefer not to discuss it." She cast her gaze downward. Darius didn't know about the Leemans. This revelation confirmed that Tabor must have been the rat who turned her in.

"You prefer not to talk about it because they will share a cell next to you." The glee in Malvo's eyes sent chills down her spine.

"No, because it's painful. Arrest them. They deserve to be arrested."

"They deserve to be arrested because they believe?"

"No." She shot him a deadly look. No one *deserved* to be arrested for believing.

"I'm ready to send officers to their house if you don't convince me of a reason that doesn't involve them believing."

"Do it."

"Why did you go to their home?"

"Mr. Leeman has some"—she made a show of swallowing hard—"fetishes."

"Like what? Kinky sex?" His excitement repulsed her.

She wrung her hands. "He likes to slap women around."

213

He stood with his hands on the table and stared at her. "Okay, I'll play along. What was in this for you? Why let him slap you?"

"Food." She opened her mouth to say more but then closed it. Jaxon warned her to keep lies short and sweet.

"You expect me to believe you allowed yourself to be slapped for food?"

She narrowed her eyes at him. "The Order says they take care of citizens and provide their basic needs. They don't. You don't know what it's like to be poor and hungry. I'm sure you have all the food you can eat. You probably waste food. Many of us don't have that luxury." Her jaw held a hard line.

He slapped the table, and she jumped. "You don't know anything about me. I was dirt poor before the Order. No one helped me, not a god and not church. I pulled myself up on my own. I have plenty, because I'm loyal to the Order. You should try it."

"I tried *it* for twenty years, and it left me hungry. Hungry enough to allow someone to beat me."

Malvo paced for a minute then turned to face her. "And Athelene Leeman what? Looked the other way while her husband hit you?"

Rory's expression turned as hard as granite. "No, she watched."

"How were these meetings arranged? They just invited you over and started smacking you around?"

"An arranger on Walton Street set it up." Luckily, all arrangers insisted on anonymity. He would never be able to check it out.

"You must have had visible bruises afterward. How did you explain that?"

He tried to give her enough rope to hang herself. Did it really matter? They were going to execute her anyway, but she didn't want to hang the Leemans beside her.

"He knew what he was doing. He hit me where the bruises wouldn't show, except he got carried away once and choked me, leaving bruises on my neck. I told my colleagues I'd been mugged." If they checked it out, Dr. Bourland would verify her bruises and her story.

Malvo smiled. "You're a clever liar. Almost clever enough to make me believe you, but I don't. How do you reconcile lying and being a believer? Lying is against your religion. Just admit they're believers."

"They're perverts. So sure, they're believers. Arrest them, put them in the cell next to me, and execute them. They get off on hurting people. They deserve to die more than me. I kept my beliefs to myself. I didn't hurt anyone."

"You are hurting people. You're attempting to lead a revolt. Many people will die."

"Don't you hear how ridiculous that sounds? I don't know the first thing about leading anything. I'm not a soldier."

"My sources say you are the Lion of Judah."

"Okay, I'm the Lion. Roar." She held her hands in a claw-like fashion. "Tell the truth. You arrested me because my name sounds like a lion's roar, didn't you?"

Malvo's red face and bulging veins made him look ready to explode. He took a deep breath. "Who told you there is a god?"

"He died recently. He was in the hospital—"

He snapped his fingers. "That pharmacist we executed. What was his name, Drummond?"

A sharp pang struck her gut. "The Order executed Mr. Drummond for stealing drugs."

Commander Malvo waved his hand. "That was the official statement. The believer front had been quiet. We didn't want to stir things up, so we said it was for stealing drugs. Drummond forced our hand. He ignored repeated warnings to stop discussing his god and inciting the people."

"You warned him? I thought if you determined someone believes, you executed them, period." Were they just going to warn her? Dare she hope?

Malvo clasped his hands behind his back and nodded. "Our rhetoric supports that. Truthfully, we've gotten soft over the years. Some in the Order believed if we oppressed religious groups, it would ignite acts of rebellion. So, we tried a softer approach. We infiltrated religious groups to make sure they remained benign. Drummond brought his demise on himself. He tried to stir up the people to rebel."

Her mind churned as she struggled to catch up. Drummond was executed because he tried to carry out her calling, not because she stole the Aztavix.

"We thought he was a lone wolf. We intended to silence him without a lot of attention."

That would do it. Execution permanently silenced a person.

"The Lion is causing more of a stir than Drummond ever thought about, so we have no choice but to behead the Lion. We must demonstrate to the world that we will not tolerate traitors."

His metaphor sent a sharp pain to her throat. Her reprieve was short lived.

"So?" Malvo asked.

"So, what?"

"Is Drummond the person who told you about God?"

She stared at him blankly. "No, I never met him. It was a comatose man sent by Gibbons to the hospital. The admission orders listed a number instead of his name, but he told me his name was David Abrams."

Malvo's face turned crimson. "A man in a coma cannot tell you anything. You know that. You're a student physician. Do you take me for an idiot?"

"No, sir. I had a hard time believing it myself. I reported it, but he never spoke or opened his eyes when anyone else was in the room. And the room recording didn't pick up any of it. My supervising physician thought I was suffering from exhaustion. It wasn't exhaustion or my imagination. It was a miracle."

"Miracles are make-believe. You're fabricating this nonsense. The recording proves you're lying." He looked like he might stroke out. That would be a most appreciated miracle.

"How would I know his name if he didn't tell me? The transfer documents only listed him by number. At first, I was terrified, but the cameras didn't record any of our conversations. I checked them. I thought I was going crazy. Then I realized I knew it all along: God is real."

"Liar. Comatose men don't just wake up. You recognized him as your grandfather, and that's how you knew his name."

"My grandfather died before I was born. His name was Judas Iscariot."

He stared at her like she was an imbecile. "Judas Iscariot was the name we gave him because his name was banned."

Rory channeled her surprise from when Mrs. Leeman first dropped the bomb on her. "He never said he was my grandfather. You're lying. He would have told me."

"He didn't tell you anything. He was in a coma. You're fabricating this whole story to protect the real person, which is your parents."

"You said you know the answers. So far, you're oh-for-two. My parents forbade me to ask questions about gods and told me in no uncertain terms that gods don't exist."

"You expect me to believe that you didn't tell your family about a comatose man who told you about a god and only awoke when you were in his room?"

Rory stared into his eyes. "Why would I? They wouldn't have believed me just like you don't."

Malvo flipped through the file on the table and tapped his finger on a page. "I met with your father after your school incident. He confirmed he understood his responsibility that you never question Order teachings again. It appears he failed."

If they arrested and executed her father, he'd spend eternity separated from God. She had to do something to throw suspicion away from him.

"At the time when the Order took over, he was a minister. Even though he swore his allegiance, I always doubted his sincerity." He placed his hands together.

"Now who's playing games? He's always been a sanitation technician."

"You expect me to believe your parents never told you? Former ministers were assigned menial jobs and separated in housing assignments. We isolated them to break them."

"This explains his anger. It finally makes sense. I've always known he's too smart to be a sanitation technician. Congratulations, you broke him."

He pointed to his eyes. "Rory, look at me, focus. This is your last chance. Who told you a god is real?"

"Mr. Abrams."

"Think about this. If there is a god, why is he allowing your execution?"

"He can save me if he chooses. Whether he saves me or not, I won't deny him." Nausea gurgled in her stomach.

"There is no god to save you."

"I don't know that he'll save me, but he rescued David Abrams from execution. Mr. Abrams told me of all the failed attempts. How the lethal injection didn't kill him. The rifles misfired and injured the shooters. A commander suffered a fatal heart attack while charging him with a knife."

"I tried to help you, to reason with you. You bring this on yourself." He cradled her chin. "It doesn't have to be this way. All you have to do is tell us who tricked you into believing."

She pulled away. "I told you."

Malvo slapped her so hard her teeth rattled.

She opened her mouth to check her jaw and blinked back tears. He was really hard to love. "You said you know who told me. If that's true, then you know it was Mr. Abrams."

Malvo turned to the tall officer and ordered, "Fortis, take her to the barrel."

Chapter 29

Rory's stomach contracted as Fortis propelled her through the exit and into the bright sunshine. What was "the barrel"? It couldn't be good. Would they seal her in a barrel and suffocate her? Would they dip her in a barrel of boiling oil or acid?

They crossed a fenced yard and headed toward a small concrete block building.

Rory squinted against the sun. Birds sang a happy song. The day was beautiful. Well, it would be, if she didn't have a date with the barrel. The beautiful day didn't care that she was on her way to be tortured.

Perspiration erupted across her forehead as Fortis thrust her through the building entrance. Terror clawed her internal organs when the room of horrors came into focus. Sharp metal objects lined the walls.

Jesus, I can't do this. He had suffered horrifically, but she didn't possess his strength. If she recanted everything and begged for mercy, maybe they would take her back to her cell. Fear confiscated her voice.

Malvo placed the sharp edge of a manual drill bit against her cheek. It sliced a fine line as it slid down her jaw. She flinched as moisture trickled from the site. His face lit up at the horror in her eyes. She hated the vile man.

Gabriel was right when he'd said it was difficult to love enemies. She forced out the words she should say. "God loves you. He wants you to surrender your life to him."

He taunted, "You sound so sincere as if you care about me. But you're a liar."

The lash of his words made her wince. He wasn't wrong on either point.

He ran a finger down her cheek beside the cut. "You're supposed to love those who persecute you. Do you love me?"

She jerked her face away. "You make it difficult."

His eyes sparkled. "You ain't seen nothing yet."

That was her fear, exactly. Her stomach spun as she bit her lip.

In one corner of the room stood a metal barrel. A faucet hung above it. She prayed the faucet dispensed tepid water and not boiling liquid.

Fortis gripped her forearm firmly and pulled her toward it. When she lost her footing, he dragged her. The grate top clanged when he flipped it open. He hoisted her to her feet and nudged her toward the steps. On the top step, she hesitated, then she stepped her right foot over the edge. She lost her balance, and her left leg stretched across the top of the barrel while her right slipped inside. With her hands zip-tied, she was stuck. She couldn't push herself up. The sight would have been comical if not for the torture part.

The officer cursed under his breath. He cut the zip ties, then grabbed under her arms and boosted her until both feet slid inside. He pushed her head down. The grate slammed above her.

"How do you like it in there?" Commander Malvo kicked the side. The sound reverberated around her.

The squeak of metal was followed by a low rumble. Rory braced for scalding water. Her heart hammered against her chest. A torrent of water gushed through the grate. She flinched when it hit. Her nerve endings shrieked from the shock. Wait, the water wasn't hot. It was cold, very cold. It cascaded over her and pooled around her ankles. They intended to drown her.

Her studies came back to her. A reflex reaction caused individuals to hold their breath when drowning. Eventually, the carbon dioxide levels in the blood would rise and the individual would be forced to breathe, ingesting water. The action occurred successive times until the lungs filled with water, which deprived them of oxygen. The entire process took ten to twelve minutes for an adult.

How many people knew when they were living their last ten minutes? If she fought, she would get what, another couple of minutes? So, she surrendered and squatted low. The water rose to her calves. Her teeth chattered.

She should make the most of her last minutes and make her soul right with God. Only there was one slight problem. She had to forgive to be forgiven. These were terrible men. She hated them, and she didn't want God to forgive them.

As she cast her eyes toward heaven, she attempted to conjure a little compassion. *God, I love them and forgive them. I pray for you to forgive them.* The words rang hollow.

She shivered violently. The beating of her heart weakened. Her blood withdrew from her extremities to protect her core. Her mind blurred. She was walking home. The night was freezing. A military jeep approached. The passenger window rolled down. Something about the driver was familiar, but she couldn't place him. Water approached her chin and she jerked. She wasn't walking home. She was in a barrel that was filling with water.

Father, please forgive me, and please forgive these men. Show them the truth. Forgive Dad.

She inhaled water through her nose. It burned in her lungs. Unable to breathe, she panicked. Water flooded her mouth and nose. She coughed and struggled to breathe. More water crowded out her oxygen. *Forgive.* Silence. Darkness.

Chapter 30

Pain racked her body. Rory expelled a foul-tasting liquid from her mouth and nose. Angry voices sounded in the distance. What were they saying? A searing pain lanced through her esophagus and lungs. She struggled to breathe. Something pressed on her chest. Her eyes slit a tiny bit open. Bright light stabbed her eyes. She squinted to allow her vision to adjust.

A fuzzy image of a man knelt above her.

Where was she? What happened? Everything blurred. Her eyes strained to focus. She shivered.

"What were you doing?"

Her teeth chattered, and her body quivered violently.

A man kicked her side. She moaned.

The kneeling man stood. He wore a military uniform. Her memories slowly returned: arrest, interrogation, water, barrel.

"She's barely conscious."

She gasped for air but didn't let on that she heard. Maybe they would give up if she didn't respond.

Fortis lifted her from the floor to a chair. He pressed her shoulders against the chair's back.

Fluid erupted from her mouth. Her lungs, throat, and stomach burned. Her head flopped to the side.

"Who convinced you God is real? Who named you the Lion of Judah?" Malvo squatted close to her face. He jumped back when she regurgitated again. He angrily kicked the fluid off his shoe. He pulled her head up by her hair. "Don't be a fool. Who else believes? The Leemans? Your parents?"

Pain stabbed her lungs when she breathed. Surely, they could see she was in no condition to answer.

"Interrogating her is a waste of time. She doesn't comprehend."

"And whose fault is that?" Malvo released her hair and approached Fortis.

"I obeyed orders, your orders."

"You were supposed to make her think we were drowning her, not actually drown her, you idiot."

The restraint in Fortis's voice was palpable. "She voluntarily breathed in water. Apparently, she's not afraid to die."

"Take her to her cell and dry her out. Inform me as soon as she's cognizant." Malvo stormed from the room.

Fortis scooped Rory in his arms and carried her out the door and across the yard.

The sun caressed her skin with warmth. She closed her eyes as she soaked it up. Earlier, she'd erred when she thought the day didn't care. It had prepared for this moment, to bathe her in its comfort. *God, please take me. Beam me up with this glorious feeling.*

If only Fortis would lay her on the grass and leave her to absorb the sun. But his long strides prevented them from lingering. A blast of cold air slapped her when the door to the main building opened. Her teeth began chattering again.

People snickered and spoke in the background as he carried her through the corridor.

The clanging slide of the cell door announced their arrival. Fortis laid her on the cot and removed her wet shoes and socks. He tossed them to the floor. Rory grabbed at his hand when he unzipped her jumpsuit and mumbled, "No."

"I'm getting you out of these wet clothes." His voice was uncharacteristically kind. He propped her against the wall and pulled her arms from the sleeves. Then he gently lowered her back to the bed and pulled the jumpsuit off. He removed her underwear. So what if he leered. At least she was free of the wet clothes. He wrapped her in a blanket in mummy fashion. The coarse blanket provided warmth. Her shivering became less violent. But something weighed on her chest and made it difficult to breathe.

Her eyelids refused to open. She drifted in and out of sleep.

Heat radiated from her skin like a furnace. She wiggled and kicked at the blanket to break free from the tightly wrapped cocoon. Shortly thereafter, she shivered and struggled to tuck it back around her.

Fitful slumber came and went.

***

Malvo's sinister grin awakened Rory with a jerk. Complete darkness enveloped her. She sighed. It had been a nightmare. A cough sparked burning pain in her chest. Her skin baked. It was like the cell was an oven, and she was the main course. She grabbed at her clothes, but she was already naked. Instinctively, she stretched her limbs away from her body to reduce the heat of skin against skin. Perspiration slickened her body and ran down her sides. Her muscles ached, and her forehead throbbed. The darkness was suffocating. Seriously, she couldn't breathe.

Was cranking up the heat phase two of the torture? How was it possible to make a cell this hot? Maybe if she sat on the concrete floor, she could cool off. But she couldn't rise from the cot.

She gasped for oxygen. *Oh, no.* She had died in the barrel, and she was not in heaven. *Crites.* She was in hell. God knew she hadn't meant it when she said she forgave Malvo and Fortis. At the time, it seemed important to refuse to forgive them. Now it was obvious that the grudge she harbored destroyed her, not them.

God, can you hear me? You probably choose not to hear because people in hell would constantly beg you to save them.

Tears stung her eyes. She would never see Jaxon or her family again. Except maybe her dad. He was as stubborn as she, or she was as stubborn as he. Either way, he refused to believe.

If she could do it over, she'd plead with him more, but from a place of compassion, not anger. And she'd forgive Malvo and Fortis. Her anger and pride had landed her here. She had stubbornly refused to respect God's grace.

Her sobs ignited her cough and spread pain through her lungs. The loneliness throbbed more than the pain.

She was in hell because Jesus was a harsh god. No, that was the devil whispering to her. Jesus wasn't harsh, he was compassionate. *She* was the angry one.

A sound piqued her attention. Her coughing drowned it out. During a lull, she identified the sound of squeaking wheels. As the squeak drew closer, low voices mumbled nearby. Were demons coming to torment her? Or did the voices belong to other poor schmucks who were doomed like her?

The lights burst on, and the glare temporarily blinded her. She squinted, and her cell slowly came into focus. Thank God, she was still in Gibbons. She closed her eyes, and her lips curled upward. Gratitude for incarceration was absurd. Still, she wasn't dead, and she wasn't in hell. She thanked Jesus for the second chance, then took a moment to pray and forgive Malvo and the other officers. This time she really forgave them.

The cell door clamored open. Two uniformed guards wheeled a gurney up to her cot. Hands grabbed her arms and legs. She struggled. Due to her sweaty skin, they almost dropped her. After adjusting their grip, they hoisted her onto the gurney. A guard secured her right wrist to the rail, then he threw the blanket over her. The gurney lurched into motion.

"Where are you taking me?" The screech of the wheels drowned out her weakened voice.

The activity rekindled her cough. She attempted to rise, but a hand pushed her down. The motion nauseated her. She closed her eyes and sucked in a slow breath. A familiar buzzer sounded. She opened her eyes. The gurney paused while a set of doors opened.

After two more buzzers followed by two sets of doors, the motion finally stopped. Her wrist was loosed. Hands grasped the sheet on the gurney and transferred her to a bed. A woman in a white lab coat jabbed a needle into her left arm. Awareness slipped away.

Chapter 31

Beep … beep … beep …

What was that noise?

Rory clawed her way to consciousness. Why couldn't she move her arm? She opened her eyes with effort. Ah, her right wrist was handcuffed to a rail. A vital sign monitor beeped to her left. An IV line protruded from the top of her left hand.

Voices caught her attention. A pain gnawed at her stomach at the sound of that horrible man's voice. The voices drifted from somewhere out of sight. She eavesdropped. The female voice must belong to a doctor.

"Get her ready to return to D block," Commander Malvo ordered.

"You're right, no point in wasting medical care. She'll expire in a few days. You'll save yourself the trouble of staging her execution."

"Send the medication with her. She must survive to be executed."

Survive to be executed sounded like an oxymoron.

"With or without medication, she'll die if she leaves the infirmary."

"Why?"

"Her pneumonia isn't responding to antibiotics. She may expire, even if she remains here. We're not equipped for serious illnesses. If you want her to recover, send her to a hospital."

The commander cursed.

Of course, the fluid in her lungs from breathing in the water had caused pneumonia. Before antibiotics, pneumonia was referred to as the old man's friend—a relatively swift, painless way to die. It sounded good to her. While they were absorbed in their conversation, she stretched her IV-clad left hand to her restrained right and pulled out the needle.

"You're going to execute her. Why do you care if she dies of pneumonia?"

"Those zealots believe she'll lead them to overthrow the Order. They need to see their Lion executed to squash the revolution momentum once and for all."

"Are you sure you have the right person? How can anyone believe she can lead a revolution? The people won't believe she is a—what did you call her?—a lion?"

"According to my source, she's the leader they're waiting for."

"Are you sure it's not a bait and switch? Look at her."

"My source has too much to lose to lie."

Perspiration erupted on Rory's face. What did Tabor have to lose? Maybe he hadn't wanted to turn her in, but they'd threatened him. Henry had warned Jaxon that the Order threatened loved ones to make people talk, but Tabor had no family.

"Her name is Rory. Do you think that's a coincidence?"

"What are you talking about?"

"What do lions do?"

"Eat people?"

"They roar, hence Rory."

She'd been right. He'd arrested her because her name sounded like roar.

"That's quite a stretch. You think when her parents first saw her, they said, 'This baby will grow up to overthrow the Order, so let's name her something to indicate she's a lion? I know, let's call her Rory.' You don't really believe that, do you?"

"I think they groomed her for this. Remember who her grandfather was. He probably brainwashed them, convinced them their first born would deliver their people. They named her Rory and brainwashed her."

Rory's pulse quickened. He believed her parents were a part of this. Her family was never supposed to be involved. If she didn't deny God, her family would be arrested and executed with her. Their deaths would be on her.

"Surely, you see how ridiculous this is."

"Your job is to make her well."

"Let her die from pneumonia. That proves she's not a lion. A god wouldn't allow his chosen one to die of natural causes. Her death derails their hope."

The doctor's words struck a chord of truth. A natural death wouldn't ignite a revolution. God needed a public death. He needed her to face execution. A lump formed in her throat.

"What part do you not understand? People need to witness her execution. They need to see that no god saves her. Her death must be a deterrent. Something horrific, something that makes a lasting impression."

Rory's mouth went dry as the chamber of horrors flashed before her eyes. The Order understood horrific. Lightheaded, she struggled to breathe. She kept her eyes closed in case they started her way or could see her on a monitor.

"Are you afraid a lethal injection won't kill her?"

"Her grandfather survived two lethal injections. It might be some hereditary resistance. That would be all I need. For the whole world to watch me give her an injection, and it doesn't kill her." Malvo snapped.

"Her best chance for survival is to transfer her to a full hospital. Her next best is to remain here."

He cursed.

"Why are you so against her recovering here?"

"The infirmary is less secure if someone attempts to break her out."

"Who in their right mind would try to break someone out of here?"

"These people are not in their right minds."

"She's cuffed to the bed, and an officer is stationed outside the door. Even if someone was crazy enough to try, they would fail."

"The last person you insisted on sending to a hospital was her grandfather. She claims she met him there, and he told her about this god of hers."

God used this doctor to allow her to meet Grandfather. Maybe the doctor would help her. Gabriel had cautioned her against getting ahead of God's plan, but she couldn't help it.

"He was in a coma. He couldn't tell anyone anything."

"She knows things only he could have told her. Unless someone from Gibbons informed her. You know the things. Maybe you're the traitor."

"You're paranoid. I'm no more a spy than you. What did he allegedly tell her?" the doctor asked.

"That's classified."

"If I know, why is it classified from me?"

"Because you don't know what she knows."

"Excuse me, I need to attend to my patient now."

"I'm holding you personally responsible if anything happens to her. If she escapes, or if she dies, you will take her place."

The doctor's voice was thick with contempt. "She wouldn't need medical care if you hadn't attempted to drown her."

"That was your brother."

The tapping of the commander's shoes against the tile floor announced his approach.

Rory remained perfectly still as her heart beat wildly.

A hand shook her shoulder. She kept her eyes closed.

"The drug's effects haven't worn off."

"At least that infernal glow's gone," Malvo said.

"Glow? What do you mean, glow?"

"Her face was glowing when I first saw her. Looks like the barrel washed it off."

"What do you mean, glowing? Flushed?"

"No, she was glowing like a light bulb. Look at the interrogation recording."

"What caused it?" The doctor's voice sounded intrigued.

"She said an angel touched her that first night in lockup."

"Did you watch the security footage for her cell during that time period?"

"Of course. Nothing was picked up except a fuzzy glow, probably a bad spot in the chip. What's that look? Don't tell me you believe an angel touched her."

"Of course not," she replied quickly.

The sound of Malvo's footsteps faded from the room.

The doctor murmured, "Jerk."

Rory slowly opened her eyes and blinked.

"Good, the drugs are wearing off." The doctor flicked a penlight to check Rory's pupil dilation. "I'm Dr. Glynn. You're in the infirmary, because you have pneumonia. We sedated you, and you've been out for a couple of days. How do you feel?"

"Like someone tried to drown me." Her raspy voice sounded unnatural.

The doctor raised her eyebrows and nodded her head. She was tall for a female. Her bobbed dark hair swept away from her angular face. The woman reminded her of someone.

"Why was I sedated? That isn't pneumonia protocol."

The doctor pushed the tray aside and turned her full attention to Rory. "That's right, you're a physician student. The treatment isn't standard, but this is not your standard hospital environment. You experienced trauma and were under a great deal of stress. The medicated state allowed your body to heal without the added strain of incarceration."

Rory's mind was slow, a side effect of the trauma, the drugs, or both. After a few moments, she grasped the rationale. "Makes sense, but why don't they let nature take its course and let me die of pneumonia? They're just going to kill me anyway."

Dr. Glynn ignored her question. "What's your last memory?"

Rory closed her eyes. Sweat popped on her brow as the intense heat and despair flickered in her mind. Peace had surrounded her when she had forgiven Malus and Fortis. She wouldn't fall into the hate trap again, even though Malus planned a terrible death for her. She opened her eyes. "I guess, when I arrived here and someone stuck a needle in my arm."

"Do you remember when the guards transported you? They said you looked a little wild-eyed." Dr. Glynn glanced at her e-notebook.

"Well, yeah, they didn't say who they were or where they were taking me."

"I'm sorry, they should have identified themselves and informed you that they were bringing you here." She struck a few keys on the keyboard and then looked at Rory. "Colonel Fortis thinks you purposely attempted to drown."

"I thought I was cooperating. Wasn't that the intent of the barrel, to drown me?"

The doctor started to reply, then spied the dangling IV line. "I need to replace your IV."

"Let's not."

"You're dehydrated. You need fluids."

Rory grabbed the doctor's wrist.

"What are you doing?"

It was no contest. Larger and stronger, Dr. Glynn easily broke free of her grasp.

"I don't want the IV."

"Commander Malvo says if you die, I take your place."

Yeah, threat of death was a motivator she couldn't compete with. She slipped her free hand beneath her back.

"Don't force me to restrain both your wrists." The doctor disappeared from sight.

Dr. Glynn reappeared on Rory's right side and jabbed a needle into her deltoid.

"Why can't you just leave me alone?" Rory flailed, which forced the needle deeper. "Ow!"

Dr. Glynn leaned in and whispered in her ear, "I'm not your enemy."

"Could have fooled me." Rory thrashed to fight the drowsiness until she couldn't.

***

After the sedation wore off, Rory opened her eyes to find both wrists restrained and an IV reinserted into her left hand. She futilely grabbed at the IV line with her teeth. After several failed attempts, she plopped back against the pillow. The IV prolonged her life. Physically, she had improved, mentally, not so much. At least, the medicated sleep allowed time to pass stress-free.

God didn't intend for her to die of natural causes. There was nothing she could do about it. She focused on forgiving everyone. She would honor the way God had forgiven her by forgiving them.

Familiar footsteps echoed in the hallway. What did God want her to say to him? She had a few choice words, but they weren't God approved. The Holy Spirit had better come through.

The one-she-used-to-hate spoke. "Well, well, what do we have here?"

"Hello, Commander, kind of you to check on me."

He sneered. "Have you come to your senses?"

"That's debatable."

"Are you going to tell me who told you about your god?"

"God loves you. He does not desire for any to perish, even you. Confess your sins, and he will save you."

"Blasphemy against the Order. You have a death wish."

"Consider the risk and return." Her restrained wrists prevented her from emphasizing her words with hand gestures.

"What are you talking about?"

"Believing in God and heaven makes life under the Order tolerable. If I'm wrong, when I die, nothing happens. I'm no worse off. You, on the other hand, enjoy this life while believing God doesn't exist. If you're wrong, when you die, you suffer torment for eternity."

Malvo raised his brows. "How could a loving god sentence people to eternal torment for simply not believing in him?"

His question threw her for a moment. Then the answer became obvious. "He gives you your desire. When you reject him, he allows you to do it. He removes his presence, and torment is what's left. Kind of like how darkness is the absence of light. Torment is the absence of God."

Her words incited a rabid-dog look in Malvo's eyes. Not that she had ever seen a rabid dog, but its eyes probably looked exactly like his. Sharp looks had never scared her, but this was different. It was as if she gazed into the eyes of the devil.

"I'll give you something to think about. We are going to put a stop to this revolutionary nonsense once and for all. We will announce that we have captured the Lion of Judah, and we'll execute you publicly." He rested his palms together. "I think it only fitting for you to be executed like your precious Jesus. We'll strip you to your underwear and nail you to a cross for all to see. This will put an end to any belief in a god almighty."

The bottom dropped out of the room. Rory whirled out of control. The monitors beeped rapidly. This was the culmination of her worst fears. No wonder Gabriel wouldn't tell her how she would die. She gasped for air.

"After the prisoner's hands and feet are nailed to the cross, it's raised and dropped into place. The victim's organs shut down from trauma and stress ... eventually. Some have lived for days before they died." Malvo offered a faux sympathetic look.

Every ounce of strength evaporated. The monitors betrayed her as she tried to hide her terror. Was he even human? A layer of ice coated her spine at the delight on his face. It was impossible for her to hate him more.

"Do you want to change your mind? Give me those names, and perhaps I will allow you a less painful death."

Not even the threat of crucifixion would cause her to put anyone else's fate in the hands of this monster. "I told you everything." Before she could regain control, her eyes fired daggers through his heart.

"Oh, I recognize that look—pure hatred. You would kill me if you could. I thought you believers had to love everyone. If you're right and God is real, it looks like you'll suffer for eternity beside me." His laughter ricocheted off the walls and avalanched around her.

She wouldn't physically kill him, but if God struck him dead, she wouldn't be sad. Except that was the same thing, right? *Ugh.* She just couldn't summon any love for him. He was cruel. He didn't deserve to be loved. She wasn't cruel like him. Even so, she didn't deserve God's love either. *God, help me.*

The monitor continued to beep. She felt lightheaded as her blood pressure rose dangerously.

Dr. Glynn rushed in and glanced at the monitor. She ordered Malvo to leave.

"I don't follow orders from you." He crossed his arms and planted his feet.

"Do you want me to keep her alive? Whatever you said is sending her into cardiac arrest." Dr. Glynn held her ground and stood between the commander and Rory.

"I'll leave, but watch how you talk to me." He nodded to Rory. "You have a date to meet your maker. In other words, I'm putting you in the ground."

She stared at the ceiling.

"What did he say?" Dr. Glynn hit some buttons and silenced the alarms.

"Why do you care?" She tried to turn away from the doctor but couldn't with her wrists restrained.

"As your doctor, I need to know what upset you."

"They're going to execute me. Isn't that reason enough?"

"I suppose." The doctor struck some keys on her e-notebook, then glanced at Rory. "Now that you're awake, you need to eat. What can I order for you?"

"I'm not hungry."
"You haven't eaten in days."
"I'm not hungry."
"You need to build your strength."
"I'm not eating."
"Have it your way." The doctor turned to leave.
"You think this is my way? Hardly."

Rory's vision blurred with hatred and tears. The thought of crucifixion strangled her intestines. Where was God? Why was he allowing this?

The apostle Paul offered to give up his eternity in heaven if his brethren would believe. But even Paul wouldn't offer to trade places with Malvo. The man was evil. How could God love him?

When she'd told Malvo God loved him, he rejected her words. He didn't want to believe. Nothing she could do would change his mind.

She had agreed to die for Jesus, but not in this way. Yes, Christ had needed to die on a cross, but he was the sacrifice for all mankind. Her death was just to stir people up. She didn't want to die on the cross. No one wanted to die like that.

Chapter 32

Five days after Rory had awoken in the infirmary, Dr. Glynn raised the blinds to allow the morning sunlight to illuminate the room.

Rory closed her eyes. Her mood was too dark to enjoy the sunshine.

The doctor removed her IV and handcuffs. She tossed a jumpsuit onto the bed. "Change into this. It's remarkable how well you're doing. I've called transport. They'll take you back to D block."

The news was unwelcome. The D block cell was more austere than the infirmary, and Dr. Glynn was more congenial than the guards. But at least in the cell, she wouldn't have an IV to hydrate her. Dehydration would speed her death on the cross.

The sudden motion of swinging her legs down made her woozy. She grabbed the rail for support. Tentatively, she stood and dropped the gown, then stepped into the jumpsuit.

She looked at Dr. Glynn, who had turned her back to give Rory privacy. "Jesus loves you. He wants you to know him."

Dr. Glynn wheeled around to face Rory. "Shut up. You might have a death wish, but I don't." She stormed from the room.

Jesus, did you hear? I'm trying, but nobody cares.

Rory lay down on the cot to wait. Transport and her friend, Fortis, arrived.

"Can you stand?" Fortis was stoic as ever.

Rory didn't answer, but slowly swung her legs to the side and stood.

Her legs were wobbly. Fortis assisted her to the gurney. What a gentleman. He shackled her right wrist to the rail.

She ran a finger across the cuff. "Aw, a silver bracelet. You shouldn't have. If I didn't know better, I'd say you're sweet on me, Colonel."

Her sarcasm received an icy stare from Fortis. Way past the point of caring, his stare didn't faze her. She was going to be crucified, what could be worse?

"I don't think he's interested, blue eyes. But me, you know, I'm a compassionate guy. I'll pay you a little visit and give you a night to remember," one of the men promised.

The other transport officers laughed.

Her pulse increased.

Fortis leaned his face close to hers. "Keep your mouth shut unless you are giving me believers' names. Don't provoke me."

She returned his icy stare. Hatred boiled through her veins.

"Forget about her. She's nothing but skin and bones. Now, move it," Fortis barked to the officers.

The men grumbled and the gurney rolled into motion. She closed her eyes to avoid the stares along the way.

Inside the cell, Fortis uncuffed her, lifted her like a rag doll, and set her on the cot. He ordered the transport officers out of the cell.

"Later," one of the men promised.

Her stomach knotted.

Fortis followed the men.

Were they making plans to return?

Jesus had remained silent after his arrest. She should have followed his example. Well, God didn't want her to remain silent. He wanted her to share his love, but she had done the opposite.

Unable to hurt them physically, she'd punched them with words. It had backfired.

She dragged her feet off the cot and stood, leaning against the wall for support. One lap around her cell wiped her out. Lying on the cot again, she breathed heavily. She wasn't strong enough to defend herself.

What was Jaxon doing? Closing her eyes, she pictured his handsome face with an afternoon shadow of stubble. The thought of him was bittersweet. She would never feel his touch or kiss again. They would never share a life together.

Voices awakened her. She had drifted off. With effort, she stood. The cell door scraped open, and two of the transport officers entered. She backed away. Barely able to stand, she silently prayed for assistance.

"This is your lucky day." One of the men smiled as he approached slowly.

Her mind whirred, running through the self-defense moves Jaxon had taught her. She would knee the man between his legs.

The first man nodded at the other. "Look, Emil, she's going to fight. This will be fun." He lunged at her.

Rory leaned into him. Her knee connected, powerfully on target.

A painful howl pierced the air. He released her and dropped to his knees. "You slut!" he squeaked.

Emil sprinted in her direction.

With the adrenaline rush over, she couldn't summon the strength for a repeat strike.

"What's going on?" Fortis growled from the cell door.

"The skank attacked me." The man's voice was still high.

"I told you to forget about her. She's mine," he boomed.

"You said you weren't interested." The man stood with difficulty.

"I changed my mind. Get out."

The two men scrambled from the cell. Rory's momentary relief dissipated at the storm brewing in the colonel's eyes. Her stomach boiled as he approached. She didn't stand a chance against this beast of a man.

Fortis threw her roughly onto the cot. With one hand pressed against her chest, he held her down while he unzipped her jumpsuit.

Her eyes opened wide. She dry-heaved but had nothing in her stomach to expel.

Fortis unzipped his trousers, lowered himself over her, and covered her mouth with his hand.

Pinned, she couldn't move. She closed her eyes, choked back a sob, and prayed for God to strike him down.

Fortis's face rested on his hand, which covered her mouth. He writhed and groaned above her but never touched her.

What was happening? Time crawled. They didn't engage in intercourse but rage roared inside her.

His warm breath against her ear was repulsive. If given the opportunity, she would scratch out his eyes.

He whispered, "Do not breathe a word of this to anyone, or I will return and finish what I started. Nod if you understand."

Her nod was barely perceptible with his hand bearing down on her mouth.

"When I get up, turn away from the door and assume a fetal position. Don't look toward the door. Understand?" He lessened the pressure on her mouth.

Wild-eyed, she nodded.

Standing, he glared at her as he zipped his pants.

Pure hatred exploded inside her. She aimed it at him for several seconds before she turned toward the wall and curled into a ball. The sound of the cell door closing made her jerk. A torrent of pent-up tears flowed freely.

The terror from Maneson's assault flooded back. If Brave could have jumped from the shadows, he would have protected her. What if the other men returned? She would never be able to fight them off. With eyes closed, she rocked slowly back and forth. She swallowed down the dirty taste in her mouth.

Jesus commanded her to love those who hurt her, but she just couldn't.

Chapter 33

The sliding of the cell door awakened Rory the next morning. Fortis and Malvo stood in the hall. Her gag reflex kicked in. She closed her eyes.

This was her chance, but she didn't want to love them.

The sound of footsteps drew close.

"Look at me," Malvo ordered.

She ignored him. But what about all she'd promised God about forgiving? She rolled her eyes beneath her closed lids. After a deep breath, she opened her eyes and slowly sat up. Automatically, she fired a lethal look at Fortis but immediately regretted it.

"A little lover's quarrel?" Malvo mocked.

Which man did she hate more? Their cropped hair, straight posture, perfectly pressed uniforms, and callous looks were disgusting.

"I'm supposed to tell you God loves you, and he wants you to surrender your lives to him." *Me, not so much.*

Malvo tilted his head. "Your eyes betray you. Eyes are the windows to the soul. They don't lie, and yours scream hatred."

"I said God loves you. I never said I do."

"According to your doctrine, if you don't love me, you're no better than me, a lowly sinner." His words stung of truth.

"I'm working on it. You're tough to love." Surely, God understood that she was trying.

Malvo's eyes shined in triumph. "If you serve this all-powerful, just god, why does he let me torture you? Why doesn't he strike me down?"

"I ask that question all the time. God's plans are bigger than you and me. Somehow my experience here matters. After my death, I'll reside in heaven, so a win-win for me."

"Is it?" He tilted her chin up.

His touch turned her stomach. She jerked her chin from his hand.

"Will you go to heaven since you hate me?"

His words cut sharper than a scalpel. He played on her worst fear that she would miss out on heaven after all this. But God knew her heart, and he would show her mercy.

The commander clasped his hands behind his back and jutted his chin. "We can easily put this behind us. Admit you're wrong. There is no god. Give me the names of all of those who are also mistaken. You will receive a reduced prison sentence and can go about your life."

The offer was tempting. She longed for the nightmare to end, but she wouldn't deny God. "I'm not wrong. He speaks to me. God is real whether you believe in him or not."

Fury kidnapped Malvo's face. He reared back and slapped her.

With her cheek smarting, Rory stood and braced herself for a second blow. She dug deep inside to force out her next words. "I forgive you."

With his finger in her face, Malvo ranted, "You don't forgive me. You're just saying that, hoping you won't go to hell after you're crucified. Go ahead and hate me. There's no hell. You'll just cease to exist." He strolled over to the bars, then glanced over his shoulder. "Stryker, bring him in."

Two soldiers dragged a severely beaten man into the cell. His head hung against his chest while his feet trailed behind. Rory flinched. Even at the hospital, she had never seen anyone this badly beaten. One eye was swollen shut, and the other was barely open. The redness and swelling indicated his injuries occurred within the last twenty hours. No blue or purple bruising was visible yet. Her medical training and adrenaline kicked in. She approached the man and inventoried his injuries.

"Take him to a hospital right now, not your infirmary, a real hospital. He has a concussion. Why did you bring him here? To show me what you'll do to me? I get the message but take him to a hospital."

Malvo's lips spread into an evil grin. "Don't you recognize him?"

"No, why would I?"

The poor man's face was battered beyond identification.

"Rory—" The voice was barely audible but familiar.

Recognition knocked her to her knees. A shocking chill shot to the depths of her soul. Her heart exploded into tiny, jagged pieces.

"Jaxon! No! What have you done to him?"

In physician mode, Rory placed her index and middle fingers above his carotid artery. She detected a weak pulse. "Jaxon, look at me."

His open eye drifted in her direction. She tore open his shirt. His chest was marred from blunt force trauma. Contusions around his navel confirmed internal bleeding.

She glared at Malvo. "He needs medical attention now."

Jaxon murmured, "It's ... okay."

A lump formed in her throat too large to swallow. It wasn't okay. If Jaxon lived, she promised God to never ask for anything again.

He raised his hand toward her. She grasped it and brought it to her lips.

"Jaxon, can you hear me? I love you, and I'm going to marry you, right here, right now, with God as our witness." She blinked back tears.

His mouth turned up into a slight smile. Moisture accumulated in his open eye. Jaxon's vulnerability delivered a blow to her chest. She gasped for breath.

Gently, she held his face in her hands. "Before God in heaven, I, Rory Rydell, promise to love you now and forever as your wife. I take you, Jaxon Jeffries, the most beautiful man I know, as my husband."

"I ... love ... you," Jaxon mumbled. He coughed weakly.

"Shh. Save your strength. Don't say anything." She tenderly kissed his swollen lips and tasted metal, a sign of traces of blood. Tears trickled down her cheeks. She tried to be strong, but she couldn't.

Commander Malvo clapped slowly. "How sweet. The shortest marriage on record."

"Take him to a hospital!"

"He's an enemy of the Order. This is what traitors deserve. His treachery is worse than yours. He swore fealty to the Order and tossed it away. He gained unauthorized access to the surveillance vault and was captured after he destroyed recordings from the homes of persons of interest." Malvo looked down at Jaxon with a look that could almost be admiration. "He's a tough one. I'll give him that. He refused to tell us whose recordings he targeted, or who told him how to delete the files. We discovered numerous recordings of the two of you together outside the hospital and your family's apartment building. The pieces fell together. As military, he knew the first thing we'd do after your arrest would be to activate the surveillance monitors in your family's apartment. So, we know he was protecting your family from incriminating themselves. We just don't know who helped him. But you do, don't you?"

She couldn't breathe. The world around her crumbled. Jaxon was here hemorrhaging because he'd protected her family.

"It was a suicide mission. He knew alarms would sound as soon as he entered the vault without clearance. But he managed to delete all the recordings before we could stop him. Jaxon, it didn't have to end like this. All you had to do was tell us who you conspired with." Malvo turned Jaxon's face toward him.

"Don't touch him." Rory jerked Malvo's hand from Jaxon.

He shoved her aside. "Fortis, restrain her."

"Let me go." She struggled as Fortis pulled her away by her upper arms.

Positioning himself between Jaxon and Rory, Malvo addressed her. "Who assisted him?"

"I don't know. I swear."

Malvo punched Jaxon in the face. A grunt escaped as his head swung violently.

"No! Stop!" Her voice was hoarse and wild. She lunged, but she couldn't get to Jaxon. Fortis's grip was too strong.

"You're lying."

Henry was a bigwig computer programmer. She'd bet her life that he had access to protocols and passwords and was probably the one who helped Jaxon. Henry was already on Malvo's radar. She could save Jaxon. All she had to do was sacrifice Henry. Before she uttered his name an icy chill spread down her spine. She would be trading the life of the man Athelene loved for the man she loved, and she wasn't even sure if Henry was the guilty party. Jaxon hadn't betrayed anyone, and she couldn't either.

Malvo punched Jaxon in the stomach so hard that it knocked the wind from Rory. Her whole body went limp when Jaxon made no sound. Fortis's firm hold prevented her from dropping to the floor. Blood seeped from the corner of Jaxon's mouth and trickled down his chin. His open eye glassed over. She summoned all her strength for another lunge but couldn't break free of Fortis's Herculean grip.

"Let her go." Malvo said.

Rory flew to Jaxon. Her blood froze when she detected no pulse. "Lay him down."

The officers who held him looked to Commander Malvo for approval, then they stretched Jaxon on the floor.

Rory shoved on his chest in compressions. "Jaxon, don't leave me. I love you." She begged God to restart his heart.

Working quickly, she tilted his head, opened his mouth, and tried to force life into him. She alternated compressions and breaths. When he still had no pulse, she thumped his chest with her fist and prayed for a miracle. She continued compressions until she could push no longer. Her world imploded as she collapsed onto Jaxon's lifeless chest.

"According to you, I cannot kill unless your god allows it. Either your god doesn't exist, or he doesn't care about you and lover boy. I'm not sure which is worse. Either way, I'd renounce him."

Her fingers balled into tight fists and ached to strike Malvo's despicable face again and again, until it was unrecognizable, until his breath dwindled to nothing. Her vision blurred, eclipsed by rage and tears.

"No wonder you broke up with your fiancé. I'll let him know you were banging Officer Jeffries, oh, and Colonel Fortis too." Malvo chuckled.

A bloodcurdling, primitive scream pierced the air. Shockingly, the sound originated from her. With an unnatural agility, Rory pounced on Malvo. She tackled him below the knees and knocked him backward. His head thudded against the iron bars. He lay stunned while she climbed on top of him and pummeled his face with her fists.

"You evil, little man! I'll gladly take you to hell!"

Strong hands grabbed her from behind and pulled her off Malvo. She kicked wildly but only connected with air.

One of the officers, who had dragged Jaxon into the cell, assisted Malvo to his feet. Malvo adjusted his uniform, then pulled his pistol from its holster and pressed the cool, steel barrel against her forehead. "You little witch, how dare you attack me."

"Do it. Shoot me. I'll wait for you in hell. I'll gladly watch you suffer for eternity. Stop hiding behind that gun. Tell him to let me go. Are you afraid to fight me?" She spat at him. He had better be afraid because she would rip his heart out with her bare hands if Fortis released her.

"Don't fire," Fortis said nervously.

Malvo shoved the barrel harder against her forehead. "I'm not going to shoot you. That would be too kind. I want you to suffer. It's your fault he's dead. You're a traitor, and you refused to cooperate." Malvo's eyes burned with loathing.

Everything inside her detonated in grief—her heart, lungs, and brain. She couldn't breathe. She couldn't think. She was more of a wild animal than a human.

The butt of Malvo's gun hurled toward her head, striking her cheek. A flash of bright lights followed the sickening crack of shattering bone. Her knees buckled. Pain rocketed from her cheek to the pit of her stomach. After a sharp pang of nausea, all feeling vanished.

Chapter 34

"Ohhhh ..." Searing pain propelled Rory into consciousness. Her face ached like it had been struck by a sledgehammer. *Oh God, no.* It wasn't a sledgehammer. It was a gun.

Jaxon's broken body haunted her. Ripping all her skin off would have hurt less. At least the physical pain from crucifixion would lessen the emotional pain clawing at her.

It turned out that she could hate Malvo more than when he'd told her she would be crucified. *God, please let me kill him.*

Malvo murdered her love. Jaxon and she would never marry, never have children. Without Jaxon, she couldn't go on. Why did he have to die?

The left side of her head throbbed at a fifteen out of ten. Her left eye was swollen shut. Each breath stabbed her lungs, an indication of fractured ribs. She slid her tongue against her teeth but couldn't determine if any were loose. Her hands ached from hitting Malvo. If only they hurt more because it would mean Malvo suffered more.

They hadn't transferred her to the infirmary. She still lay on her hard cot. Malvo had left her to perish from her injuries. She would gladly die—but not until after she killed him.

An attempt to rise fired fierce pain through her face and chest. The pain nauseated her. She released a round of unintelligible expletives. Perspiration drenched her jumpsuit.

Malvo's words taunted her. *Either your god doesn't exist, or he doesn't care about you and lover boy.*

249

Why had God let Jaxon die? And why had he made her watch? It was wrong to question the creator of the universe. But Jaxon didn't deserve to die. It was supposed to be her.

Believers should rejoice in death. But she and Jaxon were supposed to have a life first.

Numbness slowly crept over her.

The sliding of the door captured her attention. Who was there? Pain pounded in her cheek and eye when she attempted to turn toward the sound. It was too dark to see anything. Faint footsteps alerted her of someone's approach. It was more than one person.

Only guttural sounds emerged when she tried to question the identity of the visitors. A hand hesitantly touched her forehead and stroked her hair. Tears formed at the act of kindness. She missed human touch. The hand was large and rough. Whose was it? Gabriel's hand never felt rough when he touched her. Could this be Jaxon? She sucked in a ragged breath. Did God send him to bring her home? Her heart cramped. But he wouldn't have needed to open the cell door. Who was it? Who had access to her cell and would exhibit kindness?

The jab of a needle in her right arm made her jerk. What did they inject? The hand no longer stroked her hair. It wasn't an act of kindness. It was a diversion. The person stood and watched as her thoughts slowed. Was she dying? She panicked. She hadn't killed Malvo yet.

***

Voices swirled in the distance. Rory fought to awaken. The dull pain intensified as the voices grew clearer. At this level of pain, she wasn't dead. Good, she still had time to kill Malvo. With effort, her right eye opened.

"Good afternoon."

Hate coursed through her veins at the sound of Malvo's voice. If she could just strangle him and watch his life slip away. An attempted lunge failed. Her pain pinned her to the cot. Not even hatred provided enough adrenaline for an attack.

Malvo bent before her open eye. "Look what you did to me yesterday." He pointed to the bruises on his face beneath a shadow of stubble.

"It's an improvement, you slug." He couldn't enjoy her insults because her words came out as grunts.

"What's wrong? The cat got your tongue?" He leaned closer.

As he narrowed the distance, she groaned and grabbed for his gun. He easily sidestepped her attempt and slapped her swollen cheek. The slap ignited a light show before her open eye and nauseating pain shot to her core.

"You're still feisty, but not for long. I'll break you soon enough."

Rory closed her good eye and concentrated on breathing. Her face and ear pulsed with pain. She saluted him with her middle finger.

Malvo laughed.

What was so funny? She heard a click.

"Thank you for the photo op. When we announce your execution date, we'll use this." Malvo held his phone so she could view the image. "This is proof that you disrespect the Order. What kind of believer flips people off?" His laughter faded as he departed.

His words knocked the breath from her. She dropped her hand. What a fool she was. Malvo didn't break her. She broke herself by creating distance between her and God. She'd disgraced God when she waved the obscene gesture. Now Malvo would show it to the world.

Perfect love conquers all.

The biblical words caressed her. But to love, she had to forgive. It sounded simple. How could she while Jaxon's death continuously played in her mind, tearing the wound open each time?

Anyway, she couldn't speak, so she couldn't tell Malvo she forgave him. Would it change anything even if she could? Would Malvo believe?

251

Jaxon had told her that she was only responsible for herself. She was called to do the right thing, regardless of what anyone else did. *I forgive Malvo.* But the words did nothing to calm the hatred that boiled within.

Several hours later, Malvo entered Rory's cell and rubbed salt in her wound. "That was a beautiful picture I took."

She attempted to speak, but garbled sounds were all that came out.

"What are you trying to say?" Malvo asked.

She held her finger in the air and mimed that she wished to write.

He handed her a pen and held a pad.

She scratched on the pad. The words were barely legible: I 4 give u.

"You forgive me?" He looked incredulous.

She winced and slowly nodded.

"No, you don't. You hate me. I killed your lover. I dragged him in for you to watch him die. You want to kill me. I saw it in your eyes. You think you need to forgive me to go to heaven. Go ahead and hate me because there is no heaven." He rubbed his chin. "I have another surprise for you. This will rid you of any stupid idea that you forgive me." He spoke into his radio. "Bring them in."

Footsteps halted outside her cell.

"Rory, Rory, oh my word."

The sound of her mother's voice delivered a blow to her chest. Reflexively, she jerked her head toward the sound. Pain pulsed through her face. She tried to say, "Mom," but the word didn't articulate.

"Your whole family is here—mom, dad, and sister. They turned themselves in. After they learned of your arrest, they decided to believe too. Convenient, don't you think? We both know they believed all along, and you protected them. It was just a matter of time before we gathered enough evidence to arrest them. You should have turned them in."

A vise squeezed her heart. Every time she forgave Malvo, he attacked her harder. He was the devil himself.

Perfect love conquers all.

God loves everyone in spite of their actions. A freezing sensation started at the base of her skull and glided through her brain. Her open eye drifted to Malvo. His skin was sallow, and one of his eyes spasmed with a nervous twitch. He was a power-hungry, insecure man who feared the truth. The man held no power over her.

The unlovable need love the most.

Her vision blurred for a second. When it cleared, Malvo's face transformed to that of a terrified child. She blinked a few times. His austere countenance returned. Was her vision playing tricks, or was God trying to tell her that Malvo had experienced an atrocity as a child? The chains that bound her heart in hatred loosened, just a little. She formed a heart with her hands.

"Stop it. You don't love me." A rabid look infested Malvo's eyes. He was not in control, and it terrified him.

A shuffling sound in the hallway was followed by her father's voice. "What did you do to her?"

Malvo walked toward the bars between the corridor and the cell. "You should ask what she did to me? See these bruises? She attacked me. I had to defend myself."

"What did you do to provoke her?" The anger in Dad's voice was palpable.

"I merely let her see her lover once more before he died."

Her family gasped. A pain stabbed Rory's chest.

"I thought she would want to say goodbye, but this is how she repaid me."

It suddenly became clear. What Malvo had used to break her—Jaxon's death—had been orchestrated by God. In his loving wisdom, God used Malvo to give her the opportunity to confess her love to Jaxon before he died. Ashamed of her anger with God, tears welled.

"You could have easily subdued her. Do you feel like a big man, beating a defenseless girl?"

"Defenseless? She's a beast. She screamed like a banshee, knocked me down, and attacked me. I had to knock her out to make her stop. Oh, that look is the same look she gives me all the time, pure hatred. The apple doesn't fall far from the tree."

The truth of Malvo's words stung. If she could just warn her dad not to fall into the hate trap. She was only just starting to crawl out of it herself. *Please God, protect Dad from falling prey to hate.*

Malvo made it difficult to love him, but with God, nothing was impossible. She surrendered her will to Jesus and finally began to experience the power of loving the unlovable.

"Now, are any of you going to come to your senses and admit your god doesn't exist?"

"No," they responded in unison, without pause.

Her heart swelled at their refusal to deny Christ and at her father's return to faith.

"Fine. You'll face the firing squad together. It will be a family affair."

Firing squad? He said firing squad, not crucifixion. *Thank you, Jesus!* She closed her eye and wept tears of joy, tinged with sadness. Jesus had changed Malvo's mind. He had answered her prayer for a quick death. But now her family would share her fate.

"Lock them up."

Cell doors slid open and closed, and the guards' footsteps faded.

"Rory, I'm so sorry, baby." Her mom's voice sounded like it originated from across the corridor.

She lifted her hand to wave.

"Rory, I need to apologize." Her father sounded like he was in the cell adjoining hers.

The desperation in his voice tugged at her heart.

"After you questioned the world's origin, and they took me to the base, they didn't hold me. After I left the base, I spent a couple of nights on a bench at the Sanitary Works Facility."

What? All these years, she had beaten herself up for a lie.

"I was afraid for you. You always asked so many questions. I thought you would be more careful if you thought I'd been arrested. I was wrong. I should have been honest with you. I'm sorry."

His sobs doused her anger. Tears stung her eyes. He'd done the best he could. The only thing that mattered was that he believed now. She formed a heart with her hands.

"Rydge, she signed that she loves you." Her mom relayed the information.

Her father sobbed harder.

Rory pointed to herself, put her palms together, and held them beside her cheek.

Her mother guessed correctly. "You need to rest."

Rory flashed a thumbs up.

They encouraged her to rest and voiced their love.

Mom passed along to Dad and Ruby that she touched her lips and blew them a kiss.

Conflicting thoughts battled. Relief that she no longer faced incarceration alone. Grief that her family would die beside her. Elation that they would not suffer crucifixion.

Ruby declared, "I believe Jesus will rescue us."

Poor, naïve Ruby. Even if she could speak, Rory didn't have the heart to burst her sister's bubble. Luckily, once they arrived in heaven, this wouldn't even be a memory. Her heart fluttered at the thought of reuniting with Jaxon.

Chapter 35

On the third day following her family's arrest, the cacophony of multiple boots striking the corridor tiles alerted Rory of the impending doom. *Thank you, Jesus.* The nightmare would finally end.

Two soldiers entered her cell, roughly lifted her, and sat her in a wheelchair. She gasped as pain torpedoed through her chest and face. An officer restrained her wrists to the arms of the chair as though she could flee.

Her family stood somberly in the corridor as she was wheeled from her cell. They ran to her and hugged her. Pain was a small price to pay for the luxury of their touch.

Guards pulled her family aside and shackled their wrists. A guard shoved her dad to the lead, and her mom and Ruby followed. Rory brought up the rear in the wheelchair.

The entourage halted at the doors to the courtyard. Ruby trembled. If only Rory could comfort her sister.

"Such a touching scene." Commander Malvo appeared, adorned in full military regalia. Concealer camouflaged the bruises on his cleanly shaven face. Resembling a master of ceremonies, his brown eyes danced at the thrill of introducing the main attraction.

She looked away from him. When she'd refused to love Malvo and the others, it was because they had hurt her. Soon she'd be in a place with no hurt or wrongs of any kind. If she'd forgiven them earlier, things might have turned out different, better. A ragged breath shot a sharp pain through her chest.

"Do you know what today is?" Commander Malvo asked. His face beamed.

Her dad verbalized her thought. "Execution day."

"Besides that." His annoyance was obvious. "April 3, Easter. What kind of believers are you? You don't even know the day you claim your god rose from the dead? You are going to die on Easter. You're welcome." Malvo strutted like a peacock. "It was originally scheduled for next week, but after I realized today is Easter, I escalated it. The grandstands are filling to capacity. So many are eager to watch the spectacle in person. It's being streamed around the globe. You are notorious. It's mandatory for every citizen to watch. You're an example to deter traitors." He turned to Colonel Fortis. "Can she stand?"

"Not by herself, sir." Fortis stood at attention in his dress uniform.

Rory formed a heart with her hands so that Fortis could see.

The normally unmoved Fortis darted his eyes away. Perhaps chinks existed in his armor. She should have spoken kind words to him instead of her sarcasm. *Jesus, please speak to his heart.* Paul originally persecuted Christians, so there was a chance for him.

"Mom, Dad, help her up the steps and support her on the platform." Malvo covered her head with a burlap hood. "We don't want your injuries to make any of our spectators feel squeamish. We'll flash the picture of you flipping me off." He chuckled.

If she could just take back the gesture.

The hood's putrid smell of vomit and sweat soured her stomach. How many others had worn it? Her heart quickened as the hood triggered claustrophobia.

The wheelchair bumped over the threshold, causing sharp pain to shoot through her chest and head. Perspiration dripped from her nose under the stifling hood. The group halted, and her wrists were freed. Each of her parents gently took one of her arms. They whispered loving words as they helped her to the stairs. Tears brimmed in her eyes. *Jesus, thank you that Dad believes. I cannot ask for anything more.*

Each movement shot searing pain through her lungs. She slowly tapped her foot to locate the next step. The gigantic problems that had loomed over her shrank and became insignificant. The only thing that mattered was that people's eyes would be opened, and they would come to know Jesus after they witnessed her death.

Rory clenched her jaw. The effort expended ascending the steep steps rocketed her pain level off the charts. She erupted in sweat, and her stomach swam in nausea. As dizziness threatened to spawn her collapse, her mother's words sparked a small adrenaline surge. "This is the last step."

On the stage, she was barely able to shuffle with assistance. At last, her parents halted. Her breath escaped in heavy huffs.

"Thank you, for joining us," Malvo's voice boomed over the loudspeakers. "The United World Order will not tolerate traitors!"

A deafening cheer erupted from the crowd. *God, forgive them.*

"Rory Rydell, also known as the Lion of Judah, stands before you. In collusion with her family, she plotted to overthrow the United World Order. These traitors plotted to destroy life as you know it. If their deity existed, it would prevent their execution."

"Kill the Lion!" the crowd chanted. The platform vibrated from the cheers and stomping.

Jesus, these people need you. Please reveal yourself that they may be saved.

The hair on her arms stood on end as an electric current buzzed through the air. A burst of strength allowed her to stand independently. But she didn't stop at standing straight. She continued to rise. Her feet left the solid platform as if she were a hot air balloon. Weightless, Rory levitated above the stage. She flexed her feet, but they only touched air. A tingling feeling coursed throughout her body. What was happening? Was God swooping her to heaven in view of the spectators? *Yes! Please swoop my family too.*

"What the—" Malvo shouted in alarm.

Her pain dissipated, her mouth loosened, and her words rang loud and clear. "I represent the Great I Am. The God of heaven and earth. He loves you with an undying love.

"Commander Malvo called me the Lion of Judah. That is not true. The Lion of Judah is Jesus Christ, the Son of God. He died an agonizing death on the cross for you. Through his mercy, you can enjoy eternal life if you surrender your heart to him. Ask forgiveness of your sins and accept Jesus as your Lord and Savior."

A gasp ascended from the crowd, followed by foreboding silence. A rumble in the distance, like a freight train, launched the crowd into mass hysteria. Voices screamed and feet pounded. Hands grasped her for support, probably Ruby and her parents, as they struggled to stand. God served as her anchor while she hovered a short distance above the stage.

Her voice carried above the noise. "I praise you, Lord. You are my protector and deliverer. Your love anchors me. Your peace surrounds me." God sheltered her from the wind that howled viciously through the crowd.

"Turn off the PA system!" Malvo attempted to shout above the deafening noise.

A roar like a mighty ocean wave shook the earth. Spectators screamed and stampeded.

"The heavens rumble with God's fury." The volume of her voice wasn't affected by the PA system. "Even though you turned your backs on him, he invites you to return. His anger rains down as hailstones on those who refuse to accept him."

God unleashed his wrath. Hail clattered as it bounced off the platform.

"The Lord hurls lightning on those who persecute his followers. Accept his mercy. Repent and worship him."

Several sharp cracks tore through the air, followed by peals of thunder. With her head covered by the hood, she could only imagine the spectacle surrounding her.

"Jesus loves you and yearns for you to come home. The ruler of the world loves you. Rejoice as he delivers you by his mighty power."

"Aim! Fire! Fire!" Commander Malvo shrieked.

Shielded by God, an explosion of bullets whizzed around her. God's exhibition of might filled her with joy. If only she could see it.

"You are witness to God's power. Do not hesitate. Accept his invitation."

Electricity hummed in close proximity, warming the air. A bolt of scorching heat was followed by a blood curdling scream. The smell of burning flesh turned her stomach.

Rory descended to the platform. Strong hands seized her and hoisted her across a broad shoulder. Her family screamed her name. The individual carrying her bounded down the platform stairs and sprinted. As she was jostled roughly, the hood fell from her head and revealed the back of an Order uniform. No, she was still a prisoner. The superhuman strength vanished. Pain detonated through her face and ribs. The chaos diminished and consciousness slipped away.

Chapter 36

A series of beeps summoned Rory. A faint memory of the back of an Order uniform shocked her awake into the midst of acute pain in the left side of her face and body. Panic morphed into confusion. The room's décor was that of the patient rooms at University Hospital. She lifted her arms. Her wrists were unrestrained.

"Rory," her mom cried, "you're awake." She ran to Rory and kissed her right cheek.

"What … hap …. happened?" Rory's voice crackled as her jaw moved like a rusted hinge.

"God delivered us from the Order." Her mother stroked Rory's arm as joyful tears streamed down her cheeks.

God had delivered them, and she'd lived. This was unexpected. "Ruby? Dad?"

"Yes, we're all alive and well, better than well. We've been so worried about you."

Grief trampled her heart. They weren't all alive and well. Unless Jaxon hadn't really died. Maybe he was just so weak that she hadn't felt his pulse. "Jaxon?"

Darkness clouded her mom's face. An answer wasn't necessary.

"Honey, I'm sorry, Jaxon didn't make it. They told us he died after he was beaten. He sacrificed himself to protect us. I'm so sorry." She squeezed Rory's hand.

Her heart imploded all over again. A piercing chest pain doubled her over. The monitor chirped loudly.

"Amber!" her mom yelled.

Nurse Amber slipped on nitrile gloves as she raced into the room. She hit a button that silenced the monitor. "Are you in pain?"

Rory nodded. The pain was emotional, but it was more intense than physical.

Amber adjusted the controls on the IV and rested a gloved hand on Rory's shoulder. "That should help. It's good to see you awake. Can I get you anything?"

Rory shook her head.

"Thank you for everything you did." The nurse's brown eyes glistened.

Rory nodded and closed her eyes.

"Get some rest. That's what you need, plenty of rest. Of course, you know that." Amber pulled off the gloves and deposited them into the trash. "Call me if you need anything."

She didn't need anything the nurse could provide.

With the sedative taking the edge off, she worked up the courage to ask, "What about Darius?"

"He is as zealous for God as he was for the Order. He asks about you every day," her mom replied. "I'll let him know you're awake. He'll want to see you."

Rory placed a hand over her heart. "I'd like that."

God had it all under control. He'd transformed Darius. She hadn't needed to confess to him. Still, maybe it had helped in some way.

"A lot of people want to visit you. We'll limit visits while you're in the hospital. After you're released and up to it, we'll have a reception for you."

She would never be up to it. Changing the subject, she asked, "What happened to Brave?"

"Jaxon's parents took him. We thought you'd like to have him when you're stronger. They said they're happy to care for him as long as needed."

She'd never met Jaxon's parents. As difficult as it was to fathom, they must hurt as horrifically as she.

Her mom slid her hand under the blanket and clasped Rory's hand. "God is good. He held you firm above the platform. You supported us. The winds whipped all around you, but you stood solid like a rock. So many people dedicated their lives to God after seeing his display."

"Did all nonbelievers die?" Rory's mouth moved a little easier, maybe due to the increased pain medication.

"We believe they all died in our zone." Their zone consisted of the areas formerly known as North, South, and Central America. "The other zones suffered natural disasters and many loyal Order citizens died, but not like here. Thank God, many more people accepted Jesus than died. Several former Order officials are now believers. Isn't that wonderful? It's such a miracle."

"Commander Malvo?"

Her mom studied Rory carefully. "He was struck by lightning right before you were whisked from the platform."

The hair on her arms tingled. She perspired from the intense heat, and the stench of burned flesh filled her nostrils. A scream of agony echoed in her head. Commander Malvo had been the source of the scream. He'd met the wrath of God. There was a time when his fate would have pleased her, but his death didn't ease the pain of losing Jaxon. Still, it was sad that he hadn't repented. Vengeance was best left to God.

"You were taken directly from the prison to the hospital. You passed out on the way. They operated immediately. The doctors said they were doing all they could—" Her mom choked up. "I knew God wouldn't let you die after all you went through." She squeezed Rory's hand.

Dying would have been better than remaining here, abandoned and broken beyond repair.

"Dr. Bourland observed the surgery and kept us informed. He stayed the night and monitored you. He's a very nice man."

Rory perked up. "Dr. Bourland believes?"

"Yes. He thinks a lot of you and was quite concerned."

She had always known he would make a great believer.

"With the Order defeated, at least in our zone, this is a wonderful time. There's a lot of work ahead, setting up a new government and everything. Your father's one of the advisory members on the council that's forming the new government. Can you believe it? His transformation is amazing. He's the man I fell in love with."

A few weeks ago, her dad had rejected God, and now he was helping to form the new government. As amazing as the news was, it couldn't rouse emotion in her hollow heart.

Her mom beamed while she shared information. She continued to speak, but Rory didn't hear her words.

A light knock came at the door. "Amber told me you're awake. Let's have a look at you." Dr. Heppernan, the hospital's craniofacial surgeon, entered. The doctor was a short, full-figured woman. She flipped on an exam light and leaned in as she assessed Rory's left cheek. "Do you know where you are?"

"University Hospital."

"What year is it?"

"2079."

The doctor shot a sharp look at her.

"Darn, still 2078? I had hoped it was a new year already."

The doctor sighed. "Good to see you haven't lost that dry wit. In a sense, it is a new year." She switched off the light. "You gave us quite a scare when you failed to wake after the anesthesia should have worn off. Your brain scans looked good, vitals were strong, but you didn't wake. We couldn't find a medical reason, so we waited." She glanced at her e-notebook. "Today makes day seven. You were a mess when you came in—battered, dehydrated, and malnourished. You're healing well. Your cheekbone was fractured, and you have three broken ribs. How's your pain level?"

"Six or seven."

"Amber adjusted the medication a few minutes ago," her mom volunteered.

"The more you work your jaw, the faster the pain will diminish. Let me know if it doesn't. Don't blow your nose for three days. If air escapes from your sinuses into your skin, it will increase the swelling around your eyes. The bruising and swelling should lessen significantly in another week or two. Expect pain from your ribs for four to five weeks. You're a fighter. I am honored to treat you. We're all very grateful to you."

It wasn't like she had volunteered. If offered a choice, she would have backed out.

The doctor touched Rory's head. "You're lucky. If the blow had made contact on the top of your head, it would have killed you or been severely debilitating. If your eye had received the direct hit, it would have blinded it." The doctor shared surgery details, but Rory tuned her out.

"I'll check on you in the morning. If you need anything before then, have them call me."

"Thank you, Doctor." Her mom escorted Dr. Heppernan from the room.

A few hours later, Ruby and her dad visited. They chattered excitedly about life since the fall of the Order. Citizens of all classes were working together to keep necessary services operating. Her dad was a member of the Kingdom Advisory Council, along with eleven others. Rory didn't recognize the names. The council was creating the new government and optimizing the privatization of services and businesses. The people and the council believed Rory should play a vital role in the new government.

God hadn't given her any indication that he desired her to lead the new nation. Martyrdom should have fulfilled her destiny. She wasn't even supposed to be here. She should have been in heaven with Jaxon.

"Rory, are you okay?" her dad asked.

"Yeah, it's just ... overwhelming."

"I know." He bowed his head. "We're all overwhelmed, but we didn't go through as much as you."

"Is there a recording of us on the platform?"

"Yes," he replied. "The council has viewed it several times."

"I want to see it."

Her parents exchanged wide-eyed glances.

"It's pretty intense, sweetheart," Dad said.

"I was there. I know it was intense, but I had a hood over my head. I want to see what everyone else saw."

"You probably need to be a little stronger before you watch it. Some parts of it are amazing, like when you floated above the stage, and your face shined through the hood." His face beamed and then darkened. "But other parts can be disturbing."

Whoa, her face shined through the hood! God's miracles exceeded the capabilities of her limited imagination. The inability to picture her experience left her with an itch that she couldn't scratch.

Mom touched her shoulder. "We should ask your doctor first. You just came to. You need to give yourself some time."

"I'll ask her tomorrow." Rory would pressure the doctor if necessary. "Oh, and who turned me in?"

"Henry Leeman," Dad answered.

He must have misunderstood. Rory enunciated slowly. "No. Who reported me to the Order?"

Patiently, he waited for her to form the words before he answered. "Henry Leeman told the Order you were the Lion of Judah. Turns out, he was a long-time Order informant. He was the perfect spy. Since all the believers trusted him, he knew everything that was going on."

He'd threatened her, and he was the snitch? Jaxon had died because she'd withheld their names. How could he do this? He was worse than Malvo. He pretended to be a Christian, and all the while, he was the traitor.

"Leeman confessed and has been arrested. He's waiting for sentencing."

"Punishment?"

"The council is discussing. I know what I want." Anger radiated in his eyes.

"I want to speak to him."

Her mom placed a hand on her shoulder. "I don't think it's a good idea."

"I need to." She balled her hands into fists.

Her dad sighed. "I'll discuss with the council, but you need time to heal before you do anything. Wait until your speech improves and you can walk."

A knock at the door interrupted the discussion. Her mom called, "Come in."

Rory stared mindlessly out the window. She would not rest until she spoke to Leeman.

"Dawson, good to see you. How late did you guys stay last night?" Dad asked.

"Until 0200."

A chill raced up her spine at the sound of the all too familiar voice. She whipped her head in the direction of the speaker. His face resurrected her worst memories from Gibbons. "He's with the Order!" Her hands trembled.

Fortis froze mid-handshake and looked to her dad for direction.

Rory's dad approached and took her hand. He motioned toward Fortis. "It's okay, sweetheart. Dawson's one of us. It's a long story, but he was your guardian angel at Gibbons. He carried you to safety from the platform."

"He stayed with you, until we arrived," her mom added.

Guardian angel? They were crazy. Her heart beat rapidly. "You don't know what he did—" Rory gasped for breath as she inched up the bed to get as far from Fortis as possible. The medical equipment beeped loudly.

Just like in Gibbons, Colonel Fortis's stone face remained unreadable.

"I shouldn't have disturbed you." Fortis turned on his heels and exited.

"Dawson." Her dad trailed after him.

Amber burst in and ushered her mom and Ruby out. She injected Rory's IV with a sedative, which dulled her anxiety and allowed her to escape into a deep sleep.

Chapter 37

The effects of the sedative began to wear off. The room was silent. Everyone must have left. But when Rory opened her eyes, her family was seated somberly by her side like they were at a funeral.

Her mom took her hand. "Sweetheart, are you feeling better?"

"Guess so. The machine's not beeping." Her jaw moved easier and hurt less.

"I'm sorry. We should have realized seeing Dawson would upset you. He's not who you thought he was. You've missed a lot while you were in the coma," her mom said.

"Apparently." He was Dawson to them. Use of his first name indicated an intimacy that stabbed of betrayal.

"You've been through so much. Just concentrate on getting better," her mom added.

First impressions were hard to overcome. She couldn't reconcile Fortis as a good guy. Their praise for him rubbed her the wrong way. He'd prevented the other men from raping her. But that image of him above her was so vivid, so hard to forget. Since God had spared him, he'd either believed all along, or his heart had changed on the platform. Unable to deal with him at the moment, she changed the subject. "Can I see a mirror, please?"

Ruby jumped up, opened the lid of the rolling tray, and pushed it to her.

"Dr. Heppernan says you're healing nicely. In a few months, you won't be able to tell," her mother said.

The image that stared from the mirror made her flinch. She angled her head to view her right profile. It looked good. Well, maybe good was generous, but normal. Her left profile was not good. Her colorful skin displayed various shades of purple, green, and blue. Maybe others wouldn't be able to tell, but Rory always would.

"You're beautiful, even with those bruises," Ruby announced.

"Let's put the mirror away." Her mom reached for the tray.

It didn't matter that she looked hideous. She felt hideous. She ripped her eyes from the mirror, closed the lid, and pushed the tray toward her mother.

Her family made small talk. Rory closed her eyes. It was odd to hear her father call her mother Ruth. Many people who had been forced to change their names by the Order were opting to return to their pre-Order names, including her mother.

Someone touched her shoulder. Rory opened her eyes.

"It looks like you need some rest. We're going to the cafeteria to get something to eat. We'll be back," her mom said.

"You've been here a long time. You've got to be tired. Go home and get some rest. Come back tomorrow."

"We don't want to leave you alone." Her mom glanced nervously at her dad.

"I'm not. There's a floor full of nurses and assistants." Rory held up the call button. "If I need anything, I'll push the button." She attempted to smile, but the pain in her cheek made her wince.

Her parents spoke quietly, then her dad turned to her. "I guess we'll see you tomorrow, then."

They took turns and kissed Rory's forehead before they left.

The silence blared in her head once she was alone. She missed the idle chatter. A cloud passed over the sun and darkness filled the room. Her breathing became ragged. Why had she asked them to leave?

Disuse of her skeletal muscles had quickly led to atrophy and loss of muscle mass. After being bedridden for weeks, she couldn't get out of bed, much less stand. How could they want her to be instrumental in the government? No one wanted to look at her. She was hideous. Why hadn't God just let her die?

Rory reached for the call button, but accidentally knocked it to the floor. It fell just out of reach. Great, just great. She fumbled with the rail but couldn't lower it. She struck it with her open palm.

People treated her like she was close to God, like she knew his will. Maybe she had for a short time. But now, she was utterly alone and abandoned. She closed her eyes.

I am here.

Rory popped her eyes open. A form, surrounded by a bright light, stood before her. Her heart quickened. "Where have you been?"

Cradling you while you recovered. I placed you in a deep sleep to allow your body time to heal.

Jesus was the reason she hadn't awakened after surgery. "Why haven't I felt your presence?"

You have been angry with me. You have not allowed me near you.

She stared at the floor and started to deny the accusation, then stopped. Denying it was pointless. Jesus knew everything.

You blame me for Jaxon's death.

Rory drew in a sharp breath. "It's hard to live with this gaping hole in my chest. Why didn't I die when the Order fell? Why did the plan change?"

The plan never changed. You decided you had to be martyred due to your lack of ability. That was never my plan. Your obsessive tendency to worry stemmed from not trusting in me and caused you additional suffering. You suffered with pneumonia because you purposely breathed in water in the barrel. You weakened your body when you refused to eat and drink, making your recovery more difficult. I never needed your abilities to defeat the Order. You just needed to trust me.

"But no one told me what to expect. If someone had told me, I would have reacted differently."

It is not trust if you know the outcome. But even if you had known, you would have worried because you didn't believe my plan was better than yours.

"But Grandfather and Gabriel implied I would die. They said things so I wouldn't fear death."

Their words were to comfort you, to help you accept Jaxon's death.

The words knocked her breath away. She replayed the references from this new perspective. "Jaxon was going to die all along?"

Yes.

Lightheaded, she asked, "Why wasn't I told he would die?"

Had you known, would you have enjoyed your time with him?

"No, I wouldn't have been able to function. Why did I meet him if he was just going to be torn away? Why didn't I study with someone else?"

Do you wish you never knew him? Jaxon feels blessed to have loved you.

Tears streamed down her face. Rory stuffed tissues in her nostrils because she wasn't supposed to blow her nose. She was forced to breathe through her mouth.

To love another is always good. Your love for Jaxon shaped the person you are. The love you shared with him does not die, it lives on.

"Did Jaxon die because of something I did?" The guilt had been crushing her.

No.

"Was there anything I could have done to prevent his death?"

No. Residing in heaven is Jaxon's reward. Why do you wish to take it from him?

"I don't want to take it, just postpone it. I miss him so much."

After you work through your grief, you will feel his presence.

"Is he happy?"

Happiness is fleeting. Joy is eternal. Rest assured, Jaxon experiences inexpressible joy.

If granted one desire, it would have been for Jaxon to be happy. Jesus confirmed he was beyond happy. He deserved to remain in paradise.

You were not alone at Gibbons. I was with you, and I placed people to protect you.

"Was Colonel Fortis one?"

He was. I revealed myself to you multiple times. I allowed the sun to warm you after you almost drowned. I gave you strength to resist the guard. I held you above the platform and shielded you from the storm that raged all around. I was always with you.

"I didn't realize. I'm so sorry."

Rory, you have a choice. You can live consumed with grief, even though Jaxon lives in paradise, or you can trust me and lead my people along the path of righteousness. They will quickly forget that I alone delivered them from the United World Order and will need to be reminded. You can teach them to trust me.

"But I didn't trust you."

Start now. Focus on me. Allow me to guide you through the many choices you will face one step at a time. I do my best work through thankful people who trust in me. The world will encourage you to become self-sufficient. Do not listen to them. Surrender your will to me.

"I surrender."

In time, you will love again.

A lump in her throat prevented her from swallowing. She would never love like she'd loved Jaxon. She closed her eyes and pictured his beautiful face.

You will meet again.

Her heart skipped a beat.

Allow others to help you overcome your grief.

"I don't like to talk about my pain."

You deny others a blessing when you refuse their help. You desired friends. Many wish to befriend you. Allow them to love you.

"I'm not worthy of love."

That is the devil's lie. He attacks you and seeks to destroy you. He does so because he knows you will be a great leader.

"He knows exactly how to fuel my doubt. How do I resist him?"

Seek me constantly and surround yourself with others strong in faith.

"I will try. Will you tell Jaxon I love him?"

He knows, and he loves you.

Her tears flowed harder. She changed out the tissues. Jesus spoke of Jaxon in the present tense, not the past. She needed to do the same.

"I love you, and I'm sorry I blamed you for Jaxon's death."

I love you. Love others as I love you. He reached out and touched her. *I will provide you a helpmate.*

"What?" A peacefulness flowed to her core.

"Time to take your temperature." Amber entered and glanced around the room. "Who were you talking to?"

Rory blinked. Jesus was gone. Had she fallen asleep and dreamed it? Tissues were stuffed in her nose. She removed and tossed them into the trash.

"Are you all right?" The nurse's eyebrows lifted. She scanned Rory's forehead with the thermometer. "Your face … it's glowing. Did an angel visit? Is that why your face is glowing?"

It hadn't been a dream. "Jesus was here."

"Oh, my word!" Amber dropped the thermometer, then quickly retrieved it. She trembled when she took Rory's hand. "I just felt something. Like a shock went through my body when I touched you. Is my face glowing?"

"Maybe a little." Or was Amber just blushing?

273

"You shared your glow with me. I can't believe it." Amber stomped her feet quickly in place. "Thank you and thank you for all you did for us. I always thought God was real, but I was too afraid to ask anyone about him."

"You're giving me too much credit. It's Christ's perfect love you are thankful for. After everything I went through, I understand it better, but I still struggle." She attempted a smile.

"I know you went through a lot. I'm sorry for all you've lost. Everyone is praying for you. We all love you." Amber squeezed her hand.

The gaping hole in Rory's chest shrank just a little. "Thank you."

Amber's pager chirped. She glanced at it. "Sorry, I need to check on a patient, but I'll be back."

Bright sunlight warmed the room. A new day dawned for her and all the survivors. Even after her many failures, the creator of the world never gave up on her. He'd protected her when she hadn't believed he would. The crushing load she'd been carrying lifted. God shouldered it. She had been such a fool to refuse to release the burden. But she had learned her lesson. She trusted God.

The thought of Jaxon struck her with a pang of remorse, but he was content. He lived in heaven. A tingling in her brain confirmed that Jaxon's love blanketed her.

The victory had cost her dearly. It had required the life of the man she loved. As much as she believed freedom to worship God was worth the price of her life, Jaxon had believed it worth his. He would be ... He *is* thrilled at the number of people who had been lost and now were found.

She closed her eyes and smiled. Forming a new nation wouldn't be easy, but how would they grow in faith if it was? Peace, that only came from God, enveloped her.

Acknowledgements

Publishing *The Lion Within* was quite the learning experience. I would like to thank all my family and friends who encouraged me as I muddled through the process.

To beta reader and beautiful sister, Kim, you were my biggest cheerleader. You read my first draft and loved it as only a sister could. Thank you for your support and for taking on the role of unpaid publicist.

To beta reader and handsome love of my life, Jay, thanks for identifying areas where the story lost momentum and for your great suggestions. I am so thankful that God allowed us to travel through life's adventures together.

To my two gorgeous and intelligent daughters, Jaime and Courtney, I thank you for your helpful suggestions and support during the writing process and website setup. I thank God for giving me such wonderful daughters.

To my many friends who anxiously waited to acquire a copy of *The Lion Within*, thanks for your support.

To editor, Janice Boekhoff, thank you for helping me improve the story and characters. Your encouraging suggestions were true to the story and my voice. You graciously answered the many questions I had as a novice writer. You also answered questions I didn't know to ask. You were a godsend.

I highly recommend Janice as an editor. To learn more about her editing services, visit her website at JaniceBoekhoff.com.

Any errors found in the published manuscript are all mine. After the final edit, I tweaked the document several times, and I formatted it for publication.

Most of all, I thank you, the reader, for spending your precious time reading *The Lion Within*. There are an infinite number of good books available, and I am humbled that you took a chance and read this novel. Book reviews are very important for all authors but especially for independent authors. Reviews help readers decide the books where they will invest their valuable time and money. If you would be kind enough to leave a review of *The Lion Within* on Amazon, I would greatly appreciate your effort.

About the Author

Angela Gold grew up in a small Oklahoma town with a population of 300. Because she never stepped foot outside of the state, until she was fifteen, reading provided her with a necessary outlet to discover different lands, cultures, and most importantly, ideas.

Stories swirled in her head her entire life, but she pushed them aside as she worked full-time and cared for her handsome husband, Jay, and two wonderful daughters, Jaime and Courtney.

After becoming an empty nester, the idea for her debut novel, *The Lion Within*, incubated and grew. While still working full-time, the part-time writing process was slow. As fate would have it, early retirement, a move from Texas to Coastal Oregon, and sheltering at home provided time to devote to her manuscript.

An avid lover of fiction, Angela believes good fiction immerses the reader into situations they otherwise might never consider and introduces them to new perspectives. After all, it's impossible to take too many breathtaking fictional adventures!

Angela would love to hear from you. Visit her website. at AngelaLGold.com.

Made in the USA
Middletown, DE
29 September 2021